Who was she?

And what had she been doing in the San Francisco Bay at ten o'clock on a very cold night? Noah wondered.

She'd obviously jumped in, trying to commit suicide. There could be no other explanation for her fighting his rescue.

The adrenaline that had fed his muscles as he had tried to save her from drowning was long gone. It took every ounce of his resolve to stagger up the flight of stairs to his house, with the near-frozen woman in his arms.

Inside, he lay her down gently on the couch, and tried to dry her face and hair with a towel. He found her pulse, slow but steady. Removing her cold, soggy clothes took all his remaining strength. He grabbed the knitted comforter folded across the back of the sofa and threw it over her. Then he fell to the carpet...unconscious.

Dear Reader,

When I wrote Samantha and Scotty's story in *For Love or Money*, my sleuths solved the mystery of a murdered heiress. But at the end of that story, an unanswered question remained—a question that has haunted me ever since.

Who was that woman calling herself Jane Williams who came to Riddle Investigations in San Francisco looking for her birth certificate?

This story is the answer to that question. And I confess to you now that until I added the last period to the last paragraph of Jane Williams's story, even I didn't quite know what to expect next from that mysterious lady!

May you be as thoroughly surprised.

Warmest regards,

M.J.

M.J. Rodgers

M.J. Rodgers
Who Is Jane Williams?

Harlequin Books

TORONTO • NEW YORK • LONDON
AMSTERDAM • PARIS • SYDNEY • HAMBURG
STOCKHOLM • ATHENS • TOKYO • MILAN
MADRID • WARSAW • BUDAPEST • AUCKLAND

For my very special niece, Alicia Marie

ISBN 0-373-22290-4

WHO IS JANE WILLIAMS?

Copyright © 1994 by Mary Johnson

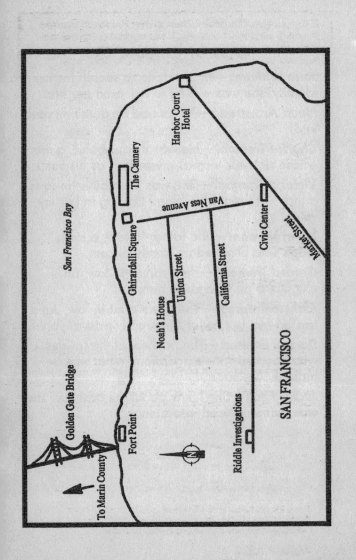

CAST OF CHARACTERS

Jane Williams—In a desperate search for her identity, she was willing to risk even her life.

Noah Armstrong—What had he gotten himself into?

Charles Tremont—He was the husband, a man whose sickness was as mysterious as his son's.

Victoria Tremont—She was the mother-in-law, a lady with real blue blood flowing in her icy veins.

Loren Tremont—The father-in-law, a stern judge who brooked no family dissent.

Gerard Tremont—The brother-in-law, an enigma to all who knew him.

Melissa Tremont—The great aunt-in-law. Jane trusted her, but could Jane really trust anyone?

Dorsey Edelson—The nephew of the lawyer who handled Jane's adoption. What was he hiding?

Judith Fitch—She knew about the past, but she was being coerced into silence.

Prologue

They had followed her. She felt it in the pressure at the back of her head, the skipping pulse beneath her skin, the wisps of shadow at the corners of her eyes, which quickly darted out of sight whenever she whirled around suddenly.

Like now.

They were back there—somewhere in the dark September night. Did they hide inside the closed courtyard of the old fort beneath the Golden Gate Bridge? Or were they lurking within that silver Jaguar on the far side of the parking lot?

They couldn't be inside the Jaguar. That had been parked here before she pulled in. And they couldn't have known she was coming here. Could they?

A quiver ran through her stomach and down her legs. The quiet, steady voice of reason told her she was imagining things. She had lost them. Hours before when she'd left the airport, she'd seen their white Mazda get stuck behind that tourist bus. She'd *seen* it.

So why couldn't she accept it? What was it that made her feel them back there still?

She drew in a deep breath, willing it to steady her nerves and disperse the annoying shadows.

The stagnant air in the rented Toyota Tercel smelled strongly of vinyl, plastics and preserving chemicals from the automotive assembly line. After ten minutes in the closed-in car, her nostrils were beginning to burn.

She looked over her shoulder, peering into the night once more. The plaguing ghosts continued to dance just on the periphery of her sight, skipping down the vertebrae of her neck, choreographed to the pulsing beat in her blood and bones.

They were there . . . watching . . . waiting.

No! This is foolish. I can't let myself be afraid of shadows. No one is there. No one has followed me.

Determined to respond to reason, she yanked on the handle, pushed open the driver's side door and jumped out. Yet despite her determination, despite all the stout assurances she'd given herself, she quickly slammed and locked the car door, her eyes darting through the darkness all around her.

Was that a flicker of movement? There? Or was it over there?

Damn. I've got to get hold of myself. She pulled the hood of her raincoat close around her face. A spray of wet, salty air bathed her cheeks. She inhaled deeply, allowing the cool, refreshing taste to roll across her palate and settle at the back of her throat.

It was chilly, but so clean and refreshing after the closed-in car. She drew in another deep breath, wishing she dared leave a window open to air out the interior of her rented vehicle.

She didn't dare.

She looked around again—very, very carefully.

Fort Point's old brick buildings lay beneath the southern arch of the Golden Gate Bridge, like a worn, ancient sentry still at its post. The fort's shiny, slick parking lot stretched before her, a quiet, dark expanse of pavement. The place seemed deserted this late at night. It should be deserted.

It *should* be.

Decision time. Should she stay close to the relative safety of the car? Or should she walk along the seawall and stretch her aching muscles, sore from so many hours of sitting?

A cool, stiff breeze whipped up from the water. She'd freeze if she didn't either walk or get back into the car. Clearly, the car was the safe choice. But safe choices had their dangers, too.

She cinched the tie at her waist a little tighter, thankful for the raincoat's warm fleece lining. The strap of her shoulder bag beneath her coat tightened across her chest.

She reminded herself she'd only have to flip her hand beneath the skirt folds of her raincoat to reach her bag and what was inside. She shoved her bare hands into the raincoat's pockets. Her fingers rubbed nervously against the jagged edges of her car key as she took one final look around.

The wind blew against the raincoat's hood, plastering it to the side of her head. She hurried across the parking lot, relying on the deep tread of her boot soles to grip the sea-slick pavement.

It felt good to be moving her cramped muscles. The air sweeping off San Francisco Bay tasted so sweet.

Still, every few steps she stole a glance behind her.

Nothing. Nothing tangible, anyway.

You just needed air and a little exercise. The only thing following you for the last hour has been your imagination.

She stepped up on the stone abutment beside the bay and walked along its edge, following the thick, heavy guardrail chain that looped over sturdy posts. Noisy waves pounded the rock wall, releasing gusts of salty spray to mist her face and clothing. She stopped and turned to face the dynamic, surging ocean at her feet. It crashed again and again against the rock, beating it into submission with its powerful, white-capped strokes.

She lifted her eyes to the famous bridge magnificently lit above the mouth of the bay. It sat like a jeweled crown on the headwaters of this immense royal body of water that forcibly lay claim to the Arctic, the Antarctic, the Americas, Asia and Australia.

Yet for all its power, this great Pacific Ocean did not determine its own direction. From 240,000 miles away the moon's silent, strong hand shoved these waves against these stones, an outside despot molding another entity to its will.

That image furrowed her brow. Once she had been like this ocean. Not anymore. *She* decided her own direction now. *She* determined what limitations she would accept, if any.

Brave, bold words. She knew nothing less would do. A woman needed her life raft full of just such brave, bold words when she was tossed through the rough seas of so many restricting memories.

She looked away from the dark waters back to the bridge, a glorious tribute to the ingenuity of the human mind challenging the natural elements to produce something functional and beautiful. She found it a truly impressive sight on this dark night.

She tried to imagine a man and woman with a child standing on this very spot twenty-eight years before, looking at this famous bridge. The woman would be holding her child's small hand. Her long dark hair would rustle against her coat as she bent to tell the little girl that this was the Golden Gate Bridge.

The little girl's face would tilt up to study the bridge, and she would think about her mother's words. Her young eyes would tell her this bridge didn't look golden at all. It looked red.

It should, since its protective coat of paint *was* red. No wonder children grew up confused. No sooner were they taught something was true than they were presented with a glaring inconsistency.

But then, perhaps that was life's greatest truth—that it was riddled with inconsistencies. And learning *that* truth early on prepared the child to keep an open mind.

Had it prepared her? Was being aware of life's inconsistencies early on what finally made her wake up and challenge the so-called truths others had tried to make her believe?

She let the sea spray bathe her face as her eyes followed the graceful lines of the bridge, towering so regally above her. Whatever had given her the impetus to challenge and break away, she was grateful. Because without it, she wouldn't be here tonight.

And being here tonight was important—for her psyche, for her sanity, for her soul.

Her attention was so focused on the bridge that she didn't hear the footsteps coming up behind her. She didn't feel the strong hands grab her... until it was too late.

Chapter One

Noah Armstrong hurt. With every lift of his legs and every swing of his arms he hurt. And he felt winded, too—already. Damn, he'd been jogging for only ten minutes. He swung his wrist forward to have another look at the illuminated green glow on the face of his sports watch. Correction, make that nine minutes, thirty seconds. Great. Just great.

He reminded himself that eight days ago he hadn't been able to jog at all. But the reminder didn't help, because he also remembered that eight weeks ago he could have run forever.

A lot can happen to a man's body in eight weeks. A lot *had* happened.

He slowed to a stop, collapsed onto the stone platform and let the ocean spray cool his sweating forehead. He wheezed into the wind, the roar of the waves matching the roar of the blood pulsing in his ears.

It would take time, the doctors had said. He must proceed slowly. He must be patient.

Noah had never been a patient man, now even less so than before. Because now he understood how precious and fleeting life was. How it could literally be gone in the blink of an eye. How criminal it was to waste one precious second of it.

The dying had taught him that. Sad how he had needed the dying to teach him the most important point of living.

He sucked in the salty air greedily as he concentrated on filling lungs gone shallow from his lengthy convalescence. As the seconds slid by, the aches in his legs and chest began to ease.

All a matter of time—rare, precious time.

He'd gotten everything out of his first thirty years that he'd put in. He'd been on the go every minute, pushing himself to the limits, striving for success. In retrospect, a good thirty years. But he realized there had been a lot of waste, too.

That life was behind him now; and, he vowed, so was the waste. He intended to be selective—*very* selective.

Noah raised his head to stare at the brightly lit bridge above him. He could see the red taillights of the cars heading from San Francisco to Marin County—bumper-to-bumper even at this late hour. It reminded him of an immense treadmill on which humans marched, from home to work, from work to home, faster and faster, until their lives were worn. And they were gone.

And only the treadmill went on.

Of one thing he was certain. Sitting at some desk in some dreary eight-to-five job between trips of inhaling too much carbon monoxide wasn't right for him.

He looked away from the bridge and stared into the full face of the incoming tide, inhaling deeply and gratefully of its clean, sharp scent. His thoughts journeyed back to when he was a youngster and his dad had taken him into a sporting goods store to buy him his first sled—and he'd come out swinging his first tennis racket, instead.

He'd known the tennis racket was the right choice. When it came to those choices that truly mattered in his life, he'd always known.

It wasn't something he could explain, not in logical terms, anyway. All he knew was that some sense within him pulled like the opposite pole of a magnet toward those things he was meant to do—toward a destiny he was meant to complete. Now, twenty years after selecting that tennis racket, the time had come to select something new.

The lights from the bridge laid an emerald sheen on the surface of the sea. To his eyes, this bay was so much more beautiful than that man-made treadmill above it. It wore the unchanging face of eternity on its smooth, undulating brow. Nature did nothing unimportant. Like this great Pacific Ocean, its every ebb and flow ended in a deeply calculated, meaningful wave.

He would let nature be his guide—he, too, would do nothing unimportant.

He took another deep breath, filling his lungs—his whole being—with enthusiasm for the inherent energy and rightness in that thought. Perhaps his next profession should have something to do with the sea. As a marine biologist, he might be able to save a dying species or discover an exciting new one. The mythical mermaid, perhaps? He laughed into the kiss of a salty spray.

But the laughter died a quick death as Noah straightened and stiffened all in one move.

What the hell is that?

He peered out into the dark night, straining to catch a glimpse of what he was sure he could not have seen. Then he saw it again . . . an arm . . . then another—clumsily cleaving through the waves. Then he spotted a bobbing head, shooting briefly out of the water until another crashing wave buried it.

Someone was out there! Someone was drowning!

Noah tore off his running shoes and socks. He scrambled to his feet, stepped over the restricting line of heavy chain guardrail and dived headfirst into a crashing wave. He went under into a shock of freezing, inky blackness. He struggled to the surface, guided by the reflecting light of the Golden Gate, breaking through the water with a gasp.

He struck out, fighting against the surging waves threatening to throw him against the slick stone abutment that fed onto the land he had just abandoned. He strained his eyes to pick up the flailing figure in the dark waters. But what he had seen from the elevated shoreline seconds before was now obscured by the rippling of the waves on the uneven surface.

He battled the fierce incoming tide, his pumping arms ripping through its icy edges. He charged its southward plunge and joined its easterly drift, reasoning that whoever else was caught in it would be pulled in that direction, too.

But it was so damn hard to see in the undulating waves. His breath tore through weakened lungs. His shoulder, arm and leg muscles already ached badly. And it was so damn cold. He knew in minutes, maybe seconds, hypothermia would begin to set in. There was so little time.

He could not give up and turn back—a precious life hung in the balance. He sucked in painful breaths, gritted his teeth against the chilling cold and pressed tortured muscles into continued service.

He wrestled with the turbulent sea for what seemed like an eternity, lifting leaden arms and legs by the sheer force of will. Finally he glimpsed a small white hand breaking through the surging tide—clawing at the air.

Hope lifted his spirits and added fuel to his spent cells. He struck out in the direction of the hand. A few more strokes and he saw the head bobbing above the waves. He yelled as he approached, "Don't struggle! Float!"

But the hand continued to flail in the swelling waves. Had his voice been swallowed by the thunder of the crashing waves?

He swam alongside, grabbing at one flailing arm.

"Don't struggle!"

"Let me go!"

It was a woman's voice. Even as his brain registered that fact, Noah felt the blow against the side of his head from her fist. Next, he felt the kick of her legs far too close to his sore ribs. Neither blow had had much force behind it, thankfully, but enough to make her intent clear.

There was only one thing to do, and he wasted no time in doing it. He yanked her to him and delivered a short, sharp punch to her jaw.

Her head fell back and she went limp. He pulled her unresisting body to him, flipping her onto her back. He wrapped his arm around her shoulders, dragging her beside him, trying to keep her face above water as he struck out for shore in a clumsy sidestroke.

He knew they never would have made it if the tide hadn't helped them along. Still, it seemed like an eternity before they were pushed up against the black rock face. He clawed at the sea-slick stone, but his numb hand slipped clumsily. Desperately he groped for a handhold, found a tiny break in the rock, held on.

He had no strength or breath left to pull himself out, much less her. He clung to the flattened stones of the sea-wall, sucking air into lungs that ached horribly, trying to keep his head and hers above water until his strength returned.

And every second he could feel the force of the waves beating against them and the numbing coldness settling into his muscles, into his bones.

He couldn't wait any longer. Breath or no breath, strength or no strength, he had to pull them out—now. Another few seconds and the cold would ensure neither of them would ever be coming out.

He dragged his body over the slick stone, pulling hers with him. How he did it, he wasn't sure, but by the time he finally had the seawall supporting their weight, blood was dripping from cuts on his palms and his knees, and his entire body throbbed with pain. Every labored breath that tore through his mouth and nose seared through his chest like a hot poker.

He collapsed onto his back—beyond pain, beyond exhaustion. He blacked out...for seconds...maybe minutes. When he opened his eyes again, he felt the weight and warmth of her lying on top of him. Was she still alive? He lifted his head and turned his body to rest his ear against her chest. After what seemed like a very long moment, he heard the light, steady beat of her heart.

His own heart lightened.

Then a blast of icy breeze shot a dreadful shiver through his bones. He could rest no longer. He had to get them to the car, out of this wind and out of these wet clothes.

Easier decided than done. Time after time he struggled to lift her, only to fall back onto the sea slick stone in a wheezing heap. Kneeling, he finally managed to work her limp form over his shoulder. Grasping the heavy chain guardrail beside him for support and using the strength of his legs, he finally staggered to his feet. Her bare white ankles bobbed in front of him as he stumbled beneath her weight toward his Jaguar on the far side of the parking lot.

By the time he reached it and retrieved the keys from where he'd hidden them inside the left rear tire wheel, his muscles were screaming and his lungs felt like two razor-sharp knives slicing through his chest.

He unlocked the driver's side door, pushed the seat forward with his elbow and deposited her on the back seat. Then he twisted toward the front, slid into the driver's seat and slammed the door shut on the icy wind. He yanked his sopping jogging shirt off his back and threw it onto the passenger seat.

With fingers shaking and clumsy from the cold, he inserted the ignition key and started the engine. It was only then that he realized his feet were bare and he hadn't stopped to retrieve his shoes or socks.

He wasn't about to go back for them now. He gunned the engine and turned on the heater full blast as he shifted into Reverse and laid rubber behind the screech of his tires.

He shook all over from muscles spent and cold. The supposedly unbreakable crystal on his watch was so smashed he couldn't read the time. The thought of driving them both to the emergency room flashed fleetingly across his mind.

He rejected it. First, he hadn't the faintest idea where the nearest hospital was. Second, any emergency room would ask questions he was sure he wouldn't be comfortable answering. Like who she was and what she was doing in San Francisco Bay at ten o'clock on a very cold night.

Not that he *couldn't* answer that last question. She'd obviously jumped in, trying to commit suicide. There was no other explanation for her fighting his rescue.

Noah shoved the gearshift into Second with a vehemence that had nothing to do with the frustration and discomfort from his cold, aching and badly abused body. Might serve her right to be arrested and thrown into prison. Might wake her up to the value of what she had so carelessly tried to throw away. Or it might just convince her to try it again, he thought with a frown. What terrible thing had happened to drive her to such insanity?

He adjusted the rearview mirror to try to see her in the back seat. All he could make out was a white face surrounded by dark, dripping hair.

Another few blocks and he turned up the familiar incline of his street. The house was the last one at the top and on the left. He hit the control to the automatic garage door opener as soon as he was halfway up the block.

He zipped his car into the small garage and leaned over the back seat as the door noisily began its descent behind him. By the time it shuddered to a stop against the pavement, Noah had lifted her out of the back seat.

The ride home had helped him get his breath back, but the adrenaline that had fed his muscles earlier during the emergency was long gone. He felt thoroughly chilled and sapped of strength. It took every ounce of his resolve to stagger with his burden up the flight of stairs that led into the house.

When he opened the door and the warm interior air rushed over him, he sucked it in with blessed relief. He switched on a nearby lamp, slammed the door to the garage behind him with his foot and ended up literally dropping her onto the nearby sofa, knowing he couldn't carry her a step farther.

He pulled off his wet jogging pants and briefs as he stumbled into the bathroom, fighting a white whirl of dizziness. He dropped to the floor by the edge of the tub, tore off what remained of his watch and dunked his head between his knees, trying to coax some blood back into his upper extremities so he wouldn't pass out.

He rose shakily, grabbing at the terry-cloth robe that hung on the door and a dry bath towel off the rack. He cinched the robe around him as he stumbled back into the living room.

He knelt beside the couch and tried to dry her face and hair with the towel. He found the pulse in her neck, slow but steady. Removing her soggy clothes took all his remaining strength. He grabbed the knitted comforter folded across the back of the sofa and threw it over her. Then he fell to the carpet . . . unconscious.

THE FIRST THING SHE WAS aware of was the light streaming onto her face through her closed lids . . . a warm morning light, cajoling her awake. The next was the ache in her jaw that pulsed up her cheek into her eye. She moaned slightly as she raised a hand to gently cup the tender side.

Ouch. Why was her jaw aching this way? Felt as if she'd run into a door—or a fist.

A fast-forward button flooded her mind with sudden and alarming images. Her eyes flew open and she bolted upright.

Sunlight blinded her.

She squinted frantically until her eyes adjusted sufficiently for her surroundings to come into focus. She found herself in some strange, exotic jungle. Rubber trees and ferns grew in healthy, vibrant profusion around her, and through the leaves stared the eyes of a golden tiger.

Startled, she blinked in disbelief, then in relief. The tiger was one dimensional, just part of an amazing wall-to-wall, floor-to-ceiling mural of some incredibly verdant jungle full of ferns and foliage and exotic birds and animals.

She could see now that a lot of the greenery in the foreground was apparently real, like the giant rubber plant next to her. A large, thick leaf brushed against the arm of the bamboo-framed sofa on which she lay. A soft, buff-colored knitted throw had been draped over her.

She was in someone's living room—but not anyone she'd ever met. Disoriented she might be, but she was clear on this. No one she'd ever met would have the guts or gall to decorate a room fit for Tarzan.

The room was cluttered with plants. A giant, gnarled tree trunk supported a rectangular, glass-topped coffee table, and more plants grew out of wicker baskets on its top. Bamboo chairs jutted out among a riotous growth of other potted plants. The seats of the chairs were upholstered in the same furry beige material as the sofa she was lying on.

Still, she'd forgive the decorator all for leaving that glorious curved bay window untouched so that sunlight streamed in, bathing everything in the room in such a healthy, lovely glow.

So where was this Tarzan, and what was she doing in his lair? Well, she wasn't going to find out lying around.

She swung her legs over the sofa, her bare feet immediately connecting with something warm and alive. In shock and alarm she quickly snatched her feet back beneath her on the sofa.

Cautiously she peeked over the edge to look down. And there he was—Tarzan in the flesh.

She relaxed immediately when she saw his lips slightly parted and heard the sound of his exhaled breath, slow and deep. He was asleep.

But her first real impression was of his length—and lots of it. His head of brown hair extended inches beyond the edge of the bamboo-framed sofa. His large bare feet sprawled beyond the opposite end. Since she judged the sofa to be about six feet long, she knew he must be tall.

Her eyes made another sweep over the flesh not covered by the robe cinched at his waist. He had lean, athletic legs and forearms that gave evidence of frequent use. There was another well-formed line of muscle development beneath the mat of soft-looking, curly brown hair on his exposed chest. He certainly looked as if he wouldn't have much trouble swinging from a few vines.

Then she started noticing the details she'd missed. A pinkish, puckered scar snaked his left forearm and a couple more scars dug across both collarbones. Still another deep pink line ran along his inner right thigh, disappearing beneath the robe.

It looked as if he'd fallen from a few vines recently—and landed rather hard. The wounds were still healing.

Who was this man? And what was she doing here with him?

When her eyes finally returned to his face, she began to think that there was something familiar about that deep widow's peak at the top of his forehead. Or was it the broadness to his forehead? Or the surprise of that light brush of freckles across that sturdy, no-nonsense nose?

His breath deepened into a grunt as he twitched in his sleep.

She shifted her position on the sofa to get a better look, tucking the knitted throw securely above her breasts. Then she made an uncomfortable discovery.

She was nude beneath the blanket.

Someone had undressed her. Had it been this stranger, sleeping so soundly on the floor beside this sofa?

All the alarm circuits tripped in her brain as a collage of unthinkable images flashed through her thoughts. No, it couldn't be. He wasn't one of them. She knew exactly what *they* looked like.

You fool. He could be one of them. There could be more than two. Hell, there could be a dozen, for all you know.

Her eyes darted around her, noticing things she had missed before—a large brown towel lay just beyond his head; her panties and bra were in a heap on top of her slacks and blouse just beyond his feet.

This latest observation did nothing to assuage her earlier frightful imaginings.

Her heart began hammering against her ribs as the adrenaline poured through her arteries. There was only one thing she could do. She had to get up and get a weapon before he came to. She could just make out the edge of a kitchen cabinet off to the right.

Good. A kitchen meant knives.

THE FIRST THING NOAH SAW when he opened his eyes was a very shapely knee stretching seductively past him. He was still half-asleep and acted on pure and simple instinct to this interesting stimulus starting his day. He grabbed for it.

And ended up totally surprised when he found himself with not just a knee, but an armful of woman. And what a woman.

She knocked the breath out of him; literally, as she landed on his chest; figuratively, as he looked into her face and found eyes as mysterious as an azure sea, framed by long, silky dark hair spilling over creamy white shoulders.

Where had this vision come from?

He barely had time for the question, let alone the answer, because the next second he felt that sharp, shapely knee he had so recently admired digging between his legs, far too near his nether region.

Fortunately, his tight hold on her ruined her aim. Her kneecap connected with his inner thigh instead of its intended destination. Otherwise, Noah knew this scuffle would have come to an immediate and painful end. As it was, that first blow hit a spot tender enough to reverberate through his body and set his kidneys to vibrating.

Immediately his fighting reflexes took over. He rolled her onto her back, pinning both her arms and legs with his before she could use any of those shapely extremities as more accurately aimed missiles.

She fought back with an amazing strength and determination. He dropped most of his weight on top of her, both to keep her in place and because he was sorely feeling the abuse he'd put his body through the night before.

Now fully awake, he remembered who she was, of course. He began to regret his decision to bring her to his home instead of taking her to the emergency room. He hadn't exactly expected gratitude from her, but he could certainly have done without this wrestling match.

Well, on the other hand, he had to admit it had certain compensations. Even through the throw he was aware of her soft suppleness and exciting feminine heat. And he was also aware of his body responding to it with far too much enthusiasm.

Damn, he wished she'd stop struggling beneath him. It was getting more and more difficult to hold her without hurting her and without letting himself get any more aroused.

In growing desperation he spoke into her ear.

"Look, I'm not up to this wrestling match. Give us both a break. You continue to fight me and you're going to get hurt."

Her limbs stiffened beneath him, as hard and rigid as steel. He raised his head to see her face. Her eyes shot defiance into his, like bolts of blue-hot fire.

"I will fight you. With everything in me."

She meant it, too. That surprisingly husky voice had been pure threat. Her cheeks were flushed and her lips were set. For a moment Noah felt mesmerized by the incredible strength and beauty in that face, so much so that it took him another moment to realize that behind that strength and beauty lay fear—pure female fear.

Well, of course she's afraid. She obviously hasn't the faintest idea of who I am or what I intend.

He took a deep breath and let it out slowly. "Look, I'm not trying to attack you. I've never forced myself on a woman, and I certainly don't intend to start now. You don't have to fight me."

She wasn't buying it. Her husky voice rippled with accusation. "Right. That's why you grabbed me."

He took another deep breath and pushed himself up, moving the bulk of his weight off her while still securely keeping her arms and legs pinned. He had to put some distance between them to prove his words. But he did so reluctantly, both because of the strain it put on his healing arm and leg muscles and because it put him out of contact with the seductive, soft heat of her breasts and hips.

He tried switching to a light, reassuring tone. "I just woke up. I saw something I wasn't expecting—namely your knee—and my reflexes reacted. That's all."

"Your reflex action is to grab what you aren't expecting?"

Noah tried to ignore the complaining discomfort already beginning to whine through his straining muscles, particularly those of his arms.

"Look, my name is Noah Armstrong. I live here. Alone. You're safe—virtue and all. There's nothing here to harm you."

Those azure eyes studied him very carefully and thoroughly. Their guard did not lower one iota.

"Why are my clothes in a heap over there on the floor?"

"They were sopping wet. You were unconscious, and I had to get them off you."

And, damn it, I must really have been in a bad way not to be able to remember what tantalizing sights lay beneath.

"Why were you asleep beside the sofa?"

The muscles in his arms had begun to ache something fierce now, as he steadfastly held his position above her. He gritted his teeth against the strain and the pain.

"Because after I got our wet clothes off, I had just enough strength left to pass out on the floor."

"*Our* wet clothes?"

"Yes. I brought you here last night after I fished you out of the bay."

He tried to read the thoughts behind her eyes, but they remained as rigid and unyielding as the rest of her.

"Why didn't you take me to a hospital?"

His arms had begun to shake. He couldn't get them to stop. "Would you have preferred awakening in one and having to answer their questions as to what you were doing swimming around in the bay?"

She had no answer to that. He didn't think she would. Her eyes darted to his shaking arms, settling on the prominent scar on his forearm, getting pinker by the second. She refocused on his eyes.

"So what now?"

He took another deep breath. This one snaked through his lungs in a sigh as shaky as his extremities.

"Now I'd like to get up and get some coffee."

The guarded look never left her eyes.

"You're going to release me?"

"As long as you promise no more commando attacks. I'm not eager to fight anymore this morning. Particularly not before my coffee."

Her guarded eyes told him she hadn't bought everything he'd said, although her body did seem to relax a bit beneath him. Still, she said nothing; she just stared at him.

His arm muscles were now vibrating like tuning forks, shouting their protest.

"Look, you don't have to believe my good intentions. You can bolt out of the house and run next door to Mrs. Truetree, my eighty-year-old neighbor, who will be happy to grant you asylum, but who will also make you pay the price. You'll be forced to consume her stale Christmas fruitcake and warm beer, while she regales you with the unabridged history of every single picture in her fifty-two family albums. And, believe me, *she* won't let you escape."

He could feel it again—another barely perceptible easing of the muscles of her arms pinned beneath his hands. But the suspicion still remained in her eyes.

"What about my clothes?"

"They're probably still wet, not to mention full of sea salt. You can wear that throw you've got tied around you until they take a spin in the washer and dryer. Look, I can't hold myself up this way much longer. I'm about to collapse on top of you, and I'm warning you, I weigh one-ninety. Can we both get up now?"

She paused only a moment more before nodding. But it was the further relaxation of her muscles that really told him he'd finally gotten through.

He raised himself completely off her then, freeing her arms and legs. A sigh of profound relief registered in his arms and was echoed by his shoulder, back and leg muscles. At the same time, other parts of his body registered a conflicting and intense reluctance to distance themselves from her exciting warmth.

The moment she was free she scrambled to her feet. She looked ready to bolt at his first false move—or to go on the attack again. She wasn't completely convinced of his honorable intentions, that was for certain.

If she'd only known the kind of shape he was in, she would have relaxed. His arms felt like two lead pipes swinging from his torso, and his legs weren't much better. He hoped she didn't get spooked again and decide to fight. He'd hate to get trounced by a woman.

And not that big of a one, either, he noticed for the first time. She was no more than five foot five and probably didn't weigh much more than 115 pounds. Her arms and legs were lean and surprisingly muscular. The knitted throw tucked just above her breasts and extending to her midthigh hugged some nice curves.

She looked to be somewhere in her twenties. Her skin was creamy white and was set off by the dark richness of her long hair that flowed in silky disarray down to her well-formed biceps. Her prominent cheekbones balanced nicely with her slightly square jaw, which was sporting a blue bruise from his sock to it the night before. Somehow that bruise didn't seem so out of place on a woman with a great husky voice who could wrestle the way she could.

Her eyes were her most incredible feature, though. Their special, one-of-a-kind azure color was arresting. But it was what projected from behind them that really perplexed him.

He'd become rather good at recognizing the signs over the past few weeks, and they were definitely there. Those eyes had the look of a lady with purpose and meaning to her life, which was rather incongruous, considering how they had met.

"I'd like to wash up."

He came out of his daze and realized that he'd been blatantly staring.

He turned his back on her deliberately, hoping to engender trust by showing some. He leaned down to pick up her damp clothing from the floor, and pointed behind him.

"There's a bathroom down the hall. First door on the right. It locks from the inside. I'll be in the kitchen when you're finished."

He left the room, his back still to her, but listening intently. She still might decide to play it safe and choose Mrs. Truetree and that stale fruitcake.

When he heard her bare feet pad down the hall, he smiled. So, the lady wasn't the kind to play it safe. Somewhere deep in his stomach he felt a small nerve twitch in both satisfaction and anticipation.

He detoured to the utility room on his way to the kitchen. One by one he tossed her clothes into the washer. The sandalwood-colored corduroy slacks went in first, followed by a rouge knit top with a lace collar.

He paused to finger the tantalizing wisps of pink nylon edged in lace that were her panties and bra, trying to conjure up any memory of his removing them the night before. Damn. Nothing.

After starting the washer he headed for the kitchen, making a quick detour to the half bath beside the kitchen to wash the grit out of his eyes and the sleep from his mouth.

He was glad, for several reasons, she'd decided not to bolt. First, he wanted to be sure she was going to be okay. Second, he couldn't deny his physical reaction to her. Then there was that interesting third reason, perhaps the most compelling of the three.

Noah had always known what to expect from a woman, but he had absolutely no idea what this woman might do next—and he found that amazingly exciting. He was eagerly looking forward to finding out all about this mermaid he'd plucked from the sea.

His smile turned into a yawn. Damn, he needed that coffee. He didn't know how long she'd be washing up, but if she was like ninety-nine percent of other women, he should have time for one or two eye-opening cupfuls.

He should have known she'd be in the one percent. Still, when he walked into the kitchen he was startled to find her so unexpectedly standing in its center, waiting for him.

But his jaw really dropped when he caught the flash of the butcher knife she wielded in her hand.

Chapter Two

"You lied to me. Noah Armstrong doesn't live here. Some guy named Eric Ellison does. Now I want the truth. Who are you and why did you bring me here?"

She watched the initial surprised look on his face gradually fade into something that suspiciously resembled a suppressed grin.

"I didn't lie to you. I am Noah Armstrong. I do live here. And I need my coffee. It's beginning to look like this is going to be one of those three-cup mornings."

She backed away cautiously, uncertainly, as he moved over to the cupboard plastered with the familiar jungle mural that was spread across every inch of wall in the house. More evidence of his unusually bizarre taste. Or was it his?

He reached for a bag of Blue Jamaican coffee beans, drew out a couple of handfuls and dumped them into a grinder. He scooped the newly ground beans into the drip coffeemaker and poured in bottled water.

As she watched, she stayed ready for anything, the same plaguing question revolving inside her brain.

Moments before, when she'd been pinned beneath that impressive body and had felt his arousal during their struggle, she'd thought she had the answer. But then he had deliberately held himself away from her and sought both through his words and actions to reassure her.

And she had been reassured. Particularly after he'd stood staring at her with such blatant desire afterward and had then turned away from that desire once again to put her clothes in the washer.

Damn, he'd almost made her believe he was the chivalrous man who had somehow saved her from the sea. Now she wasn't so sure. Maybe he *was* really in league with the others, trying to play some sinister game of manic roulette with her mind.

She watched him take out four different cellophane sacks filled with the kind of grains that came from the natural food bins in the back of the grocery store. He dumped them into a bowl, adding raisins, walnuts and water.

Then he slipped the bowl into the microwave, and as its sound hummed through the kitchen, he turned to another cupboard, where he retrieved a cocoa-colored earthenware mug. Into it he poured some of the freshly brewed coffee.

On his way to the small, glass-topped, bamboo kitchen table, he retrieved a pint of real cream from the refrigerator. He sat on one of the two bamboo chairs and poured cream into the mug. Then he gulped it down like a man with a mighty thirst.

He looked at her again. His voice was calm, like the expression on his face and in his eyes.

"You want some coffee?"

Did she want some coffee? About now she would have killed for a cup. The wonderful, rich aroma of those freshly brewed beans smelled so good it was making her dizzy.

But she held her ground, continuing to brandish the butcher knife.

"If you are Noah Armstrong, who is Eric Ellison and where is he now?"

He sipped some more coffee and reached for a tennis ball lying on the table. He squeezed it with his hand, not answering right away. But when he did, his voice had a quieter quality to it.

"Eric was my friend. He died eight weeks ago."

His light, clear amber eyes underlined every quiet syllable with a loud and deeply felt meaning.

She exhaled a breath, full of a shaky kind of relief. Slowly she laid the butcher knife on the counter and helped herself to some coffee. She refilled his cup, then added a dash of cream to hers, set the carafe between them on a woven grass coaster and dropped onto the bamboo chair opposite him. He watched her quietly as he squeezed the tennis ball in his hand.

The coffee tasted the way it smelled—rich, creamy, heavenly. She savored it on her tongue and then let it slide luxuriously down her throat. She closed her eyes and concentrated on the exquisite feel of its evaporating warmth through her chest. Her peaceful state was interrupted by the beeping of the microwave, signaling that the hot cereal was ready.

He got up, dished equal shares into two bowls that matched the earthenware coffee mugs and returned to the table carrying cereal, spoons and a couple of paper napkins. He poured some cream into the first bowl before offering it to her.

"Did you find something of Eric's in the bathroom?"

She nodded as she took the offered bowl and spoon from his hand.

"The medicine chest is full of his prescription bottles."

"I haven't had much time to clean things out yet."

"I...I'm sorry about the knife. I jumped to the wrong conclusion. This has been a pretty jumpy morning for me all around."

"I can imagine. It's okay."

She watched his face as he stood before her. A lot of people said something was okay, but you could tell they were just being polite. Noah Armstrong wasn't just being polite. She looked directly into his eyes and finally recognized why his word could be accepted.

This man did not deal in trivialities, nor in subterfuge. Something in his life had taught him to move beyond them. She wondered what it had been.

"Had your friend been ill long?"

The ends of Noah's mouth twisted into an unexpected grin. The faint lines at the corners of his eyes crinkled attractively with good humor.

"Eric Ellison was never ill a day in his life. He was just a hypochondriac."

She understood the grin, which was not incongruous at all to his grief. It had come from a fond memory of a friend. Noah slipped back onto his bamboo chair.

"This was Eric's place?"

"Yes. I was the closest thing he had to a family, so he left it to me."

"The decor is . . . unusual."

As his eyes climbed the walls around them, his grin got bigger.

"He had it decorated right after we got back from a trip to India. We'd taken a trek into the jungle there. He went ape over it. Quite literally, as you can see."

Noah focused his attention on his food and dug in with the force of the famished.

Her hands circled the warmth of her bowl as she watched him. He had a nice face under that cap of thick, flyaway brown hair. Not Hollywood handsome, but attractive in a big, athletic, clean-cut way. And there was something about that grin of his coupled with that brush of freckles across his nose, that was pure seduction. Even the morning whiskers peppering his chin added to, rather than detracted from, the impression.

She noticed that he wasn't wearing a ring, and he had said he lived here alone. With that sexy grin, those sincere amber eyes and a body like that, this guy must be fighting off women by the truckload.

The truckload?

Truckload. Eric Ellison. Noah Armstrong. Wisps of familiarity flittered across her mind. What was it about that combination? The words kept rolling around the open memory slots in her brain like marbles on a game board, searching for the right hole to fit into.

Then suddenly the marbles dropped into adjacent slots, snug and sure, and she knew. She leaned over the table, feeling the steam spiraling up from the cereal bowl to warm her chin.

"Eric Ellison and Noah Armstrong. Professional tennis players. You were coming back from a tournament when a truck lost its brakes, rammed into your open sports car and dumped its load of steel beams on top of it. You both just barely survived. Must have been, what, two months ago?"

His eyes raised to hers. He swallowed his mouthful of cereal, then cleared his throat. "About that."

His eyes said a lot more, however.

She leaned back, stuck the spoon into her bowl and stirred the cream around.

"That must have sounded pretty cold, blurting it out like that. It's just that I thought you looked familiar and then your names sounded familiar. I don't follow professional tennis, but *Newsweek* featured you on their cover, and when the accident made national news they ran your picture with the broadcast."

"Pity. The camera never catches my best side."

His comment sounded strange. She looked up in surprise. "They were both full-face pictures."

"See, what did I tell you?"

She caught on then. *He* was making *her* feel comfortable about discussing the topic. The guy had manners—the real kind.

She played with her cereal some more.

"I didn't hear that your friend had been killed."

This time Noah's answer took a little longer in coming.

"It happened a couple of days later...on the operating table."

She didn't know what to say. Condolences from strangers never seemed right somehow. She could not give voice to meaningless platitudes with this thoroughly genuine man.

She diverted her attention to the cereal, took a spoonful and found it surprisingly tasty. Of course, she'd decided a long time ago that a little cream, raisins and nuts could make just about anything taste good.

She looked up to see he had finished his cereal and was pouring himself a third cup of coffee. He poured her a second, settled back in his seat, then picked up the tennis ball and began squeezing it again. She understood he did it to strengthen his grip and probably his forearm. He watched her with eyes full of undisguised questions.

Well, he had answered hers readily enough. She supposed it was her turn. But this could get tricky. She decided it was best not to volunteer anything. Best just to wait and see what he asked. She quickly ran over the possibilities in her mind. She was ready.

Or at least she thought she was, until he finally gave voice to his first question.

"Why were you trying to kill yourself?"

She nearly spilled the cream she was pouring into her coffee cup.

"Kill myself? Where in heaven's name did you get the idea I was trying to kill myself?"

"Well, if you weren't trying to kill yourself, then why did you fight my efforts to save you?"

She set the carton of cream on the table and leaned over it. "Fight you? I fought you?"

"You punched me in the temple and tried to kick me in the ribs."

A hand went to her sore jaw as his meaning finally became clear. Her voice rose in choleric disbelief. "So it was you who socked me!"

"I see your memory is coming back."

She dropped her hand, but a certain amount of umbrage remained in her tone. "My memory never left me. I had no idea you were trying to save me. You were yelling at me to stop struggling. I assumed you were the one who threw me in.''

Whoops. It had gotten out before she could censor it.

She noticed that Noah's clear eyes quickly clouded over.

''Wait a minute. Did you just say someone *threw* you into the bay last night? As in tried to *kill* you?''

No use trying to deny it now. Her earlier rehearsed versions got a quick rewrite. She took a breath and leaned her forearms on the table.

''Actually, there may have been two of them. It happened pretty fast. One minute I was walking along looking at the bridge. The next thing I knew I was being lifted into the air and thrown into the water.''

She shivered as the awful, unspoken parts of that scenario once again filled her mind. She thought about how her boots, coat and shoulder bag had filled with water so fast they'd dragged her down with them. She recalled desperately fighting to shed the offending articles one by one, and feeling her lungs ready to burst. She remembered how she'd barely made it to the surface, gasping for air, spitting up swallowed seawater.

Then there had been the awful, endlessly cold battle with the icy sea.

''But who would do such a thing? And why?''

The demanding tone of his questions helped her to refocus. She took another gulp of the hot coffee, willing its warmth and reality to wash away the last of those frigid, frightful images.

''I don't know.''

''You don't know?''

''I told you, it happened so fast I didn't see who he or they were.''

Noah was up and out of his chair. ''We've got to call the police.''

She rose quickly to stay his hand, catching it just before it reached the cordless telephone sitting on the kitchen counter. He smelled warm and potently male. He felt that way, too, beneath her grasp.

Suddenly the heat of him swept through her, quickening the beat of her blood. For one very unexpected and surprising moment she totally forgot what she was going to say.

"Why are you trying to stop me?"

His question brought her mind forcibly back to the issue at hand. Tardily she reclaimed her lost thoughts.

"Why are you insisting on calling the police?"

"Why? You just told me someone, maybe two someones, tried to kill you!"

"Yes, but what can the police do now? I mean, who do they look for? I didn't see who did it, did you?"

"Well, no. I didn't see anyone except you. But—"

"It's over with, Noah. And I'm okay, thanks to you."

Divert his attention. That's what she had to do. She deliberately leaned closer, looked deep into his eyes and smiled.

"And I do thank you. Most sincerely. You're a chivalrous knight in shining terry cloth."

She watched the warmth climb into his neck as the light spray of freckles across his rugged nose deepened. Damn. How could a big hunk of a guy like this, with such natural raw vitality, come across so incredibly cute and sexy when taken unawares?

Did he have any idea what that did to a woman?

Apparently not. He cleared his throat and growled as if slightly peeved. "I think we'd best get back to the point here. There's a would-be murderer, or murderers, out there throwing people into the bay. If this guy, or these guys, get away with doing it to you, he, or they, might do it to others. They may already have, for all we know. You must report it."

Well, since feminine wiles seemed to be failing, that left only one thing—shock treatment. Her fingers clasped his arm firmly. She had to talk him out of this, and she had to do it fast.

"Noah, I don't want to go to the police. I *can't* go to the police."

Noah battled against succumbing to the warmth of her nearness, the mesmerizing blue of her eyes, the entreaty of her words. But his stomach really curled into a tight ball when he heard her husky voice pronounce his name and watched it form on her lips, coming together on the first syllable, then easing apart on the second as though getting ready to smile.

He couldn't ever remember his name looking like that on another woman's lips.

"Noah, I know this is difficult for you to understand."

Difficult? Impossible. He forced himself to look away from those lips and wondered what in the hell was wrong with him. This woman had just told him she couldn't go to the police. His mind should be filling with all the unsavory images of the kind of illegal activities that wouldn't allow her to seek the help of the proper authorities.

But the images filling his mind were more tantalizing ones of her saying his name like that, over and over again, as he slowly undressed her, this time both of them fully awake and aware.

He took a deep breath and tried to reclaim what was left of his slipping sanity so he could ask the questions he knew he must.

"Why can't you go to the police? Who are you? What are you involved in?"

She coaxed him back onto his bamboo chair and filled his mug for his fourth cup of coffee. He'd obviously underestimated when he'd predicted needing three cups this morning. With this much caffeine in him, he'd soon be trying to climb the vines painted on Eric's walls.

She sat across from him again, but her eyes didn't meet his this time. Instead they stared at the rich liquid in her cup. Her fingers tightened around it. She seemed to be struggling with something. Finally she let out a long, loud sigh as though she'd reach some sort of a draw in the fight with herself.

"My name is Jane Williams. I live in New Jersey. I ar-rived in San Francisco yesterday afternoon. My...family doesn't know that I've come or why and they must never find out."

He took a moment to try to sift through the meaning of her words, only to find himself as confused as ever.

"Let's take this one step at a time. Why are you here?"

"To find out the truth about my birth."

"I don't understand."

"No, of course you don't." She took a deep breath and let it out slowly. She continued to study the coffee in her cup, avoiding his searching eyes.

"Twenty-eight years ago my parents were killed in a bus crash back East. Their bodies and identification were burned beyond recognition. I was two, and one of the few fortunate survivors of that accident. Apparently all I could tell the authorities was that my name was Jane Williams and that I came from a place with a big bridge that my mother called golden, but which I thought looked red."

"San Francisco. The Golden Gate."

Her eyes rose to his then. "Yes. That's what the author-ities decided it had to mean. When no relatives could be found, I was adopted by a couple from New Jersey. Now I've come to San Francisco to find the records of my birth and discover who I am."

"You say this all happened twenty-eight years ago. Why did you come now? Why not before?"

"I came to San Francisco six years ago to attend the fu-neral of an aunt of my adopted parents. I took the oppor-tunity to contact Riddle Investigations, a local P.I. firm. One of their investigators found a birth certificate for Jane Williams, and I went home thinking it was mine. Unfortu-nately, after further inquiry, the investigator discovered the birth certificate belonged to someone else. So I've come back to see if I can locate the right one this time."

"Why is it so important that your family doesn't find out you're here?"

"My family would be hurt if they found out I was trying to learn about my real parents."

"You could be selling your family short, Jane. It's only natural that as an adopted child you'd be curious about who your birth parents are. Surely in this enlightened day and age they would understand—"

She shook her head vehemently, cutting him off in mid-sentence. "I will not hurt my family."

And that was that. Her stubbornness was apparent in her husky voice, her steady gaze and the tight clench of her square, bruised jaw. The woman wasn't about to budge.

Damn, what was a man supposed to do faced with a woman who could be so obstinate and yet so incredibly appealing at the same time? He decided this man was going to take another sip of his coffee. And try to reorder his thoughts and feelings.

"So, you're in San Francisco to find out about your biological parents. What were you doing walking around Fort Point so late at night?"

"When I arrived at the airport I rented a car, drove to my hotel and called Riddle Investigations. The receptionist arranged an appointment for today with Sam and Scott Lawrence, the owners. Then I had some dinner and decided to just drive around. I ended up at Fort Point, and the rest you know."

"So your rental car is back at the Fort Point lot?"

"Yes. But the key to it, and my coat, shoes and purse are either at the bottom of the bay or washed out to sea by now. I had to shed them to keep afloat. Was your car the Jaguar?"

He nodded.

"Did you see a Toyota Tercel or any other cars when you returned to your Jaguar?"

"No, but I wasn't looking. My attention was focused on other things."

Her forehead furrowed into a frown, and the next words she spoke were more or less to herself. "Yours was the only other car I saw in the lot when I pulled in. Whoever came up behind me and threw me into the water must have either driven in later or they were already there."

How could she discuss this so calmly? Someone had attempted to murder her! He leaned across the table and put his hand on her arm.

"Look, Jane, you have to report this. Do so anonymously if you insist, but report it. If you don't, I'm going to have to. You may not be the only victim of this man or men. Your silence could endanger others. You understand that, don't you?"

She appeared to be studying his face, and that guarded look was back in her eyes. He hadn't a clue what was going on behind it. Then finally she smiled and seemed to completely capitulate.

"Yes. You're right. I wouldn't want anyone else to become a victim because I failed to speak up."

"Then you'll report the incident?"

"Later. Anonymously, as you suggested. From a pay phone."

He leaned back in his chair, only momentarily placated as he reconsidered his own suggestion.

"You might as well give them your name, Jane. You're going to have to contact your family, anyway."

"Why do you say that?"

"You said you lost your purse in the sea. How are you going to get back into your hotel room without your room key, and how are you going to drive around without a driver's license? And what about your credit cards? Or am I wrong in thinking they are also gone?"

As the reality of his questions sank in, a momentary shadow crossed her lovely face.

"Damn. I forgot about that. Oh, well. I guess I'll just have to make do."

He shook his head in disbelief.

"Make do? You're in a strange city, without money or identification. You've got to call your family. Explain things to them. You might be surprised at how understanding they'll be."

She shook her head with a new vehemence. "No. Noah, I told you. I can't call my family."

"But how are you—"

"I have some cash tucked away in a drawer in my hotel room, enough to get me by for a few days, anyway. The hotel already has all the information they need to bill my credit card. So does the car rental place. I'll just tell the desk clerk I lost my key. I'll tell the car rental place the same thing, of course, and explain that the car is at Fort Point. They can pick it up there."

"But you can't rent another car. You've lost your license, too, remember?"

"I'll take taxis. Once I put this business back in the hands of Riddle Investigations, I won't really need a car. They'll be the ones doing the running around."

"But none of this is necessary. You can come back another time to find out about—"

"No! I'm not going to go back not knowing. It was difficult for me to arrange to get away this time without questions. I won't live with this uncertainty anymore. I need to know...now. Look, Noah, I realize your heart is in the right place, but you needn't be concerned. This is just a minor setback. I'll be fine."

A minor setback? She'll be fine? Noah had known a lot of self-sufficient women in his time, but none who would have termed being deliberately thrown into San Francisco Bay and barely escaping with her life a minor setback.

This lady was getting more unpredictable and fascinating by the second. Heaven help him.

"I would like to use your phone to call Riddle Investigations, if you don't mind. They're on Geary. Near Franklin. Is that a toll call from here?"

"Doesn't matter. You think I'm the kind of a knight in shining terry cloth who would demand reimbursement from the fair damsel in distress?"

She smiled as she got up and took the phone from his hand. "You've really been . . . very gallant. I'll try not to tie up your line for too long."

"Don't give it another thought. The only people who have this number are AT&T, MCI and Sprint, and I'm holding out until one of them gets desperate enough to offer free maid service as a promotion."

Her smile followed him out of the room, but he noticed that she didn't punch in her call until he was out of earshot.

"YOU MISSED THE STREET," she said. "You should have turned right back there."

Noah shot her a quizzical glance. "How do you know? I thought you just arrived in San Francisco yesterday?"

"I studied a map when I rented the car and learned some of the more prominent landmarks and streets. See Coit Tower up there on the left? That's Telegraph Hill. My hotel is the Harbor Court at the end of Market Street between Mission and Howard. Due south."

"Okay, I'll take the next right if it's not one-way. Got to deliver the damsel safely back to her castle if I'm to live up to my billing."

She could tell he had liked being given the knight image. He seemed to find it amusing, as if it were a new role for him, which it probably was. This attractive bachelor with a sexy smile, who was also a globe-trotting tennis star, was probably so surrounded by women he hadn't had much opportunity to notice—much less rescue—any distressed damsels before.

"I take it you and your steed haven't lived in the city long?"

"A week. Give or take a few hours."

"And no one but the long-distance telephone companies know an internationally famous tennis star has taken up residence. Which must mean you came here to get away."

"Actually, just the opposite—to get in touch."

His answer confused her, and he seemed to sense that. His small laugh was directed at himself as he downshifted the Jaguar into Second to take the next right turn.

She wanted to ask him to explain, but she held back. She reminded herself that there was no reason to try to find out any more about him, and there were lots of reasons not to.

She forced her eyes away from that nice profile of his, trying to tell herself that as soon as she said goodbye to him in a few minutes she'd forget all about him. She had to. He had nothing to do with this mess.

And what a mess it was. Certainly nothing like she had anticipated. What in the hell had last night been all about? Why hadn't Scotty answered the phone this morning? Where was he?

She took a deep breath and let it out slowly. Worrying wasn't going to help. She concentrated on looking out the window. It was a lovely September day in San Francisco— warm, brilliantly clear and still. Summer had finally broken through the fog that had held the city hostage through most of the previous months.

"When is your appointment?"

His question caught her off guard. "Appointment?"

"With Riddle Investigations. The one you made yesterday for today."

"Oh, yes. Of course. Ten-thirty."

"It's just about nine-thirty now. I'll wait for you while you change, and then drive you to your appointment. Afterward we'll get some lunch, and you can let me know how things went."

She tried to make her voice sound as dismissive as possible. "Thank you, but that won't be necessary."

He ignored the coolness in her tone and kept his own light and playful. "Save on taxi fare. Besides, I've always hated getting involved with a story and then not knowing what happens at the end.''

''The end?''

''When you locate your real birth certificate and find out who you are. Who knows? It might turn out that your parents were visiting royalty who were traveling incognito when they disappeared twenty-eight years ago. Then I can tell everyone that I met a princess. Or, it might turn out that they were heirs to a fabulous fortune that had gone unclaimed until you were discovered. Then I can tell everyone that I met a billionairess.''

''You have a very vivid imagination.''

''Plus, those socks you're wearing are sentimental favorites of mine. I don't intend to lose them.''

She looked down at the borrowed socks peeking out of the bottoms of her corduroy slacks. They were brand-new, passionate pink argyles that were far too large for her. These were his sentimental favorites?

''You're kidding, of course.''

''On the contrary. Those socks, Miss Williams, represent a bet I lost. Had my career not taken such a sudden, unexpected turn, I would have been wearing them at my next match.''

She smiled as her eyes skidded across the brazen pink color. That would have been something to see.

''What was the bet about?''

''I bet my manager that a lady who knocked on my door one night, looking for something she lost, had the wrong room.''

From the disreputable grin on Noah's face, Jane guessed that despite what he'd said about losing the bet, the lady really hadn't lost anything in his room.

She looked out the side window of the Jaguar. The sky was the color of a refreshing blue mint. Natives lined the busy sidewalks in their shorts and T-shirts and smiles. ''I suppose you can't wait to get back into condition so you can get out on the courts again.''

Her question was greeted with a slight but significant pause that brought her eyes back to his profile.

"I won't be playing tennis anymore. Not professionally."

His voice was not quite as playful. But, even so, it remained even, his expression calm.

Her eyes darted to his forearms, exposed because of his rolled-up blue shirtsleeves. Her scrutiny confirmed that the pinkish, puckered scar snaked over his left arm. He followed her eyes and answered the question before she could ask it.

"I'm left-handed."

Of course he was. She'd seen him wield his cereal spoon with his left hand and raise his coffee cup to his lips with it. Still, she was reluctant to accept the meaning in his words.

"You're going to be all right."

"Month or two more, the bone will be like new and I'll have nearly ninety percent of my strength back."

She understood. No use pretending she didn't. "Except professional tennis requires a hundred percent."

"And then some."

He flashed her a smile, his warm eyes clear and unconcerned. Their message was unmistakable. He'd lost his profession as well as his friend. Yet, somehow, he'd confronted these life-altering realities and come completely to terms with them. As she faced the full force of that strength in this flesh-and-blood man, she found it more than impressive. She found it amazingly arousing.

Quickly, she looked away.

Damn. She'd always been a sucker for a really gutsy guy, the kind who could take life's blows, even those below the belt, and still walk away straight and tall. She knew she shouldn't have been so inquisitive. Why had she asked all these questions?

Good thing they were about to part company. Damn good thing.

He drew up to the front of her hotel. When he started to get out with her, she rested a restraining hand on his arm.

"This is where we say goodbye, Noah. I have your address. I'll send the socks back. Now I—"

"I'm seeing you to your room."

It was a statement, not a question. He was out of the Jaguar and had handed his keys to the parking attendant before she was able to even form a protest on her lips.

She exhaled in frustration. He wasn't going to make this easy.

She led the way into the hotel, a former YMCA, which had been transformed into one of the Embarcadero's newest, cushiest upscale establishments, with sparkling water views of the Oakland Bay Bridge.

The luxurious lobby—spreading nearly two thousand square feet around a cast-stone fireplace, was full of men and women in dark blue business suits sipping coffee and making deals on the overstuffed sofas and chairs of muted greens, beiges and corals.

She felt their glances, all finally coming to rest on her bright pink shoeless feet. Then she felt Noah's arm slipping inside hers for a reassuring squeeze. She looked up to catch the smile in his eyes, the grin lifting his lips. *Brazen it out,* he seemed to be saying.

In her mind she could see his long, lean legs running across a tennis court in these socks, with fans crowding the sidelines and cameras rolling and that grin on his face. A private smile played at the sides of her mouth.

She stepped up to the desk and explained in a courteous but nonapologetic voice that she had lost her purse and would require another key to her room.

The young, neat desk clerk sent her a smile.

"I'd be happy to produce a duplicate key, Ms. Williams—" then he added in a voice that sounded like someone committing an act of questionable taste "—but I will need to see some identification."

"My identification was in that purse I lost. Surely someone must remember me registering yesterday?"

His brow sprouted a regretful frown.

"I hate to inconvenience you this way, Ms. Williams, but the man on duty yesterday left on vacation. I'm sure you understand that these rules are for the safety of all. I must protect our guests from theft and improper intrusion into their rooms by any unauthorized individual. I'm afraid that without proper identification—"

"Take mine," Noah said as he stepped forward. He handed the desk clerk his driver's license and two credit cards.

"I'll vouch for Ms. Williams and indemnify the hotel against any loss. Both American Express and Visa have sufficient limits to cover any—"

"Noah Armstrong! Of course. Forgive me for not recognizing you, sir. If *you* wish to sign an acceptance of liability in case of—"

"That won't be necessary," she interrupted, quickly handing Noah back his identification and credit cards. "If you will call Riddle Investigations, a local private investigative firm, they will vouch for me and indemnify your hotel against any loss."

She gave the clerk the number. He nodded as he stepped away to use the phone.

She felt Noah move close to her side. He lowered his voice so it wouldn't carry. "You look angry. I was only trying to help."

She let out a small sigh. "Yes, I'm sure of that. And I also recognize the fact that there aren't many knights running around these days willing to rescue damsels in distress both from drowning and the establishment."

"Then why didn't you let—"

She turned to look up into his eyes. "Noah, when you were in the hospital after the accident, did your injuries make it difficult for you to do everyday things for yourself?"

"Yes."

"Can you remember how it felt when a hospital employee had to bathe you?"

His answer emerged through gritted teeth. "Yes."

"But you submitted because you had no choice, right?"

"Right."

"Imagine how much more difficult it would have been if you were perfectly capable of bathing yourself and someone still insisted on doing it for you."

He nodded. "What you're saying is that's how I just made you feel."

"Thank you for understanding."

"Well, let's just say I'm beginning to understand that living up to this knight-in-shining-terry-cloth role is a bit more complicated than it looks."

She smiled up at him.

"Ms. Williams?"

She turned back to the clerk. "Yes."

"Riddle Investigations was most eager to vouch for you. Here is a duplicate key. Please let me know if I may be of further service."

She stood beside Noah as they took the elevator up to her floor, feeling as though she was in a hole next to his impressive height. Six foot three, at least. This was quite a man—in many ways.

It was getting harder to say goodbye by the second. Still, hard or not she had to steel herself to do it. She knew she'd have to find words that would be effective—words he wouldn't be able to argue with. She knew what words they'd have to be.

She went over them in her mind as they stepped out of the elevator and walked down the hallway to her room. She approached the door, inserted the key and pushed the door inward. She stood facing inside silently for a moment. She did not like having to say these words, but she knew she must.

She gathered her resolve and took a deep, reinforcing breath.

But when she swung around to speak to him, every rehearsed word instantly fled her mind. Because behind Noah, bearing down on them both, marched two familiar-looking men with guns drawn.

Chapter Three

Noah took one look at the expression on Jane's face and whirled around...right smack into the long barrel of an enormous pistol. Behind it stood a stocky man with dark eyes, a pinched face and an unmistakable sneer. His voice echoed the sneer.

"Get inside. Both of you. Now!"

Noah found himself being pushed backward by this belligerent man, who barely came up to his chin. He would have liked to have argued with the order, but one didn't argue with a hand-held cannon the size of the one shoved against his chest. A second look had confirmed that its extra length was due to the silencer on its end.

As he stumbled backward, Noah groped for Jane, hoping to keep her safely behind him, out of the direct line of fire.

But another man had circled around and grabbed Jane's arm. This man was tall and thin, with light wispy hair and a long face. He, too, wielded a pistol with a silencer on the end.

"Get 'em up!" the dark man ordered.

Noah's heart raced as he raised his arms. Adrenaline squirted into his muscles, making them vibrate from lack of physical release. The door closed behind the four of them. The shorter man locked and bolted it, all the time keeping his gun and eyes on Noah.

Thugs—in expensive suits, no less. From the looks of them, crime certainly did pay. What did Noah have in his wallet? Two hundred dollars? Half a dozen credit cards? Would that satisfy these creeps?

"Who are you?"

The guy wanted to know his name? This wasn't exactly what Noah envisioned when a mugging came to mind.

The short dark man moved threateningly closer. "I said, who are—"

"Noah Armstrong."

"What are you doing with her?"

A couple of things became quite clear to Noah at that moment. This was not a mugging. These men were specifically interested in Jane. Noah had always been known for thinking and moving fast. A tennis player who couldn't move fast, both mentally and physically, didn't make it as a pro. He'd made it. Now he just had to hope that these thugs weren't tennis fans.

"I'm with the San Francisco Police Department. Miss Williams is under protective custody. The other two undercover officers will be here any moment."

Not a bad bluff. For a moment, just a moment, Noah thought it might even work, as a flicker of alarm flashed in the dark eyes. But then the next order came.

"Turn around."

There wasn't much Noah could do but comply. He felt the brief punches up and down his body that served as this man's idea of a frisk. Since he was wearing pretty snug-fitting old jeans and an equally snug-fitting light blue cotton shirt, it should have been pretty clear he wasn't carrying a weapon. But this guy wasn't taking any chances. After he'd finished the weapons search, he pulled Noah's tennis ball out of his shirt pocket with a look of puzzlement and then lifted his wallet from his back pocket.

Noah took advantage of his new position to check on Jane. The tall, thin man had her stiff, resisting body drawn

to his side, his gun pointed at the side of her head. Her face
was white as chalk, her eyes enormous, bright, glassy.

Shock—she must be in shock, he thought.

"He's no cop, Vance," the sneering voice said from behind him. "The address on this driver's license is on Bel-
laire Street in North Hollywood. That's Southern California. Looks like she's latched on to a tourist."

A rough hand grabbed Noah's arm and spun him back
around. "You made your move on the wrong woman,
tourist."

"Look, I don't understand. What's this all—"

"Shut up."

Noah had no choice, since the pistol was now pointed
right at his mouth.

"What's the best way to handle this, Marty?" the other
man called from behind Noah.

The sneer never left Marty's face, nor did the wariness in
his dark eyes. "It's a good thing we decided to break into
her room to see what she left behind. Take her into the
bathroom. Somehow she managed to get out of the bay. See
she doesn't manage to get out of the tub."

"What about him?"

"We'll think up something for our tourist here later."

There was no mistaking the message in those words. The
adrenaline in Noah's body began to explode through his
arteries. These men were obviously the ones who had tried
to kill Jane the night before, and if he didn't act quickly,
they'd certainly succeed in finishing her off now.

He turned his head slightly to see Jane out of the corner
of his eye.

She was still stiff as a board, her eyes glassy, staring
straight ahead. Vance was forced to literally drag her into the
bathroom. Noah's heart constricted inside his chest.

"Eyes front and center, tourist!" Marty barked at him as
he scraped the pistol's barrel against Noah's cheek.

Noah brought his attention back to the face of his tor-
mentor. He had hoped Jane would at least try to resist

Vance, considering how spirited a fight she'd put up against him. But the awful knowledge of what these men intended must have sent a numbing fear through her body, reducing her to a virtually catatonic state.

His thoughts raced. An opening—any opening—that's all he needed. But he needed it now. He could hear the water gushing out from the faucets into the tub, and the grumble of complaint from Vance as he tried to pry the clothes off her stiff, uncooperating body. Then suddenly the bathroom door slammed shut.

Marty jumped in response. For a fraction of a second his eyes darted toward the bathroom door. Noah saw his chance and took it. His right hand came up and batted the gun out of the man's hands. Then, as hard as he could, Noah slammed his fist into Marty's jaw.

Marty crumpled to the carpet without even a peep. Noah didn't waste a second more on him. He leaned down, grabbed the gun and moved toward the closed door of the bathroom.

He could hear the water still gushing into the bathtub full force. Vance couldn't have heard the scuffle between him and Marty with that rushing water so near his ears. All Noah had to do was slowly turn the knob, push the door open and hope to hell Jane wasn't in the line of fire.

He gripped the pistol tighter in his left hand and reached forward with his right, intending to grasp the knob. But before he could seize it, he saw the knob slowly turning of its own accord.

He had just enough time to move out of the way before the bathroom door swung open and he found himself face-to-face with the business end of Vance's gun.

But it wasn't Vance on the other end of that gun. With an audible sigh Jane lowered the pistol.

"Noah. Whew! What a relief. I almost shot you. Give me a minute. I've got to shut this water off."

She swiveled then, set the gun on the rim of the tub and leaned over to turn off the spout.

Noah dropped the pistol to his side, his hand shaking, feeling almost dizzy with relief. At the same moment he was having trouble believing his eyes. Jane was all right. Perfectly all right.

He stepped into the bathroom and nearly tripped over Vance, who lay unconscious, sprawled haphazardly across the floor tile, a trickle of blood coming out of his nose.

Jane shut off the water and straightened beside Noah. Her eyes were bright, her cheeks flushed. She looked victorious and so very different from the glassy-eyed victim he'd seen only a moment before. He wondered if he could be hallucinating.

He drew her into his arms, feeling the warm, reassuring reality of her, hugging her to him in overpowering relief. She smelled of the soap and shampoo from his shower. But the familiar smells were mixed with her own distinctive scent, as exotic and mysterious and unpredictable as the woman herself.

He rested his cheek against her hair, feeling its silky softness as it rustled in his ear.

"Jane, I'm so relieved you're all right."

He felt her relax against him for the mere measure of a heartbeat before she drew slightly back to look into his face.

"I'm rather relieved to see you're okay, too, Noah."

As he watched her say his name this time, he forgot everything but how much he wanted to kiss those lips. He leaned toward her, watching that intent register in her eyes. For one wild, mad moment excitement and desire swirled there. Then it was quelled and her guard returned. She stepped back.

At the same moment disappointment filled him, he realized she was right. This was hardly the time or place.

"Jane, what happened?"

"You mean to him? Oh, he tripped. How did you manage the one called Marty?"

"His attention got diverted. Which is not what is going to happen to me. Now tell me, Jane, what exactly went on in here?"

"Noah, I don't know how long this guy is going to be out. I think we should continue this conversation after I get some shoes on, my stuff packed, and we're blocks away."

She leaned away from his hands, which were still resting on her shoulders, ducked under his arm and wiggled past him. Noah followed, certain he couldn't have heard what he'd just thought he had.

"Blocks away? Jane, we can't leave here. We have to call the police."

She took a quick look at Marty's unconscious form, stepped over it and proceeded to the closet. She slipped her feet into a pair of white running shoes and leaned down to tie the laces.

"I already told you, Noah, I can't go to the police."

"But surely that was before you found out that these men were actually trying to kill you. *You*, Jane. Not some nameless woman walking alone at night down at Fort Point. You can't expect me to believe you didn't hear what they said."

She yanked a light beige Windbreaker off a hanger and shoved her arms inside.

"I didn't need to hear what they said. When they turned up here I pretty well figured out they had to be the ones."

With one hand she yanked her remaining two outfits off their hangers and with the other she picked up a medium-size flowered suitcase off the floor of the closet. Arms full, she marched over to the bed, threw the suitcase onto the bedspread, flipped open the suitcase and unceremoniously dumped her clothes inside. Then she moved to the light wooden dresser.

"How could you know these men were the ones? I thought you told me you didn't see who threw you into the bay?"

She yanked open the top drawer.

"I didn't. But I recognized them as the two men who followed me from the airport yesterday, so it seemed to fit."

"Wait a minute. You didn't tell me you'd been followed from the airport."

She grabbed a thick black belt from under a sweater in the top drawer, pulled open a secret pocket fastened with Velcro and quickly counted the bills sticking out from it. She answered him in a somewhat preoccupied tone.

"I didn't know it mattered then. I wasn't sure it was the same men."

Noah's tone ascended into the realms of incredulity. "You didn't know it mattered? You weren't sure it was the same men? Two men follow you from the airport. Then two men throw you into the bay. And you couldn't make the connection that it might be the same two men?"

She slipped the belt around her waist, fastening it securely. "I thought I'd lost them. Besides, I told you, I didn't see who threw me in. I wasn't even sure there were two of them. It could have been someone else."

"So what you're telling me now is that maybe other people, in addition to these two, want to murder you?"

She paused from her emptying of the contents of her dresser into her suitcase to shrug her shoulders, her voice maddeningly even. "One never knows."

Noah let out a disbelieving breath. How could she possibly be standing there packing so calmly and talking so crazily at the same time?

"Jane, what in the hell is going on? Who are these men?"

"You know as much about them as I do."

"This doesn't make any sense."

She threw the final contents of the drawers into her suitcase, closed it and spun the combination lock. "Agreed. And I'm ready to discuss its lack of sense on our way out of here. Come on. Let's go."

Noah dropped the pistol he still had in his hand onto the bedspread and grabbed her shoulders to stay her retreat.

"Jane, we are not leaving here. We are calling the police and we are waiting until they get here. And when they do, we're going to tell them everything that's happened."

"Noah, I know you think that's the logical thing to do, but— "

"Not just the logical thing to do, it's the only thing to do. What's more, it's what we're going to do. Jane, listen to me. These men have tried to kill you twice. They belong behind bars, and we're going to put them there and then let the authorities sweat the reasons for this madness out of them."

She shook her head. "It's not that easy."

"Of course it's that easy. These men tried to kill you! Twice! If they go free, they'll probably just try again. Don't you understand that? Aren't you afraid?"

"Yes, I'm afraid."

And he could see the fear in her face, creating small white lines about her mouth and between her dark eyebrows.

"But that doesn't change anything," she added.

And he could see that, too. The stubbornness in her eyes and that square chin underlined her words and then some.

Noah was so frustrated he could barely get his words out. "Look, we can't just walk out of here. These men must be stopped. You may not care if they go free, but I'm not about—"

Her eyes flashed with instant sparks of blue-hot fire.

"Not care? I'd like to see these bozos behind bars forever. I'd call the police if I could. But I can't. Not now. If I contact the police and stay here to tell them my story, then I'll jeopardize everything I've been trying to do. Please, Noah. You must believe me. There are other things at stake here. Things you know nothing about."

"Then tell me about them."

"I can't. Not now. We've got to leave now, while we still have the chance. Please, just believe me when I say that these things are very important."

"Are they more important than your safety?"

Her pause was deliberate as she looked directly into his eyes. "Yes."

She meant it. Heaven help her, she meant it. And heaven help him for the feelings that kept surging through him every time he looked into those eyes. He grasped her arms tightly, stared into that lovely, serious face and prayed he could get through its shield of stubbornness.

"Jane, I can't accept that there's anything more important than your safety. I can't let you go. We're staying and seeing this thing through—both of us."

"You got that right, tourist."

Noah swung around so fast at the unexpected sound of the voice behind him that he could feel the whiplash in his neck. The sight that met his eyes caused a sharp pain to shoot through his stomach.

"You know the drill. Get 'em up."

Noah stared at the gun pointed at his chest. During the time he and Jane had been arguing, Marty had come to, gotten to his feet and sneaked into the bathroom to retrieve Vance's weapon.

As Noah saw it, he had only one chance. His eyes immediately dropped to where he had laid the other pistol on the bed. But Marty's eyes followed.

"Don't even think about it, tourist. I'd blow your hand off before you were halfway there."

Noah quickly glanced at Jane. She stood stiff and immobile beside him, glassy eyed, just as she'd been when Vance had held the gun at her head. Once again, she was like the helpless doe caught in the headlights of the hunter.

Noah tasted the acrid bile of recrimination rising up his throat. He'd let her down. If only he had hit this thug harder. If only he had tied him up. If only he had called the police right away. If only he had let Jane go when she wanted to, she might be safe now.

Not one of those if onlys was going to help them now.

"So you sneaked up on Vance, did you, tourist? Aren't you just full of surprises. Okay now, you two are going to back up. Step away from the bed and the gun. Hug that far wall with your backs. Then come this way. We're going to change positions here. You get the picture?''

Noah nodded, knowing he must play for time. He faded back as directed but noticed that Jane stayed rooted to the carpet by the bed, still holding on to the suitcase she had packed.

Marty's eyes swept over her, taking in her rigid stance and glassy eyes. His voice filled with growing impatience. "Move her or I shoot her."

Noah grabbed hold of Jane's stiff arm and gave it a gentle tug. Jane didn't resist. She came on command, like a stiff marionette without a will of her own. Noah felt another sharp pain in his stomach.

"That's right. Nice and slow now. No sudden moves. Any sudden moves and I'll shoot. Believe it."

Noah kept moving, very slowly as ordered, but his mind was racing, desperately trying to weigh the options.

"Look...Marty, isn't it? We can make a deal. I've got money. Name your price."

"I've already got a deal."

The implication of the man's words caused a chill to run up his spine to the back of his neck.

"Are you saying someone hired you to kill this woman?"

"I'm not saying nothing to you, tourist. Come on. Keep together. Keep her moving."

Jane's stiff body had begun to resist Noah's tugs. She was almost a foot apart from him now. Noah tried to bring her a little closer. She moved in jerky little spurts.

Noah watched carefully for any opportunity to present itself. But in light of his earlier mistake, Marty was playing it safe and staying on the opposite side of the small room, his pistol pointed at Noah's chest, his eyes glued to Noah's every move.

Noah understood that the man wouldn't be giving him another opening. There was only one thing to do—and Noah had to do it while there was still just one of them to contend with. He would have to rush Marty, drawing his fire, and then delay him long enough for Jane to escape . . . and pray she came out of her catatonic state long enough to recognize that she could escape.

Noah got himself ready, carefully calculating the distance between himself and the pistol-toting man. He knew he'd have to make his move at the point when they were closest to Marty. He would let out a loud yell and lunge at him, doing his best to grab the guy's arms and knock him down, if at all possible.

He didn't think about the fact that he was probably facing certain death. All he thought about was giving Jane a chance to get away safely.

He'd make his move on the count of three.

One . . . two . . .

But Noah never got to three. Because suddenly everything began without him.

A floral pattern swung past his peripheral vision as Jane's suitcase hurtled by. Marty's hand jerked upward and fired. His first shot blew a hole through the suitcase and then the ceiling, echoing in Noah's ears as a distinctive pop and hiss. His second shot struck the suitcase's metal seam, literally blasting the suitcase apart.

Noah didn't give the man time for a third shot. He leapt at him, knocked the gun out of his hand, straddled his supine body and proceeded to pound the thug's face with his fists. This time he intended to make sure he hit the bastard hard enough.

When he finished, Marty was out cold and Noah was shaking and winded, both from the physical exertion and from the release of the enormous amounts of adrenaline coursing through his body.

He felt spaced out and unreal. He only came back to himself when he felt Jane's hand on his shoulder.

"Noah? Are you all right?"

He turned and raised his eyes to hers. She gave him a look that was warm and glowing with admiration and more. He

felt the residual heat of that unspoken message surge
through his body. His hand covered hers where it rested on
his shoulder.

"Jane, I—"

She looked away immediately, withdrawing her hand and
cutting him off. Her words were clipped, nervous. "I just
checked on Vance. Looks like he'll be out a while longer.
I've dumped their pistols in this pillowcase, which I'm taking with me. You can stay if you want to, but I'm leaving."

She was already halfway to the door by the time he'd recovered. "Jane, wait."

She paused and looked at him over her shoulder. Her
cheeks were flushed with determination. Gone was the
warmth and admiration in her eyes; in its place was a sharp
impatience.

"Noah, I promise you that if you stay and talk to the police, they'll never find me to verify your story. And if you try
to keep me here, I'll deny everything."

And she meant it, too. That husky voice was attached to
the will of a woman who should have stood ten feet tall.
Where was the quiet mouse who had just been in such a
catatonic state of shock?

That's when the reality of what had *really* happened in
this hotel room finally hit Noah.

Jane had never been in shock. Not the first time when
she'd been dragged into the bathroom, nor the second time
when he had all but dragged her across this hotel room.
She'd been playing possum. She'd done it with Vance when
she had stiffened her body and somehow made the man trip,
and then again with Marty when she had deliberately lagged
behind on their slow retreat across the room, waiting until
the right moment to throw her suitcase at the man. It was
the only explanation that made sense.

Her azure eyes watched him from the depths of a cool and
quiet mystery. His first impression when he'd awakened that
morning to find her in his arms was that she was quite a

woman. He was only now beginning to appreciate how accurate an impression that was.

"Noah, I won't wait any longer."

And she wouldn't. She was crazy and reckless and stubborn and the most infuriating woman he'd ever met. Who knew what appalling secrets she kept? Who knew what she might do next?

Noah couldn't wait to find out. He took only a moment to dig through the unconscious Marty's pockets to retrieve his wallet before jumping to his feet.

"I'm ready. Let's go."

HER MIND WAS LIKE a tennis match in progress, with possibilities volleying back and forth. She barely paid attention to the streets as they rose and dipped before them. Noah had remained quiet, too, since they'd fled the hotel.

She stole a glance at him. His strong hands rested on the steering wheel. Fresh blood caked the abrasions on his knuckles. She licked the corner of her mouth as worry dried her lips. She should never have let him come up to the room. Now they knew his name and face.

Still, selfishly, she had to admit that if he hadn't been there, she might not be sitting here now. She very much doubted she'd have been able to escape from two of them.

Noah being with her had no doubt saved her life... but had he forfeited his own?

She took a deep breath, exhaling slowly. She told herself he'd be all right. He'd said no one knew he was in town. His driver's license had an address in Southern California, and they had assumed he was a tourist. They'd look for him in the registries of the hotels—as they must have looked for and found her.

Only they wouldn't find him—not in a vintage Victorian on Union Street.

She'd get the goodbyes over at the earliest possible moment, send him firmly back to his safe life and forget what his clear amber eyes had said to her back in that hotel room when he discovered her beside him, safe and unharmed. She'd forget it all and get on with what she had to do.

Resolutely she looked straight ahead again, but saw little out the window. She was still shaking inside, her stomach churning out pure acid. She consoled herself with the fact that two such close brushes with death—three, really if she counted both attempts in the hotel room—in two days were enough to give heartburn to even the stouthearted.

How stout was her heart? Could she really go on like this, after last night and this morning? She thought she'd been prepared for anything, but hired killers trying to drown her was a bit more than even her imagination had supplied.

And now that it was all over, she could barely believe it had happened. A funny kind of laugh bubbled in her throat. She couldn't understand how she could possibly be laughing. Was this the beginnings of hysteria? She immediately covered the laugh with a cough. Still, an odd, crazy kind of exuberance tingled in her cells.

Then the source of these strange feelings dawned on her— she had survived. She had faced the worst and survived. She'd kept her head and had done the right things. That was relief bubbling in her throat, life singing through her veins. That was *life* that tasted oh, so sweet!

Her attention was drawn to the cable car riding beside them. Several passengers stood on the outside steps, hanging on tight, despite the fact that there were seats inside to accommodate them. Those riders who were hanging on for dear life wore a different look from those who sat securely inside. Their faces were flushed; their eyes were bright. She understood that look. A part of her had always understood it.

"Jane, you made some pretty strange and outlandish statements back in that hotel room. Are you ready to explain what it's all about now?"

Her attention was drawn back to his face—his very nice, sane, normal face. Her fingers were still grasping the pillowcase holding the two pistols.

"Noah, we're on California Street. I know how to get to Geary and Riddle Investigations from here. And since I'm already running late for my appointment… I appreciate all you've done, more than I can say, but I'm afraid I'm going to have to ask you to let me off at the next corner."

"What?"

"Drop me off and drive away, Noah."

"You're kidding, of course."

"I've never been more serious. You don't know what's really going on, and for your own sake, it's best that you never find out."

He looked at her quietly for a moment, and the force behind the look gave her a glimpse at the kind of fierce competitor he'd been. It sent a small jolt of surprise through her.

"Jane, listen to me and believe what I say. I intend to find out what's going on. After what just happened back in that hotel room, I have a right to a full explanation. I was a witness to attempted murder, yours and mine. I should have called the police immediately. I didn't. I'm still not sure why. What I am sure of, however, is that we're in this together now, whatever this is."

"You don't understand."

"On that we both agree. But whether you agree or not, I'm sticking like a lover until I do understand."

Like a lover? She looked away from the sincerity in his eyes as the inappropriateness of her exciting physical responses to that image registered on every synapse firing in her brain.

"Noah, please. I don't want *you* hurt. I don't want to hurt you."

"You don't have to worry about me getting hurt, Jane. We knights in shining terry cloth are made of stern stuff. I'm not dropping you at some corner to fend for yourself. I'm taking you to Riddle Investigations. *And* I'm going in with you."

"No, you can't go in. I have to handle this alone."

"Jane, this has gone way beyond convincing a desk clerk to give you a duplicate key. I'm not letting you face this alone. And whether you like it or not, I'm not going away."

Oh, hell. He meant it. He was the worst kind of stubborn fool—the chivalrous kind. She gripped the ends of the pillowcase tighter and exhaled an exasperated breath.

"All right, Noah, let's see what we can do to compromise. You take me to my appointment, but I go in alone. That part is not negotiable. Afterward, I'll explain."

His expression told her that he was clearly not used to compromise. But the ensuing moment of thoughtful silence also told her he was considering it this time.

"Over lunch."

"I can't promise—"

"Over lunch. Otherwise, no compromise."

She sighed. Damn, he was an obstinate man. Still, she'd gotten him to agree on the most important point.

"All right. Over lunch."

"Good. Which way to Riddle Investigations?"

"Turn left at the next intersection."

NOAH WASN'T GOOD at waiting. For forty minutes after Jane disappeared up the stairs of the Georgian brick leading to the second-story offices of Riddle Investigations, he'd paced up and down the block more than a dozen times trying to burn off pent-up energy.

When she finally reemerged into the late-morning sun, the pillowcase and its contents were gone, and she was licking the corner of her mouth, a mannerism he'd begun to realize signaled some significant worry.

"Jane, what is it? What went wrong?"

She looked up at him and forced a small smile.

"Nothing's wrong. They're going to handle everything for me. They're even going to let me stay at their place here in the city until they find my birth certificate and trace it back to my family. I told them I'd be back just as soon as I thanked you."

Noah stiffened. "Thanked me?"

She held out her hand, her husky voice resolute with added solemnity.

"You've been wonderful, really. But everything is in capable hands now, and they need me upstairs right away to get things started. There are so many details. I'm sure you don't wish to delay them. I know your address, so I'll be sure to send the socks back to you. Goodbye, Noah."

Chapter Four

Goodbye?

Noah took her offered hand, capturing it between both of his.

"We had a deal. I was promised lunch and an explanation, and I can assure you that I'm getting both."

He felt her hand in his, trying to slip away. He held on to it firmly. She squinted up at him in the bright sun for what seemed like a very long, calculating moment.

"In a week or two I could maybe come by and—"

"No. Not in a week or two. Now. You can't put me off again. I won't let you. Even if I have to kidnap you to do it, I'm taking you to lunch and finding out what the hell all this crazy business is about. Accept it."

She sighed. "I was afraid you were going to say that."

"You were right. Now we're going to march right back up those stairs and tell your investigators that we'll be back after lunch."

Something unspoken skittered across her face so quickly he wondered if he had imagined it.

"That won't be necessary. I told them if I wasn't back right away, they should assume it was because I wasn't able to talk you out of lunch."

Noah shifted his hold on her arm, as he urged her toward the car. He opened the passenger door and started to help

her in. She got in hesitantly, and finally leaned back in res-
ignation.

Noah quickly circled the Jaguar to the driver's side, still
not sure she wouldn't bolt out the passenger door at any
moment. And if she did, would he give chase?

Hell, yes. He pounced into the driver's seat, rammed the
key into the ignition, shoved the stick into First and shot out
of the parking space before she could even think of attempting an escape. No, he was not going to let this woman
get away.

After he drove a couple of blocks and it looked as if she
was willing to remain a passenger—albeit a fidgety one—he
began to relax a bit. But the quiet between them now was
uncomfortable, full of the tension of unasked and unanswered questions.

He tried to focus on the task of finding the right place for
this lunch. "I know how to get to the restaurants around
Ghirardelli Square, but the ones I've tried there didn't im-
press me."

"Let's head in that direction, anyway. Maybe we'll get
lucky this time."

She pointed to one she said looked good, and Noah pulled
into its parking lot. Her instincts proved right. It had three
decks, with walls of windows facing the bay so that every
seat in the house had a dazzling view.

Noah slipped the maître d' ten dollars. The smiling,
heavyset man led them past a crowded room to a small, se-
cluded table for two on the upper deck. It proved warm and
sunny, a perfect complement to their dual orders of cool,
lightly seasoned spinach salad laden with superbly poached
salmon.

All through lunch Noah could sense her preoccupation
with faraway thoughts, even as she seemed focused on her
food. He waited until she consumed the last tasty bite and
brought her still-full glass of white wine to her lips.

"Explanation time, Jane."

She set down her wine and began fingering the glass, her eyes seemingly intent on its contents.

"I told you this morning about how my biological parents had died in a bus accident back East and that I was here to find my birth certificate. But there are a few things that I neglected to mention."

"So I gathered from your comments back in that hotel room."

Her tongue quickly licked the corner of her mouth as a frown formed between her eyebrows.

"It seems I'm going to have to start over in order to fill in some of the blanks."

"All of the blanks, Jane."

She neither agreed nor disagreed with his correction. She just kept circling her index finger around the rim of her wineglass, as though searching for a way out of the circle. Then finally she dropped her finger and let out something that sounded like a sigh of frustration. She continued to stare at the wine.

"My adoptive parents were a couple already in their fifties when I was placed with them. They died when I was barely twenty-one."

"Wait a minute. You mean to tell me your adoptive parents are dead?"

"Yes."

"Then what were all these impassioned declarations about how you couldn't tell your family about your search for your birth parents because you were afraid of hurting them?"

"My adoptive parents weren't the family I was referring to, Noah. The family I've been trying to keep ignorant of my quest is the family I married into six years ago—my husband's family."

Husband? Noah couldn't have been more stunned if the roof had suddenly collapsed onto his head.

A husband . . . she has a husband.

No. Impossible. She couldn't be married. He didn't feel this way toward married women. His next words carried an accusatory note he couldn't hide. "You're not wearing a ring."

She shifted in her seat, spread her hands and looked at her fingers as though noticing they were bare for the first time.

"It must have come off in the bay last night. I've lost weight recently, and it was a little loose. I kept meaning to have it resized."

Noah picked up his glass of wine and took a healthy swig. He could feel the hot pulse jumping in his veins. He was angry—very angry. She should have told him. She shouldn't have led him on.

She didn't lead you on, you fool. You've been leading yourself on.

It was a bitter realization, but he was too honest to deny it. She hadn't done anything intentional to capture his affection or prolong their relationship. On the contrary. She had tried to say goodbye to him. Several times. And he hadn't taken the hint.

Seems he was one of those guys who has to get hit over the head before anything gets through. Well, he felt the lump on his noggin now.

She still stared resolutely into her wineglass, purposely avoiding his probing eyes. He looked at the dark chocolate richness of her hair, the warm cream of her skin, the lips that could say his name with such a smiling caress.

Married . . . damn. Even in his wild, reckless youth, when he'd done his best not to disappoint the many women wanting to sleep with an internationally known tennis pro, he'd drawn the line at the married ones. And now, at this time in his life when he particularly wanted to eliminate waste, do nothing unimportant, he gets mixed up with a married woman.

What a joke. He tried to school his voice into a civil tone, knowing instantly he was only partially successful.

"So, you have a . . . family." He couldn't bring himself to say *husband* yet. When had he become such a coward?

"Yes."

"Any kids?"

She lifted her eyes to his, and he could actually feel the regret in them.

"A son. And he's really the reason for all this, if you still want to hear about it. But if you'd rather just get up and leave now, believe me, I'll understand."

He could tell that she knew all about his disappointment and the reason for it. That warm, husky gentleness in her voice was just like what he'd heard when she'd come to ask if he was all right after he'd knocked Marty unconscious.

That moment when she'd touched him on the shoulder, looked into his eyes, then turned away from what had passed so briefly between them.

Just as he should be turning away now. Noah actually came very close to getting up right then and leaving. Every ounce of self-preservation urged him to.

But another emotion—even more compelling—kept him in his chair. He pushed away his nearly full glass of wine.

"So what's the story?"

She looked away from his eyes and shifted uncomfortably in her seat. He noticed that since her first sip, she hadn't drunk any more of her wine. She was keeping a clear head, so she could keep her emotions in check—the same as he'd just decided to do.

Her eyes gazed at a distant point over his shoulder. Then her detached voice, strung into a monotone, began to relate the events of her life like a paid announcer reading from a cue card.

"When I became engaged six years ago, I told my fiancé about my having been adopted. His family was uneasy with the blank spots on the birth certificate of an adoptee. When Riddle Investigations supplied me with a normal birth certificate of a Jane Williams, born in San Francisco of a middle-class, gas-company engineer and his homemaker wife, my fiancé's family withdrew their overt opposition to the marriage.

"The wedding preparations began. The invitations went out. Then the telegram arrived from Riddle Investigations explaining that the birth certificate supplied to me belonged to another Jane Williams."

"Wait a minute. Are you telling me you learned you had the wrong birth certificate *six years ago?*"

"I didn't want to upset everything and reopen my in-laws' concerns, so I didn't show that telegram to my fiancé or his family. We married and a year ago we had a son."

Her pause was poignant, considering what followed it. "Only, something is wrong with little Charles. He's sick most of the time, seemingly without cause. The doctors have begun to wonder if it's something he's inherited."

Noah leaned forward and rested a hand on her arm. She stiffened slightly beneath his touch, but she didn't move away. He wondered how she had managed to maintain that monotone voice—so distant from the pain these discoveries must have brought.

"What can be done for him?"

"The doctors are trying to discover the answers. But they have a long way to go. If they are right, and he's inherited something, then they need the family profiles on both branches of the genetic tree in order to trace it."

Noah nodded as his understanding expanded. "Which is why you decided to conduct a new search for your birth certificate in order to trace your family."

"Yes. I went through genetic testing a month ago. It didn't supply any answers. Researchers still know very little. The genetic mapping of the human being is still very much in the beginning stages."

"What about your husband's side?"

"His family tree is well documented on both sides. As he saw it, there was no reason to take the test."

"Even so, I don't understand why your husband can't help you in this search to find your natural parents."

"My husband still doesn't know that the birth certificate I presented to him and his family six years ago isn't really mine."

Noah studied her face for a sign of distress, a sign of any emotion. He found nothing but a placid steel shield. This was one controlled lady. Only the tenseness beneath his fingers gave her away.

"Why haven't you told him?"

"I could have told the Charles I married six years ago, but I couldn't tell the man he'd become after our son was born."

"How has he changed?"

"The illness drew me to my son's side. I looked to Charles for support, but coping day to day with his son's devastating disease became more than he could take. A few months ago he suffered what at first appeared to be a severe case of gastric distress, but which the doctors later diagnosed as a complete nervous breakdown."

"What's the prognosis?"

"The doctors try to be positive, but they seem worried."

"How old is your husband?"

"Thirty-five. He's stopped practicing law. He rarely leaves the house now. Even the smallest amount of stress seems too much for him. He breaks into tears every time he sees his son, so he just doesn't see him. That's why I couldn't tell him about the birth certificate. I knew he couldn't cope with the news."

And all the burden had fallen squarely on her shoulders. No wonder she kept them so straight—were she to relax them, the weight might crush her. Noah tried to keep his voice even.

"So you decided to come to San Francisco alone to locate your family tree."

"First I went to my attorney, Judith Fitch. Her father handled my adoptive parents' affairs for years, and she took over after his death. I felt I could trust her with the truth."

"But?"

"But when I told her about Riddle Investigations and the wrong birth certificate, she seemed quite uncomfortable with my confession. She told me she'd have to think about helping me in the matter. At first I thought her reaction was only because such an investigation wasn't the normal thing a client called upon her to do."

"At first. What about later?"

"Within hours after I visited her she'd called to tell me she couldn't handle the matter. She didn't even bother to offer an explanation. When I tried to press her for one, she told me it would be much better for me to live in the present and forget the past. Then she all but hung up on me."

"If I were you, I think I'd consider looking for another lawyer."

"I'm tied to Fitch because she's the administrator of the trust fund left to me by my adoptive parents. But, yes, I certainly won't be going to her for any other matters."

"Did you try another attorney?"

"No, next I went to a private investigator in New York."

"Why not New Jersey where you live?"

"I didn't want my family finding out. The firm came highly recommended. Its senior partner was all smiles and cordiality. He took my retainer check with a promise to do his best. The next day he returned my check by messenger. A short note paper-clipped to it said he was sorry, but the firm would not be able to take my case after all."

"No other explanation?"

"I called to ask. The secretary told me no one was available to take my call. She told me that same thing morning, noon and afternoon for three days straight."

"Strange."

"It gets stranger. On the third day after I visited the New York P.I. firm, I got a threatening letter. It was typed on plain white paper and mailed in a plain white envelope. It had a New Jersey postage mark. It said that I'd better stop trying to find out who my parents were and just learn to be happy with the ones on my bogus birth certificate. It was unsigned.''

Noah felt something like a hand with very cold fingers creeping up about his spine. He once again tightened his hold on her arm.

"You have any idea who sent that letter?"

"No."

"Who knew the birth certificate you presented to your husband's family wasn't yours?"

"At that time just Riddle Investigations, my trust attorney, Judith Fitch, and the New York P.I. firm."

"At *that* time. You've told other people since?"

"You and Great-Aunt Melissa."

"Who's Great-Aunt Melissa?"

"She's my husband's great-aunt. I met Melissa at a mall when we were both reaching for the same Stephen King book. We hit it off right away. It was while visiting Melissa a week later that I met Charles."

Noah released his hold on her tense arm and leaned back in his chair. He didn't want to hear the story of how Jane met and married her husband. Accepting that this woman was tied to another man was still beyond difficult for him.

"What did Great-Aunt Melissa say when you told her about the first birth certificate not being yours?"

"I don't think she minded. She's not overly concerned with appearances, like Charles's parents are. But she did mind when I told her I was planning on coming to San Francisco and contacting Riddle Investigations again."

"Did you tell her about the threatening letter?"

"No. I didn't want to worry her. She was worried enough about my plans to reopen the investigation. She refused to loan me any money for the trip. In fact, she did her best to talk me out of it."

"Why did you have to go to her for money? Didn't you say something about having a trust fund from your adoptive parents?"

"Yes, I do. And separate bank accounts and credit cards my husband set up for me. But right after I received the anonymous threatening letter, all my funds suddenly became unavailable to me."

"Even from your parents' trust fund?"

"I had just received that monthly check and deposited it in the bank. The next day all my funds in that bank account were frozen."

"How could that happen?"

"I called the bank. They told me that the account had been closed. When I asked them where my money had gone, they said that they didn't believe I was who I said I was and that they couldn't discuss the matter further."

"Did you go in person, with identification in hand?"

"No, the bank's in New York. My son had gotten ill again. He needed me by his side. I couldn't get away."

"What about your credit cards?"

"Each one told me the account had been closed. They, too, refused to discuss the matter with me over the phone."

"What did you do?"

"I told Charles about my difficulties. The news just seemed to drag him down even more. I appealed to my in-laws, but they just brushed aside my concerns."

"They ignored the fact that you had no money?"

"My mother-in-law told me to just relax, that I didn't need any money, since she paid for all the household expenses."

"You live with your in-laws?"

"It's not always comfortable, particularly with Loren and Victoria—those are Charles's parents—always trying to control my life. But it's traditional."

"Traditional? I don't understand."

"For old families to all be under the same roof. Charles's brother, Gerard, also lives with us. Only Melissa has her own separate cottage and that's only because she got thrown out of the main house years ago. I can't complain that our privacy isn't respected, though. We were given our own wing at the estate right after the wedding."

"Estate?"

"Yes. I suppose I should have mentioned this sooner. It's part of what makes this all so difficult. My in-laws are wealthy, obviously. And they're very well-known. My married name is Jane Williams Tremont. My father-in-law is Judge Loren Tremont. Perhaps you've heard of him?"

Noah could barely believe his ears. He shifted forward in his chair.

"*The* Judge Loren Tremont? The one who's just been nominated to the Supreme Court? The one who will be sitting before the Senate in a couple of weeks to go through the confirmation process?"

"I see you have heard of him."

Noah knew this lady was full of surprises, but he was still having trouble believing how many she'd thrown at him in less than twenty-four hours. He fell back in his chair, feeling positively winded from this one.

"The Tremonts of New Jersey. Probably one of the most wealthy and influential families in America. One that can really trace its roots back to the *Mayflower!*" Noah said in astonishment.

"So the family picture gallery would tend to support."

"Jane, is the prominence of your family and your father-in-law's important appointment the reasons you haven't wanted to go to the police about these attempts on your life?"

"I don't ascribe to my father-in-law's dictum that the Tremont name must be preserved above all else. Certainly not at the sacrifice of my life."

Noah let the breath he'd been holding escape his lungs. At least the lady had that priority in order.

"But your reluctance to contact the police can't be because of that bogus birth certificate. Surely you'd tell your husband and in-laws the truth that it belonged to someone else if you had to?"

"No, I very much doubt I would."

"What?"

She was watching his face carefully as she answered, still using that disembodied tone—uninvolved and unemotional.

"That anonymous letter I told you about threatened that if I didn't leave well enough alone, the real secret surrounding my birth would be revealed to everyone, and that secret would ruin not just my life, but the life of my son."

Noah digested her words for a moment, trying to absorb all their implications. That icy hand was creeping up on his spine again.

"Ruin your life and the life of your son? It said exactly that?"

"Yes. And that is the reason I can't go to the police."

"But you can't know for sure—"

"Noah, I can't take any chances. I have to assume that whoever wrote that threatening letter is serious. I have to believe that some horrible truth surrounds my birth parents—one that can reach through the generations to hurt my son. And since I must assume that's true, I must also assume that police involvement could expose that secret."

He noticed she hadn't referred to anything about how the letter writer had also threatened to ruin her life if the truth came out. Her focus seemed totally on the protection of her child.

Was it that protective maternal instinct that generated the focused strength in her eyes and straight shoulders?

"But if you think the writer of that threatening letter could be serious, why are you still insisting on investigating?"

"First of all, if it means possibly saving my son's life, then I *must* find out the genetic background of my real parents. Secondly, I must find out the truth, quietly and discreetly, because if there is some terrible secret swinging like a pendulum over the head of my child, then I must discover what it is. I can't just sit back and hope it never descends to harm

Senate in two weeks, you should have no worries about being presented with any surprises."

"No? You think the senators won't be looking at *all* the members of my family?"

Gerard looked all too at ease despite his father's challenge—that infuriating, enigmatic smile just lifting the sides of his mouth. Loren recognized at least two of the Tremont traits in his younger son: the deep green eyes ringed in black and the rigid backbone.

"So, Father, you want me to delve into our Calamity Jane's doings, too, is that it?"

Loren Tremont shifted his erect posture on hearing his daughter-in-law's name, as though even the vibrations associated with the sound could inflict a glancing blow.

"Her affairs should have been at the top of your list! All those weird people whom she has made her friends. All those disreputable places she dragged Charles off to until he finally found the sense to say no. No telling what that woman might have contributed to or even joined. Talk about a Pandora's box of possible embarrassments! When I think of all the other women available six years ago—"

"But you forget, Father, Jane wasn't just available. She made it obvious from the first moment she saw Charles that he was what she wanted. You know how compelling that kind of focused attention from a beautiful woman can be to a man."

A small spark twinkled in Loren Tremont's deep green eyes as youthful, tangent memories intruded. When he caught the dint of Gerard's lazy, mocking look, Loren had the uncanny feeling that his younger son had all too accurately read the contents of those memories, despite the fact that logically he knew that was impossible. Loren coughed to clear both mind and throat and brought his thoughts forcibly back to the issue at hand.

"That's what concerns me most. Jane's feelings for Charles have always been excessive, possessive and obsessive. It's unnatural, unbalanced, un—"

"Tremont?" Gerard provided.

Loren watched that lazy, appraising expression in Gerard's eyes that seemed so taunting and so much a part of him. He shifted on his feet again, determined to keep his irritation in check.

"Jane's behavior is very un-Tremont. Only it took too long for Charles to finally see what his mother and I have been telling him about the woman. And just when I had him talking to the attorneys about a nice, quiet divorce, he gets sick!"

That damn enigmatic smile lifted the sides of Gerard's mouth again. "You have to at least give Jane credit for the care she's given her son and her husband since their illnesses."

"Do I? As far as I'm concerned, they'd be better off with professional help. Every nurse your mother has engaged for our Charles or little Charles, Jane has dismissed, insisting on caring for them herself. She won't even let the cook take them their meals, intercepting her on the stairs and taking their trays. Why, I've even heard Jane whistling on her way in with their trays, like she was enjoying it! It's obsessive, excessive behavior, Gerard."

"Charles seems to appreciate it."

"Charles is too sick to take the stand he should and get rid of that woman. I tell you, Gerard, I only wait for the day when he recovers to get him back on board with that divorce. And in the meantime, I want you to review every one of Jane's canceled checks."

"How am I supposed to get access to—"

"How do you think? Ask her for them, of course. She can't be so obstinate as to fight us on this."

"If she were here, she might not. But have you forgotten that she's at that children's hospital in Boston for most of the week?"

Loren Tremont's normally unshakable composure slipped slightly as he felt the heat of irritation pouring into his cheeks.

"Damn, that's right. Who knows what she might get into now that she's no longer without funds."

"You knew she was having trouble with her accounts?"

"Of course I knew."

Loren watched his younger son shift forward quite suddenly in his chair, a very quick and uncharacteristic movement.

"Father, are you telling me you were the one who deliberately had Jane's bank account closed and her credit cards canceled?"

Loren Tremont raised himself to his full six-foot-two-inch height and looked down in disdain at the man who had the gall to ask him such a question.

"I'm telling you no such thing, Gerard. I learned of it when Jane complained to your mother and me about the matter. Not that it wasn't cause for rejoicing. The less money that woman has, the less trouble she can get into. From your knowledge of the matter, I take it you had a hand in getting her funds released?"

"When she came to me about it."

"You didn't do your family any favors. You should have talked to me about it first. I'm the head of this household."

"You expect her to cause trouble in a Boston hospital while she waits to hear the results of her child's tests?"

"I've come to expect the worst from Jane, no matter where she is, and she seldom disappoints me. The best way to deal with the woman is to anticipate and block those things that will cause the worst damage. What are you shaking your head and muttering about?"

Gerard's shoulders and back slowly relaxed themselves into his distinguishing slouch.

"Nothing important. Look, about those canceled checks. Her rooms aren't locked. I could—"

"No, you could not. Ask Charles to find her checkbook for you and any other pertinent papers. I won't have you rummaging through her rooms while she's gone. We will do this the right way."

Gerard shook his head once more.

"And what is that continuing look of disapproval about?"

"You draw the line at some funny edges, Father."

"I draw the line between right and wrong. There is nothing funny about that edge."

"Since those terms carry the crispness of your definitions, obviously not."

Gerard said the words blandly enough. But Loren Tremont could feel the disapproval in his younger son's irritating smile. Yes, Gerard was strong, but if he couldn't be made to see things clearly, to what avail would that strength be?

"Loren! There you are!"

Loren's attention was immediately drawn to his wife's raised voice coming from the entrance to the library. Victoria Tremont's face was atypically flushed. Her tall, elegant figure sailed into the room on a cloud of expensive perfume and all-too-evident outrage.

"Do you know who is in my drawing room this very moment? Do you know the kind of position Jane has put me in? Yet again?"

Loren Tremont had no doubt he was about to find out. Damn that daughter-in-law of his. If it was the last thing he ever did, he was going to be rid of her!

THE IMPACT OF JANE'S LAST words flashed across Noah's face, though he fought to hide his surprise.

"Jane, you're serious? You really think your father-in-law could be behind this craziness?"

"I have to consider the possibility. I have to ask myself who is threatened by my learning the truth."

"You believe the truth could threaten Judge Loren Tremont?"

"If some dark secret surrounding my birth thirty years ago could so threaten me and my child, it would certainly also threaten my in-laws, since we are part of the family. And the most celebrated member of the family—the one who stands to lose the most from any scandal because of his position and upcoming appointment—is the honorable Judge Loren Tremont."

"But couldn't this letter writer be someone wanting to discredit your father-in-law, perhaps someone who plans to jeopardize his chances for appointment to the Supreme Court?"

"If whoever sent this threatening note wanted to try to use whatever information he has about my past to hurt my father-in-law, then why try to prevent me from learning the truth? Surely if I learned it and exposed it, I'd be doing the person's dirty work for him, wouldn't I?"

"Good point."

"No, only someone in the family could be trying to stop me. Desperately trying to stop me."

He nodded. As awful as it was to contemplate, in light of what she'd just told him, so many other things made sense.

"Desperate is the word, all right. Someone with a lot of money had to have hired those two thugs in expensive suits."

He watched her face when he said the words. She didn't flinch. She'd understood this, faced it and accepted it—by herself. Life demanded some pretty terrible tolls and this lady had paid them.

"Do you really suspect your father-in-law?"

"I have no favorite suspect in the family at the moment. Loren, Victoria, Gerard—none of them wanted me to marry Charles."

"But you don't suspect your husband?"

"It's hard to think Charles capable of such deeds. But then, until I heard what those men had to say this morning in that hotel room, I would not have thought any of the Tremonts capable of having me . . . killed. Now I can't afford to trust any of them. Not even Charles."

Her mouth didn't quiver. Her eyes didn't blink.

How had she been able to master the emotion of these shocking events and appalling conclusions?

The same way he had learned to accept the loss of his friend and his profession. Because it was the only way to survive them. And, like him, she was determined to survive no matter what came. That realization gave him his first real feeling of comfort since she'd begun her story.

"Where is your son?"

"He's at a children's hospital in Boston, undergoing some very sophisticated tests. A friend, someone I trust completely, is with him. She's about my height, age, coloring. She changed clothes with me in the ladies' room at Kennedy Airport and took my place on the plane to try to confuse anyone who might be following."

"You suspected someone might be following you even then?"

"The week prior to coming here, I felt I was being followed every time I left the estate. And I had the uncomfortable feeling my telephone calls were being monitored. I didn't want to take any chances."

"What did you tell your family?"

"That I'm staying at the hospital in one of the rooms provided for family. The trip afforded me just the right opportunity to slip away without anyone knowing. At least, I thought no one would know. Apparently, one of them does—the wrong one."

"Won't your in-laws stop by to see how you and the boy are doing?"

"No. My father-in-law's nomination to the Supreme Court has them all scurrying around in preparation. Besides, little Charles's illness has had him living in hospitals for most of his brief life. My in-laws stopped showing up after the first few months when they began to realize there was no easy fix."

"They sound like a cold lot."

"I hope you realize that my descriptions of them are skewed by suspicions."

"Mine would be, too, if I thought one of them was trying to kill me. But even before this business, not visiting a small, sick child—"

"They're not a family that deals with weakness or illness well. My father-in-law has difficulty relating to anything that doesn't involve a legal precedent. My mother-in-law is a true blue-blood socialite, jumping energetically onto the fundraising bandwagon of the latest cause, but emotionally unable to bring herself to even enter the nursery where her grandson sleeps. And as for my brother-in-law, Gerard, all he cares about is money."

"And the boy's father?"

"The birth of our child brought us closer together. But then little Charles and his father became ill. Now my time is divided between caring for them both. Even the mention of his son brings on an anxiety attack. I think Charles just wishes all the problems would go away. Maybe he believes if he can remain detached from them long enough, they will."

There was no bitterness in her voice, her face, or her eyes. She was giving him the facts, nothing more or less.

"What about Great-Aunt Melissa, Jane? I notice you didn't include her in the list of suspects."

"She's quite unlike the rest. Very loving and supportive. She'd be at the hospital every second by the boy's side if I'd let her."

"But you don't?"

"She's well into her seventies and suffers from a severe case of arthritis. I won't subject her to the physical and emotional stress of those long hours waiting for test results that generally just bring bad news. Of course, sometimes she shows up anyway."

"Will she this time?"

"She might, but I doubt it. She knows I'm not really there. I told her where I'd really be when I tried to borrow the money for this trip."

"So she knew you were coming here?"

"I can trust her not to give away my whereabouts. And she understands that these tests for little Charles require him to be unconscious most of the time, so even if she was there, he wouldn't know it."

"You said earlier that your accounts had been frozen, even your credit cards invalidated. How did you get them cleared?"

"I finally went to Gerard when appealing to the other Tremonts failed. Gerard studied finance, not law like the rest of the family. He acts as liaison with the accountants and financial managers in charge of the family money. He made several calls and straightened it out."

"What was there to straighten out?"

"Gerard said someone with the same name as mine had apparently died, and instead of the deceased's accounts being tagged, mine were. Anyway, he managed to clear my bank accounts within hours. I got new credit cards in the mail within a few days, just in time for me to make the trip."

"You actually *believe* this computer-error thing?"

"Seems too coincidental, considering it happened right after I received that threatening letter. No, I believe someone deliberately reported me dead."

"To scare you or to tie up your funds in order to prevent you from pursuing the truth about your birth?"

"Possibly both."

"And when this person found he couldn't stop you, he sent those two goons after you."

"They were waiting for me when I arrived in San Francisco. I know they weren't on the plane. I took an extra precaution by using only my maiden name when I booked the flight, checked into the hotel and rented the car. But these men were obviously given enough information about me to know to check under Williams, too. They spotted me at the San Francisco Airport.''

"I'm surprised you spotted them.''

"I didn't at first. But I got lost in the airport parking lot, and when I noticed the white Mazda behind me kept making the same wrong turns, I got suspicious.''

Noah took a moment to digest everything Jane had told him. The daughter-in-law of the renowned and respected Judge Loren Tremont was on a quest to find a dark secret surrounding her birth and had paid assassins on her trail. If she hadn't been sitting across from him now, if he hadn't heard and dealt with those men with his own fists, he wouldn't be able to accept a word of this incredible story.

He took a deep breath and let it out slowly and deliberately.

"This must be one hell of a secret surrounding your birth.''

"So it seems.''

Calm, collected, in total control of herself—this was one hell of a woman.

"Jane, I know you said Great-Aunt Melissa is elderly and friendly, but it sounds to me like she's the only one in the family who knew you were heading for San Francisco to pursue this matter.''

"I understand the implication, but it's difficult for me to think that elderly woman who has shown me nothing but kindness is behind these attempts on my life. She's not like the others. Family name and such mean nothing to her—a philosophy she expounds frequently, much to the family's chagrin, I may add.''

"All right, who other than Great-Aunt Melissa knows you're in San Francisco?''

"I told no one else.''

"What about the friend who's at the hospital with your son?''

"I'm trusting her with my son's life, Noah. Does that answer your question?''

"Does she know about this birth certificate business?"

"Other than those people I named earlier, no one else knows about my search for my biological family."

"Okay. What about the lawyer, Judith Fitch?"

"I don't know what you mean."

"You told her the truth about your earlier birth certificate not being genuine. You asked her to look into the matter for you. Don't you think that she might have figured it out that you would take things into your own hands and come to San Francisco yourself?"

"I suppose she might have suspected I would."

"And if she did, she might have called someone in the family and warned them."

"Who? She didn't have any ties with the family except through me."

"Did she handle your adoption?"

"Her father did. He's deceased now. He worked with a San Francisco lawyer, Desmond Edelson."

"San Francisco? Didn't you tell me the bus crash took place back East?"

"Yes. A little town in Vermont."

"And you were adopted by a couple from New Jersey?"

"Yes."

"So where does this San Francisco lawyer come in?"

"As I understand it, he coordinated the adoption with the child welfare services here. My adoptive parents explained that since I told everyone I was from the city with the red bridge everyone called golden, the San Francisco authorities took responsibility for me."

"Did you ever try to get in touch with him or the child welfare services?"

"When I was eighteen I asked my adoptive parents to help me try to discover what I could about my birth parents. I had seen my adoption papers, of course. Mine was not the kind of adoption that required secrecy, as many did and still do. My adoptive parents had their attorney, Walton Fitch, arrange a court order through the San Francisco attorney,

Desmond Edelson, who had handled the adoption at this end, to release the child welfare files.''

''Any response?''

''Everything they had came through Edelson in response to the court order. I read it over and over, but there wasn't anything new there. They knew only what I had told everyone at the time I was orphaned. That my name was Jane Williams. That I was two years old. And that my mother and I had lived where there was a golden bridge that I thought looked red.''

''If the San Francisco police did try to find your family, why weren't they able to uncover the birth certificate for Jane Williams that Riddle Investigations found?''

''Riddle Investigations believes that they really didn't try very hard. It was simpler for them to turn me over to child welfare and let them handle it.''

''So why didn't child welfare find that birth certificate?''

''Apparently, no one came forward to claim me after all the stories in the media. Tracing other relatives would have taken time and effort. As I understand it, they were soon contacted by Desmond Edelson, representing my adoptive parents, offering to provide a home for me, a solution that eliminated the need for further effort.''

''Placing an orphaned San Francisco child with a family in New Jersey seems a bit unusual, doesn't it?''

''Yes, but explainable. My adoptive parents were older and very well off. They told me they had tried to adopt a baby, but had been turned down because of their age. The only reason they had a chance at me was because I was already two when I was orphaned and most adopting parents want an infant. Even so, they confessed that they had to make a few 'extra contributions' to those who had arranged for me to be placed with them.''

''You mean they bribed someone to get you?''

''The acceptable age of an adopting couple was pretty well etched in stone then. Still, whatever the circumstances surrounding my adoption, I did find a warm, loving home.

And even if a few legal corners were cut, they don't seem germane to the real mystery, since the real mystery is who my biological parents were. And what it is about my birth that could possibly threaten my son.''

''Or, more precisely threaten your anonymous letter writer. It all comes down to that, doesn't it? Until you get hold of your real birth certificate and use it to track down that family of yours, you won't know what you're up against.''

''Yes. And that is what Riddle Investigations will do for me, Noah. They will discover that secret, and they will act as my bodyguards in the interim. So you see, as much as I appreciate your consideration and concern, there is nothing more you can do. The resolution of this matter now rests in their hands.''

She'd said it quietly and firmly in that husky voice of hers. What she didn't say, but implied, was that there was no need for him to be hanging around anymore. And, considering she was a married woman, there was every reason for him not to be.

The waiter sidled up to ask about dessert. Jane shook her head. Noah asked for the bill and put it on a credit card. He wondered what he'd think about all this a month from now when he got his credit card statement.

Would it seem unreal then? Would she?

Hell, it seemed unreal now.

But she didn't. For reasons he could not explain he knew she was more real than anyone he'd ever met.

They walked through the restaurant and out to the parking lot in silence. The view of the bay was impressive, but not as impressive as the woman beside him.

The sun glistened through her hair; a light breeze picked up a few dark strands to play with. She was, without a doubt, physically lovely and alluring. But it was that determination in her husky voice and the way her feet seemed to spring off the ground with each step as she carried that heavy burden that stirred his soul.

Noah deliberately looked away. He wasn't the kind of man to get involved with a married woman. And this married woman had made it quite clear she wanted him firmly out of her affairs. For his own sake, he'd better start forgetting her.

Besides, he had a life to get on with. He had a future to find.

He preceded her to the car and unlocked the passenger door. She looked up at him as she slipped inside, and he caught a brief flash of blue, as cool and mysterious as the first moment he'd awakened that morning to find her in his arms.

It couldn't have just been that morning, could it?

"Will you let me know how it all comes out, Jane?"

So much for his resolve to forget her.

"I'll write you. When I send the socks back."

He closed her door and circled around to the driver's side. He slipped into the seat and pulled on his seat belt. But when he leaned forward to put the keys into the ignition, he found he just couldn't do it.

He didn't give a damn what his logical brain told him. It felt wrong to be leaving her. It felt very wrong.

He twisted in his seat to face her, having absolutely no idea what he was about to say. "Jane—"

"Don't, Noah."

Her face and eyes remained forward. She did not look happy, but she looked resolute. He exhaled a frustrated breath, forced himself to face forward and started the Jaguar.

He joined the traffic pouring past the wharf area, but his pace was slow. He wasn't eager to retrace his route back to Riddle Investigations, because he knew that as soon as he took her back she would be gone from his life.

The Jaguar crawled along. Horns soon blared behind him, and tires squealed beside him as spaces opened up for impatient drivers to shoot past. Several colorful phrases shouted by offended drivers reached his ears.

Noah ignored them. He ignored everything. His focus was on one thing and one thing only.

How was he going to let her go?

"Noah, could you speed up a little?"

Great. Here he was proceeding with anything but enthusiasm, and she obviously couldn't wait to get rid of him.

His hands opened and closed around the steering wheel. "I'm doing the speed limit."

"No one does the speed limit in San Francisco. Besides, at the moment, a ticket is the last thing we need to be concerned about."

Her voice was calm, but it had an underlying quality to it that demanded a glance in her direction. He found her twisted in her seat, looking out the back window.

A twinge of alarm registered at the back of his neck. "What is it?"

"We're being followed."

Chapter Six

Noah checked his rearview mirror. A black Porsche tailgated him. The driver leaned on his horn to show his displeasure at Noah's legal speed limit. Just behind the Porsche Noah caught the brief flash of a white Mazda.

"That's them," Jane's voice confirmed from beside him, her husky tone vibrating through him. "Apparently they were attempting to stay far back, but your slow pace made it difficult for them to keep out of sight."

"Them?"

"Marty and Vance."

"How can it be them, Jane? We lost them at the hotel."

She turned to face him. Despite her relatively even tone, he could see her worried tongue darting at the corner of her mouth.

"That's the same car they were in when they followed me from the airport. Damn. This is my fault. We never should have gone to Riddle Investigations. They must have picked us up there. Noah, we have just one chance. We have to lose them. Do you think you can?"

She felt herself thrown back against the seat as Noah suddenly gunned the Jaguar. She grabbed the door and dashboard and held on. It was a good thing she did. The engine growled as the car dug in with rubber claws, pouncing like a silver cat, hungrily devouring the roadway. They leapt around the vehicles in front of them with swift, feline ease, many occupied by the same impatient drivers who had passed them minutes before.

Nothing passed them now. They were a silver streak of unleashed primitive speed. A roar echoed in her ears as they whizzed by vehicles and buildings alike, all relegated to mere blurs in her peripheral vision. She had driven fast in her time, but nothing like this.

She could feel the raw power of the car and the unerring reflexes within the man behind its wheel. Together they were a determined and dynamite combination—and quite an exhilarating one.

She really wanted to check out the back window to see if their pursuers were still there, but she was afraid to loosen her handholds to do it. They were flying.

A wild screech of hot, disintegrating rubber bellowed in her ears as Noah yanked the wheel into a ninety-degree turn. Her shoulder slammed into the passenger door. They bolted down an alley so narrow she was surprised they weren't scraping the sides. Then they sailed through an intersection full of suddenly beeping horns and squealing tires and leapt into the next alley.

They raced down this one and at its end Noah yanked the wheel into another ninety degree turn at what felt like ninety miles per hour.

They climbed a street that went straight up, accelerating all the way. When the car got to the top it took off into the air and flew fifty feet before touching down again.

And what a touchdown. Her head hit the roof of the Jaguar, even with her seat and shoulder belts securely fastened. The ache in her jaw, which had subsided, flared up in a sharp reverberation through her cheek. She held on for dear life as they careened down the deep incline on the other side, then swung in a screeching arc down the next one-way street . . . going the wrong way.

They dodged head-on collisions right and left at top speed until she feared she was in danger of losing her lunch. Finally she was thrown against the passenger door again as

Noah yanked the wheel left and turned onto the next two-way street.

"I think we outdistanced them," he said.

"I think we outdistanced the space shuttle," she replied, her teeth still rattling.

He flashed her a smile and reduced his speed just enough to allow him to swerve into the driveway of a car rental place, zip behind a line of parked cars and cut the engine.

"Scoot down, Jane."

She scooted, but like him she raised her head just high enough to watch the street in front of them. Less than thirty seconds later a white Mazda went whizzing by.

"Damn. Even with your incredible driving they weren't far behind."

"They're going to start backtracking when they don't find us up ahead," Noah said. "We have to get rid of this car."

He shook his head when he saw the resultant expression on her face. "No big deal. It's leased. Come on, we can rent one here, and I'll use their phone to call the company the Jaguar came from and have them pick it up right where we've parked it. I just need to get my baseball cap and sunglasses out of the glove compartment and we're ready to go."

"Let me rent the new car."

"No. You don't have any credit cards and I very much doubt these places will take cash. Even for one of these wrecks."

One of these "wrecks" actually turned out to be a brand new and very nice forest green Ford pickup, although why Noah had selected it over a regular car she couldn't imagine. They were just pulling out of the parking lot when they saw the Mazda returning up the street, slowly now like a prowling predator, looking for signs of its quarry.

"Get down, Jane."

She did. Noah slipped on his dark glasses and set the baseball cap securely over his hair. He rolled the sleeves of his shirt up even farther until they strained over his well-developed biceps. Next he shoved some gum into his mouth and punched the radio on, tuning to a country music station.

He chewed his gum in time to the beat as he rolled down his window and increased the volume to where she had to put her hands over her ears. She liked country music, but not at these eardrum-splitting decibels.

Still, she now understood Noah's selection of the Ford pickup and his subsequent actions. He was a fast thinker—and mover. If their pursuers drove by and saw him sitting behind the wheel of this forest green truck, blaring out Garth Brooks, she'd bet her life that they wouldn't recognize him.

Come to think of it, she was betting her life.

The worst part about the next few minutes was that she couldn't see a thing from her position on the floorboards. They kept a moderate pace, but she knew danger was not far behind, because Noah never once glanced down at her.

She concentrated on watching his face for any clue as he continued with his simulated sing-along with the loud noises blaring out of the speakers.

And then, finally, Noah turned the radio off and a deafening kind of quiet rang through her ears. Gratefully she removed her hands from the sides of her head.

"It's okay now," he said. "You can get up."

She scrambled into the passenger seat and fastened her seat belt. And just in time, too, because the truck made a forward lurch and took off.

"I thought they might be following us for a couple of blocks, but now I think they were just arguing about what to do next. They just did a one-eighty to retrace their steps. Sooner or later they're going to turn into that rental place and check it out."

"They'll see the Jaguar. They'll find out you rented this car. They'll be after us again."

"Which is why I plan to put as many blocks as possible between us and them while we can. Any preference as to direction?"

"Go right at this next street. I think I recognize it from the map."

Noah let her navigate as he concentrated on twisting in and out of traffic on the streets she directed him to, while at the same time keeping an eye out for a white Mazda behind them.

When he saw another car rental place up ahead on his right, he pulled in and parked around the back.

"Another vehicle?"

"They might know what this one looks like by now."

She nodded. "We have to assume the worst, I suppose. But we can't leave the Ford here for that other rental place to retrieve. It'll be too easy to find us again."

"Which is why you're going to drive it off the lot when I rent a new car. We'll abandon this pickup somewhere else."

"If we leave it in a parking lot near the ferry landing and they track it down there, we might be able to make them think we took one of the ferries over to Marin County."

Noah handed her the keys. "Sounds like a good move. I'll be right back."

Noah had the keys to a red Cadillac Sedan DeVille within twelve minutes of entering the second car rental place. A new record, no doubt facilitated by the fifty he'd slipped the clerk on the side. Everything was going as planned.

But when Jane slipped into the passenger seat of the Cadillac twenty minutes later after parking the pickup near the ferry landing, she had a definite frown on her face.

"What's wrong?"

"If they check back on the leased Jaguar, will they discover your address on Union?"

Noah pulled away from the curb and headed back in the general direction of the city. He didn't have a specific destination in mind, only an urgent feeling that they had to keep moving.

"I did it all by phone. I'm pretty sure the leasing firm used the address off my driver's license because I told them that was my legal address. But they did deliver the car to the house on Union. It must be somewhere in their records."

"Damn."

He said nothing for a moment, but the implications of her question and response buzzed in his head.

"Let's call Riddle Investigations and arrange to meet them somewhere."

"No, we can't."

"Why can't we?"

"Their phone might be bugged."

"Well, since they know about Riddle Investigations, we can't go back there. Since they could find out about the place on Union, we can't go there. As I see it, we have just one option."

"Not the police."

Noah surprised himself. For once, he hadn't even considered the police as an option. But he couldn't ignore the bargaining position her assumption provided.

"Then give me some answers, Jane. How did you know these guys followed us from Riddle Investigations? What did you learn there today that you've kept from me?"

She licked the corner of her mouth as she steadfastly stared out the windshield. Something was wrong—very wrong.

"Jane, come clean or I promise you, bug or no bug, I'll call Riddle Investigations directly and ask. Or, better yet, I'll let San Francisco's finest do the honors after I relate this tale to them."

She threw him a hard glance. He caught it and held on.

"Jane, you've trusted me this far. You might as well trust me with the rest of it."

"This is not about trust."

"No, it's about life and death—yours and mine. I never for a moment supposed we were dealing with anything less. You've put everything on the line to seek out the truth.

Don't you think I've earned the right to at least know what you've found out so far?''

She looked at him a moment more. Then she looked away, straight out the windshield. A long, deep sigh escaped from some inner cavern of her being.

"All right, Noah. What I didn't tell you before is that when I arrived at the Harbor Court Hotel yesterday, the desk clerk gave me a message I thought was from Scott Lawrence of Riddle Investigations. It cautioned me not to call the office because the line might be bugged. The note asked me to meet him in the Fort Point parking lot at ten last night."

"So you weren't at Fort Point to just walk around. You went there for an appointment. And this Scott Lawrence never showed?"

"No. But those men did. I know now that Riddle Investigations never sent me that message because Scott Lawrence wasn't even in town yesterday. Or today. He and his partner, Sam, never got back from St. Thomas in the Virgin Islands where they've been on a case."

Noah couldn't believe his ears.

"No one was at Riddle Investigations this morning? You were up there for forty minutes talking to no one?"

"Actually, I was talking with their receptionist."

"Why didn't you tell me this before?"

"Because I knew if I told you the truth you wouldn't leave. I learned from the receptionist that Sam and Scotty received threatening calls and messages while they were down in St. Thomas. They were warned not to have anything more to do with me or my case."

"And they let those threats deter them?"

"No. They hired a private plane to fly back immediately so that they would be here to help me when I arrived. But their plane is missing. No one seems to know what happened to it or them."

"Why did you pretend to have their help? What would have happened if I had just dropped you off at the corner when you asked me to?"

She turned to him then, that damned determined look in her eyes.

"You would have been out of it, Noah. You could have gone back to your life. They wouldn't have had any way to track you to your local address, because they'd never seen your leased car. But they've seen it now. Now you're in as much danger as I am."

Noah knew Jane was right and a sane man should be fearful. Certainly a part of him was. But overriding that fear was something even stronger, and that was the knowledge that this scrap of a woman had been prepared to fight this battle on her own rather than put him in danger.

Noah pulled over to the curb, put on the emergency brake and shoved the automatic into Park.

He turned to her, his blood racing.

She was married. She had lied to him about the mess she was in. He should be long gone.

But here he sat, looking at that stubborn, beautiful face, his stomach tied in knots, his heart racing as it had only raced when he'd faced his most formidable opponents.

Maybe it was his belief that what she was doing was important that drew him in. Or maybe it was the danger that surrounded her task. Then again, maybe it was the mystery that swirled out of the beautiful, bottomless blue depths of her eyes. He didn't know what, how or why, but he did know the pull was unmistakable. He *knew* that he could not leave this woman—not now.

He leaned over to grasp her shoulders with his hands.

"Jane, listen to me, because this is the way it's going to be. You and I are teaming up to find your birth certificate and trace your family."

"Noah, you can't be serious."

"I've never been more serious."

"But the danger—"

"The real danger in life is wasting it. Look, I'm already deeply involved. They've seen me. They know my name. We both know they can find my local address with a little ingenuity. So what are we even arguing about here? Let's give them a run for their money."

There was surprise in her eyes, genuine surprise.

"How can you say that so glibly in the face of what we've been through?"

He raised his left hand from her shoulder and extended his index finger to gently lift a silky strand of hair resting against the bruise on her stubborn jaw. He was aware of the worry in her eyes, and he felt the squeeze of pressure in his chest because he knew that worry was for him.

"Same way you can admit to the danger you're in so glibly. Because I'm past worrying about what I have no control over."

"But *you* have alternatives. You can fly out of here to the other side of the country. To the other side of the world, even."

His hand dropped back to her shoulder.

"I'm not the kind of man who runs from the game just because the serves are coming at me a little hot and heavy. And I'll be damned if I'll let anyone run me out of town. Besides, if I were to leave the fair damsel in distress with no champion on the horizon, I would most certainly lose my knight-in-shining-terry-cloth union card. You wouldn't want that to happen, would you?"

"Noah, please be serious. There's no reason for you to risk your neck. If you leave San Francisco without me, they'll probably just write you off. And I can disappear into the city's crowds. We both stand a better chance if we split up."

"You don't believe that any more than I do."

She seemed to deliberately load more conviction into her husky voice. "I do believe it, Noah. I'd do better alone and so would you. Now, I know I owe you—"

"You bet you do and I'm collecting."

He saw a new look flash through her eyes and quickly shook his head as he carefully removed his hands from her shoulders.

"No, Jane. Not that way. I'm not going to pretend I'm not attracted to you. And I'm certainly no saint. But I am one of those guys who still believes marriage is an important commitment two people have to live up to."

She nodded, accepting his assurance just like that. Her complete trust in him expanded like an unaccustomed warmth inside his chest and brought even more certainty to his tone.

"Jane, you might as well face it. I'm staying. With you. We're going to see this thing through together."

"But, Noah—"

"No buts. You see, if you don't let me help you, I'm going to the police and the newspapers right now, and they're both getting the complete story of Jane Williams Tremont, her quest to find the truth about her birth and the men who are trying to stop her. And I don't really care whether you verify it or not, because my notoriety as a former tennis celebrity alone will be enough to make them sit up and listen to what I have to say."

"I can't believe you'd really let the media discover a secret that might irreparably damage a sick little boy."

"Don't try strumming my heartstrings with that scenario, Jane. I don't know for certain that they would find any such secret and neither do you. What I do know for certain is that no secret is worth your life."

"You're blackmailing me."

"You better believe it."

After a very long moment she looked away. He could see her desperately trying to find a way out—and failing. Her sigh was like a deflating balloon.

"It seems I have no choice."

He rested his hand on her arm until she looked back at him. "You don't need to look so glum about it. It's all right.

I may be a dirty, rotten blackmailer, but at least I'm on your side. And I'm sticking there to the finish.''

Something that looked a lot like curiosity and another emotion he couldn't quite catch swirled at the edge of the guard in her eyes.

"Why, Noah?"

He gave her arm a small squeeze as his mouth spread into a grin.

"Let's just say you remind me of my first tennis racket."

"A tennis racket?"

He watched the comment confuse her to no end. His grin got bigger.

"I take it that was your first compliment from a tennis player?" he quipped.

Her rigid shoulders relaxed just a bit as the corners of her mouth raised the smallest sliver.

"If anything happens to you, Noah Armstrong, I don't think I will ever forgive myself."

"Believe me, I wouldn't be too pleased, either."

Her smile got reluctantly bigger. "Glad to hear you have some sense of self-preservation left."

"Not to worry. I have heaps. Okay, where do you suggest we start to look for this elusive birth certificate of yours?"

"Well, at the risk of sounding too pedestrian, how about heading for the Hall of Records at the Civic Center, since that's where they house birth records?"

Noah checked his side mirror and pulled out from the curb. "Brilliant. Now, any idea on how to get there?"

"I think we go straight ahead from here."

"Do you have a photographic memory for maps or something?"

She gave him another small smile as mysterious as the azure twinkle in her eyes. "Or something."

THEY PARKED in the Civic Center underground garage and made their way to the Hall of Records and the window labeled Birth Records. While they were standing in line, Noah leaned over to ask her a question.

"Since you don't know the date of your birth, and you don't have the names of your parents, how are you going to ask for the right birth certificate?"

"I was considering that problem myself just now. This bruise on my chin should help. I think the best story is to say that I was mugged, had my purse stolen and received a bump to my head that has given me partial amnesia. Then I'll throw myself on the clerk's mercy."

Noah glanced down the line to the large lady standing on the other side of the counter, her hands planted firmly on her hips as she scowled at the man she was currently "helping."

"I'm not sure this one has any mercy. But I like the mugging and amnesia ploy. Mind if I fly with it?"

She glanced up at him with curiosity swimming in her eyes. Those eyes could certainly be expressive on those occasions when she let her guard down.

"What do you want me to do?"

"Just sit over there on that wooden bench and try to look sort of glassy eyed and vacant. Shouldn't be much of a trick. I saw you do it quite successfully a short while ago."

A flash of something like surprise gave her away before that guard could come crashing down over her eyes.

Ah, so he could catch her off-balance now and then. He was inordinately pleased to discover that. He might as well admit it, he was just inordinately pleased to be with her.

And he was also optimistic about this doubles match they were in. They'd successfully returned three deadly serves from their opponents. Somehow they'd see their way through this danger. They'd find the secret to her past. And whatever it revealed, he'd help her through that, too. And afterward?

His optimism hit the net. He couldn't think about afterward. He could only think about now.

"One quick question," he said as she began to turn away. "What year?"

"Nineteen sixty-three," she replied in a deadpan voice, as if already beginning to enter a catatonic state.

She sat on the wooden bench as suggested, watching everything around her carefully, particularly the doorway where people milled in and out.

Would Marty and Vance check with the offices of Riddle Investigations? Would they know by now that the plane Sam and Scott Lawrence had chartered out of St. Thomas was missing?

Professionals in their nasty line of business would. And after that, professionals would check the airlines to see if she had given up and gone back. And when they found she wasn't on the next flight to Boston or New Jersey, they would start to make other assumptions.

Like she might contact another P.I. firm. Or try to find the answers on her own.

And when they ruled out the others and came to that last assumption, this Hall of Records would be their logical starting place, too. Every second she and Noah spent here increased their chances of being found.

She just hoped to hell that Marty and Vance were still chasing the trail of rental cars, trying to get a lead there. Either that or waiting outside Noah's house on Union. Anything that would keep them busy and give Noah a chance to get through this long line.

And it was long. The hands on the wall clock raced on and yet he seemed to be just inching forward. If she had been a nail-biter, she wouldn't have any left by now.

She was angry at him for insisting on staying around, of course. He'd put himself in serious danger. She kept thinking that she should have been able to discourage him. She'd used every possible argument she could think of.

Or had she? Considering her growing feelings for Noah Armstrong, had she subconsciously not done all she could to deter him from remaining at her side?

She fidgeted on the bench, then went back to watching the clock and, of course, the door. Now was no time to engage in those old self-doubts.

Finally Noah stepped up to the counter and gave the large lady a big smile. The large lady did not smile back.

Noah's and the clerk's heads turned toward her as his hand pointed toward the bench. Jane was appropriately stiff and glassy eyed by then, staring off into the distance as if far removed from reality.

She waited, resisting the impulse to closely scrutinize what was going on at that counter, reminding herself to maintain the glassy-eyed stare, wondering if whatever Noah was saying was working to win over that surly look that the clerk had treated her to so briefly.

Time dragged by so slowly now, it felt as if there was something pushing against her chest, making it difficult to draw breath. She hated not being an active participant in whatever was happening at that counter. She didn't care if Noah had a better chance of charming the clerk. This sitting on the sidelines just was not her style—not anymore.

Finally, from out of the corner of her eye, she saw Noah starting toward her. She maintained her glassy-eyed stare just in case she was still being scrutinized by the clerk, while trying at the same time to see if he carried anything. When he leaned down next to her and took her arm, his hands were empty.

Her rising expectations took a nosedive.

His voice was a whisper as he made a show of helping her to her feet. "Continue the glassy-eyed stare. My story about having found you on the street and being a doctor with the San Francisco Association of the Foraging and Unhoused, or SNAFU for short, was received with a skeptically raised eyebrow. I felt Candy's eyes on the back of my head every step I took away from that counter."

"Candy?"

A small grin lifted his lips.

"The large lady clerk who looks like she could pickle cucumbers just by staring at them. She's rather nice, really. Despite her obvious reservations regarding your amnesia and my medical credentials, she still tried to help."

The operative word here was *tried,* apparently. Jane waited until they were through the doorway and outside the Hall of Records before relinquishing her glassy-eyed stare and asking the question she was afraid she already knew the answer to.

"No luck, I take it?"

He grinned at her as he reached into his pocket and brought out two separate folded pieces of paper.

"Oh, ye of little faith. Candy found two Jane Williamses born in San Francisco during the years 1963 and 1964."

New hope sprouted in her chest as she snatched at the papers. She unfolded the first, noticing immediately the printed words Certificate of Live Birth across the top. She read the now-familiar birth certificate that Riddle Investigations had uncovered six years before made out to Jane Marie Williams. She refolded the copy.

"That the one you found out was bogus?"

She nodded as she put the sheet inside her beige Windbreaker and unfolded the second one, its white lettering bold against a black background. This one she hadn't seen before. She eagerly read it aloud.

"Jane Anne Williams. Born November 13, 1964. Ten forty-five a.m. Mary's Help Hospital. One-forty-five Guerrero Street. Residence of mother, Borica Street, San Francisco. Birthplace, California. Age, 19. Maiden name, Katya Jane Dusart. Occupation, student. Father's name Stanley Russell Williams. Birthplace, Maine. Age, 21. Occupation, cartographer."

"Aha! I knew it. You've got mapmaker genes in your blood."

She looked up and couldn't help smiling at that good-natured grin.

"Actually, I was more interested to learn that Stanley Williams was born in Maine. The bus accident took place in Vermont. That might tie in."

"You're thinking he might have taken that bus trip back there to show his wife and child the old homestead?"

"It crossed my mind. I understand why Riddle Investigations didn't come up with this birth certificate, though."

"How's that?"

"The date of birth. November 13, 1964, is not quite two years before the bus accident."

"Which means?"

"I wouldn't have been two years old yet. If I wasn't quite two, why would I tell everyone I was?"

"I see what you're saying. Still, it might be that your parents told you that you were almost two and the *almost* got lost when you repeated your age to the authorities. Not that I claim to know that much about kids. But my nephew is in the terrible twos and outside of answering every question with 'no' these days, he has a tendency to just pick out the highlights of phrases my sister says to him."

"But would a child barely two be able to give her name as well as her age and add that business about being from somewhere with a golden bridge that really looked red?" Jane asked.

"Good question. I haven't the faintest idea what the answer might be. Do you have any memories of the bus accident or your parents?"

"My mind produces vague images and impressions, but it's very difficult to tell whether they're real or the product of my adoptive parents' later explanation of why my real parents weren't coming back."

"Sort of like the mental scenes being provided to fit what you were told."

"Hmm. Sort of."

"You're frowning, Jane. What is it?"

"I'd like to think that finding the right birth certificate is just this easy."

Noah knew there was a big, unspoken "but" at the end of her sentence.

"Is that the other reason why this birth certificate bothers you? Because it was too easy to find? Would it help if I told you that it took all my powers of persuasion to talk Candy into giving me that particular copy?"

The corners of her mouth raised slightly.

"And you obviously have considerable powers there. No, that's not what's really bothering me. I'm concerned because there's nothing out of the ordinary about these two people."

"Oh, you mean like your mother's maiden name being Hitler or your father's profession being listed as something like anarchist?"

Her mouth curled into a real smile at his dramatic accuracy. "Something like that, yes."

Noah draped his arm across her shoulders as he steered her past some shops in the direction of the parking garage.

"Cheer up, Jane. Maybe when we look into the pasts of these two, we'll find they robbed a federal bank or were the ringleaders of a gang that ripped the Do Not Remove tags off pillowcases."

Her smile broadened. "One can only hope, I suppose. It's been thirty years. Finding relatives won't be easy."

"Any idea where to start?"

"Just the basic, obvious one."

"Well, if it's so basic and obvious, why am I drawing a blank?"

"The telephone directory, Noah."

"Of course. They say genius is simple. Look, there's a group of pay phones on the side of that building over there. They appear to have directories with them."

He was pointing down the street. Her eyes followed to the telephones, but she drew up sharply when they alighted on something else.

"Noah!"

She felt Noah stiffen beside her as he, too, saw the tall, thin man with the wispy light hair and the dark suit coming straight toward them.

Chapter Seven

"Quick, Jane. I don't think he's seen us yet. In here."

"Here" turned out to be a small boutique specializing in women's lingerie. Once inside the glass doors Noah grabbed Jane's hand and dragged her to a carousel of full-length robes near the window, which provided both camouflage and a view to the outside.

They hunched down behind it as they watched Vance pass by and head directly for the Hall of Records. Jane's voice whispered in his ear, sending a warm puff of breath that spread throughout his body.

"It's Vance alone. I didn't see Marty, did you?"

"No. Looks like they might have split up to cover more ground."

"Excuse me, may I help you?"

She was a young clerk with a perky smile, short, bouncing red curls and a very curious light in her hazel eyes as she looked down at the two people crouching so strangely behind the robes.

Jane straightened and surprised Noah by her answer.

"Yes. I need a few things. Darling, you keep looking for that dropped contact of yours while I shop. I may be a while. After you find your lens, perhaps you wouldn't mind watching for that friend of ours?"

Noah nodded obligingly and started scanning the carpet for the imaginary contact lens. But echoing in his ears was how the word *darling* had sounded, slipping out so casually from those lips.

Jane accompanied the clerk to another part of the boutique, their conversation immediately focused on the colors and sizes of items on display.

Noah soon straightened from his crouch behind the robes, but kept as much out of sight as possible as he watched the entry to the Hall of Records. It must have been five minutes later when Vance reemerged. He glanced around, intently studying the couples strolling by. Noah had a strong feeling that the man was actually expecting to catch a glimpse of them.

It didn't seem possible that Candy would tell Vance about Noah's inquiry regarding the birth certificates for Jane Williams. But why else would Vance be looking around like that? After a very long minute Vance seemed to give up. He crossed the street and headed back in the direction from which he had come.

A minute later Jane sidled up next to Noah, a small parcel in her hands.

Her voice was just loud enough to carry to the clerk's ears back at the counter.

"I see you found your contact lens."

Noah turned to her, wiggling his eye appropriately.

"Yes, dear. Our friend has left. Are you ready to go?"

She slipped her arm inside his and they exited the boutique. Once they were outside, they both looked around carefully before beating a hasty retreat toward the underground garage.

"Did you buy something just to divert that clerk's suspicions?"

"And to make sure we were off the street for a while. Not that these underthings won't come in handy. We're both going to have to do some serious shopping for clothes later. But right now I think we'd better get out of here."

Noah drove out of the underground garage a few moments later with what was fast becoming his typical question.

"Which way, navigator?"

"Away from the vicinity of this Civic Center. If we continue in this direction we'll eventually intersect with Geary again. The Riddle Investigations' receptionist mentioned that there was a shopping center at the other end of Geary opposite Union Square. The nice thing about shopping centers is that there is generally a crowd to get lost in. And telephone directories to consult."

They found the latter after parking the car. Jane opened the white pages, and Noah read over her shoulder. They found a page full of Williamses.

"We'll know I'm not the Jane Williams on this birth certificate if we can find her. I don't see a Jane Anne, but there could be a lot of reasons why not."

Noah nodded as he listed them. "She might be married. She might have moved out of the city. She might have just decided not to list her name in the directory. She might even be one of these J. Williamses who decided not to list her complete name."

"There are eleven of those. I only have two quarters. Before we start on the *J*'s, let's see if there is a Stanley Russell Williams listed."

There was one Stanley Williams, no middle name. Jane dialed the number.

"Hi, I hope I have the right party. I'm a schoolmate of Jane Anne Williams, daughter of Stanley Williams. I'm trying to locate her."

Noah watched the expression on Jane's face change as she listened to a brief response, thanked whoever had answered the phone and hung up. She responded immediately to the question on his face.

"No Jane Anne in the family. At least, Mrs. Stanley Williams said there had better not be, since she'd been married to Stanley for forty years and she'd given him only sons."

"So, are we ready to tackle the J. Williamses now?"

"Let's try the Dusart name first. Katya Jane Dusart was listed as Jane Anne's mother, and her birthplace was California. If we're lucky, that might be San Francisco. Perhaps we'll have a better chance of locating the maternal side of the family."

They found four Dusarts. Jane used her last quarter and then borrowed some more change from Noah. She got three nos and one answering machine on which she left a message that she was looking for Katya Jane Dusart and would call back.

"I guess I can't put it off any longer. I'm going to have to call these eleven J. Williamses, one by one. I better go get some more change."

"You start on the first J. Williams, and I'll take care of securing the quarters. I've got to find an automatic teller machine and stock up on some cash, anyway."

She nodded as she dropped her final quarter into the slot, and Noah took off to find a sales clerk and an outlet for his ATM card. By the time he'd managed his errands and returned, Jane was waiting by the phone with her report.

"The first two didn't answer. The third was a night worker by the name of John Williams, who told me in somewhat sleepy but still quite coherent terms what he thought of my waking him up."

"Cheer up, Jane. That means just eight more to go. Here's the change for your next four. I'll call the others."

They went through the final names on the list and received four more negatives and two more where no one answered. On the other two they reached answering machines, on which they left messages that they were trying to reach Jane Anne Williams and would call back later that evening.

Jane dutifully reviewed their progress.

"Let's see, that's one Dusart we have to call back and six J. Williamses, including those that didn't answer and those who had an answering machine."

She paused to look up at the clock on the wall.

"Nothing much more we can do until after six when these folks might be home. I need to buy a watch, not to mention a new wardrobe. You ready to do some shopping?"

"I guess we might as well grab a few things while we can. And don't forget luggage. When we check into a hotel later, we'll need it for appearances, if nothing else. You have enough money, Jane?"

"For my immediate needs, plenty. Let's say we meet back here at five. And, Noah, I hope you know that I will be paying you back for all these expenses."

"Don't be silly, Jane. You don't pay back friends."

She looked at him straight, with the strength he'd come to expect, with the warmth he'd always hoped for and with something new that hinted of vague discontent.

"I do. I know I'll never be able to repay you for the really important things. Heaven knows I'm not comfortable with your sticking out that obstinate neck of yours for me. But I'm not so preoccupied or ungrateful as not to notice or appreciate a heroic gesture when I come across one. And yours is the most heroic I've ever had the pleasure to appreciate."

She leaned up then and kissed his cheek—just the barest of brushes. And in that second Noah glimpsed a world full of forbidden possibilities. But just for a second. Because in the next second she had turned away and disappeared into the crowd of shoppers.

Her small kiss felt like a tuning fork struck inside him, setting every cell humming to life's deepest and most primitive rhythm.

It was at that precise moment that Noah promised himself he would one day meet this Charles Tremont if for no other reason than to look into the face of either the biggest fool or the luckiest guy on this earth.

"PLEASE, FATHER. I'm not up to this now."

Charles Tremont gulped his full glass of Scotch and stood

wobbling next to the massive Italian marble fireplace that rose to the very heights of the ornate cornices of the twenty-foot ceiling of the Tremont estate's formal drawing room.

The tapestries were Oriental, the rugs Arabian, the chandeliers English, the furniture French. The best from every part of the world was gathered within these walls, his mother was always fond of saying. The hot September sun had finally set outside its leaded-glass windows, which had once witnessed the poverty of a sixteenth-century English abbey and were now fringed by the opulence of Italian red silk draperies.

His great-great grandfather's stern countenance gazed down at Charles from above the elegant room's enormous unlit hearth. He turned his back on his ancestor, instantly feeling a cool reproving draft lick up his spine—a welcome contrast to the fire that raged in his belly.

"Charles, this issue has to be addressed," Loren Tremont said as he settled himself in his favorite Louis XV chair, directly in line with his eldest son's position beside the fireplace. "Jane has once again stepped beyond the boundaries."

A silver swath rose in the center of Victoria Tremont's dark, full head of hair like a regal crown. She lounged opposite her husband as confidently as Marie Antoinette might have once done on the couch that had belonged to the ill-fated queen two centuries before.

"Your father is right, Charles. Jane deliberately invites the... oddest assortment of people to our home and then doesn't even have the courtesy to be here when they arrive."

"Mother, I—"

"Do you know who showed up this morning at our front door? A woman running a home for destitute unwed mothers who wish to keep their babies. Jane told this person to stop by here for a donation. And this is not the first of such incidents. This last year has seen an ongoing series of such foolishness!''

Charles took a deep breath as the doctor had told him to do and let it slowly out. ''Mother, you know how sensitive Jane has become to this issue since she herself became a mother.''

Across the room Charles caught a small movement as Gerard's lips screwed up in distaste—either at him, their father, their mother, the conversation topic or all four.

Loren waved his glass of sherry in a negative sweep. ''I don't care how sensitive she's become. A Tremont masters his or her emotions. Doesn't let them run amok! Jane has never been a sensible woman, heaven knows, but this last year she seems to have lost all sense for the fitness of things.''

The deep breathing wasn't working. Charles took another gulp of his drink. ''The child—''

''We are all deeply distraught by little Charles's illness. But none of us have let it blind us to our responsibilities or used it to engage in the most outlandish and obsessive behavior. She insists on personally being at the child's side every moment like some drudge. It's not as if she's helped him, is it?''

Charles had heard it all so many times. What good was it going to do to hear it all again?

''Charles, are you listening to me?''

''Yes, Father.''

''Her defiance of our repeated requests to act with simple and basic propriety has grown by leaps and bounds over this last year. She seems to flaunt her inappropriate behavior at us like some kind of malicious dare! Now that this irrational side has fully blossomed—''

''Father, I don't think irrational is—''

''Irrational is precisely the word, son. When I think of the way she insisted—no, demanded—that *you* go through genetic testing as well as she when the boy got sick. As though *your* genes could possibly be in dispute!''

Charles took another gulp of his drink.

Victoria ran plum-colored nails against her Waterford crystal of sherry, like a hasty comma scratched at the end of her husband's sentence.

"And this unwed mother business. Jane knows I am on the board of no less than two organizations that contribute substantial amounts to these unfortunates. They are given free hospital care. Their babies are found good homes when they have the sense to put them up for adoption. Even if they choose to keep their child and mire it in the continuing cycle of poverty into which they were born, no one stands in their way."

Charles felt the burning intensify in his stomach. He slumped against the enormous mantel and downed the rest of his Scotch, leaving nothing but ice cubes clinking in the crystal tumbler.

Victoria squinted off into the distance at something distasteful and, thankfully, far away. "It is truly tragic that so many young women are beyond help by the time they reach puberty. They have no understanding of the true consequences of their actions."

"Your mother is absolutely right," Loren said, raising his chin so that the deep cleft of the Tremont men was in full, scolding evidence. "Parental standards aren't set in so many homes. The children's moral education is abrogated to the television and movie screen. Rampant sexual promiscuity in those media bombard these unfortunate young men, as well as young women. By the time they reach puberty they emulate what they see and end up with all the disastrous consequences."

"And that is why men like your father must get on the Supreme Court, dear," Victoria added. "Someone has to start setting some standards. The violence is even worse than the sex. The very continuance of this country's moral fiber is dependent upon—Gerard, where are you going?"

Charles watched his younger brother slow to a stop on his way to the door. With insolent ease he turned on his immaculately shined shoes, pushed up the white silk sleeve beneath his impeccable dinner jacket, consulted the Rolex on his tanned wrist and raised his eyes with that look of disdain that had always seemed so much a part of him.

"I have an important call to make."

Victoria's plum-colored lips thinned into a straight line.

"Make your call after dinner. Mansard will be announcing it in just a couple of minutes. We are not letting it get cold while we wait for you to return. And I would think this matter we are discussing would be of interest to you, as well."

A lazy smile appeared on Gerard's lips. "Of interest to me? This censorship speech hasn't been of interest to me since the first time I heard it, more years ago than I care to remember."

"Gerard, what are you saying?"

"I'm saying that what you and Father refuse to face is that this is not a moral issue, but a financial one. Sex and violence sells. The public is getting precisely what it's paying for."

Victoria's nails screeched against the crystal. "I find those comments most distressing. Most distressing. I did not bring you up to think this way, Gerard."

"You paid for my M.B.A. at Harvard. Did you expect me to ignore the basic tenets of demand and supply?"

"Gerard! I can see your father and I should never have indulged that whim of yours to pursue finance. You should have been made to learn the law like the rest of the men in this family and with it the respect for authority! Charles would never speak to me in such an unforgivable fashion!"

Gerard's eyes flew to his brother's, the deep disdain in them as clear and hard as green glass.

"No, of course not, Charles's guts are gone with the tranquilizers and alcohol he guzzles down, then throws up every night."

Charles felt the searing heat of his brother's words roaring through him. He clung to the marble mantel as a wave of weakness buckled his knees. There was a time when he would have broken Gerard's nose for saying far less; in fact, there *was* a time when he *had* done just that.

And now? Now, reeling from the pain in his gut, he was barely able to keep from falling to the floor and breaking his own nose. Despair rose like a black cloak around his heart.

Loren flew to his feet, his tall, well-conditioned body bounding gracefully and quickly toward his younger son. He planted himself in front of the shorter man, deliberately looking down at him.

"Gerard, enough! I will not have you talking to your mother that way or disparaging your brother in such despicable terms!"

Charles watched Gerard face their father, a combatant light in the younger man's green eyes that more than made up for the difference in their height.

"Honesty isn't always a lovable trait, is it, Father?"

There was a momentary pause, one so full of tension that Charles had difficulty drawing the room's thick air into his lungs. When he spoke again, Loren's voice was as quiet and sharply cutting as the edge of an industrial diamond.

"Gerard, you would do well to remember that this family lives up to the very highest standards of conduct. The Tremont name has been blemish free through seven generations. And it will remain that way. Do you understand me?"

Charles watched the deep green, vibrantly alive eyes of his father, the timbre of whose words echoed through the massive room. Loren Tremont still stood straight and formidable at fifty-eight. Charles found his heart pounding with pride that this strong man's genes flowed in his veins.

Charles's attention switched to his brother's face. Gerard's earlier truculent expression had faded. Charles watched in surprise to see the same emotions for his father reflected in the green light of his brother's eyes. Gerard stepped back in a gesture bespeaking both respect and reconciliation.

"Yes, Father. I do understand."

Loren looked at his younger son for a moment more before raising his hands to cup him on either shoulder. Charles could almost feel the strength in those hands, as he saw the pride in his father's eyes.

"When are you going to find the right woman and settle down, son?"

Gerard was saved an answer to this question by the appearance of Mansard, the Tremonts' tall, stiff, elderly butler, who preceded his announcement of dinner with his customary discreet introductory cough.

Charles stared at his brother and his father as they strolled into the dining room arm in arm, his stomach now the blackened hearth of a roaring furnace.

It was too soon to take another pill. He didn't care. He dug into the pocket of his dinner jacket, clasped the vial and drew it out. He cursed quietly as his fumbling hands made messy work of lining up the arrow on the childproof cap.

Victoria rose silently and came to his side.

"Dear, do you really need that?"

Charles forced his answer through lips clenched with pain. "Mother, please don't start."

Desperate now, Charles tore off the top. It twirled out of his hand and fell to the priceless, three-hundred-year-old Shiraz carpet beneath his feet. He ignored it as he spilled one of the precious pills onto his palm. The force knocked the others to the carpet. He ignored them as he stuck the pill on his tongue and downed it with the half-melted ice cubes remaining in his drink.

Victoria stepped on the dropped pills, grinding them into the carpet. She laced her formally clad arm through her son's. "Charles, it's time to go in to dinner."

She urged him forward. He resisted her pull.

"I'm not going in."

"Dear, you've lost far too much weight already. You must eat to keep up your strength."

"Mother, you don't understand. I...I can't go in there now."

Victoria's eyes filled with unaccustomed tears.

"But I do understand, dear. You are the oldest son, my firstborn. It was in your eyes that your father first saw his younger self. And, now... Oh, Charles, you were once so strong! We must find a way for you to regain that strength!"

Charles exhaled a heavy, painful breath, his shoulders sagging beneath the weight of his admission. "I don't have the stamina anymore, Mother. I want to. God knows I want to. But I feel so beaten down by everything. If I could just find a way to get free of this weakness, this...pain."

Victoria's almost colorless eyes glowed suddenly as bright as the summer sun. Her strong, elegant hands clasped her son's arm tightly.

"To get rid of the pain, dear, you must get rid of the underlying cause."

Charles sighed, a great, heavy heave of lungs and heart. "Yes, Mother. This has gone on too long. For you, for father, for us all. I must find the strength to end it."

"JANE, YOU DIDN'T EAT much. Everything all right?"

She looked up from her half-consumed halibut, baked in parchment and soaked in a walnut-parsley puree. He could tell her mind was miles away. In New Jersey? Or Boston?

"The food's fine. I guess I'm just preoccupied."

"It must be difficult being apart from him like this."

She nodded.

He hadn't specified her son, but Noah chose to believe it was the younger Charles she meant. He didn't want to dwell on any more painful thoughts than she was already plagued with. He decided to change the subject.

"You mentioned that your adoptive parents were older. Did that cause any problems while you were growing up?"

"Not because they were older, no."

"But there were problems?"

He didn't think she was going to answer at first. But then she gave a little sigh and leaned her forearms on the table.

"I was a born tomboy. Then when I was nine, I got hurt. I'd been playing baseball with a bunch of boys at school after classes, unbeknownst to either of my parents. I was the catcher. The boy who was up at bat stepped back, swung hard, missed the ball and connected with my head instead.

"I was rushed to the hospital and lay in a coma for two days. My parents went through hell. When I survived, and miraculously without permanent injury, they vowed my tomboy days were over.

"They drove me to and from school after that. I was subjected to long, impassioned and vivid descriptions of all the terrible, maiming injuries that could result from swimming, horseback riding, even girls' basketball.

"But it wasn't just physical things. The debating team was out because it would have necessitated an overnight plane trip out of state. The band for the same reason. And each time I was told no to something I wanted to try, I could hear the fear in my mother's voice and see it in my father's eyes. As the years passed I grew timid. Shy. Afraid to try anything."

"Jane, that person doesn't sound like you at all."

She sighed deeply. "I hope to hell it isn't. For most of my adult years I've worked very hard to undo that conditioned response of fear and giving in to others."

He rested his hand on hers and smiled. "And you've achieved amazing success."

The bitterness and irritation in her voice melted as she smiled in response to his comment. For a moment his eyes held hers and he could feel the warmth behind their guard. But then her eyes dropped from his as she withdrew her hand and fiddled with the silverware.

"You and Eric Ellison must have been quite close for him to have left you his place."

He recognized her question for what it was—a quick change from a topic that had let them get too close. He understood the necessity, of course, but it still disappointed him. He tried to keep that disappointment out of his tone.

"With the kind of traveling a professional tennis player does, making and keeping a good friend isn't an easy thing. You always seem to be on the road to some tournament. A lot of people hang around you just for the notoriety. You don't meet too many who are genuine."

"But Eric was."

"Yes. Grew up on an Iowa farm. His family had gotten wiped out by a freak fire when he was just twelve. I think it was only his love of tennis that kept him going after that. He believed in giving it his all. He was a damn tough competitor. His backhand could drive nails through you."

"He never married?"

"Neither of us did. Like I said, you don't meet too many genuine people on the circuit. After the accident Eric knew he'd never play again. Just before he went into that operation he made out a will, making me both the executor and beneficiary of his estate. I don't think he wanted to survive the surgery. You see, all he had was tennis."

She nodded, and from the look in her eyes he thought she understood what he was saying. "We feel badly for those who die, leaving behind family. But it must be even more difficult to have no family to leave behind."

She sounded a little sad. For Eric? Or herself?

She looked up at him. His thoughts took that turn they always did when their eyes met like this. She read their message clearly, then abruptly looked away and fumbled for the strap of her new shoulder bag slung over the back of the chair.

"I should be getting to a phone to start following up on these calls. It's after six and the people who were gone during the day could be home now. It might be easier if we got a hotel room and made the calls from there."

He had to let her retreat, but he didn't have to like it. What he would have liked was to take her in his arms and hold her very close and kiss that sadness from her lips forever.

Noah took a deep breath and scraped the bottom of the barrel for the last ounce of all that wonderful control he used to have.

"I've been giving some thought to where we should stay. We need a place that's either so cheap they're used to cash or something just offbeat enough where the management still doesn't mind dealing on a cash basis."

"I vote for the offbeat. There's the Hotel Triton across from Chinatown. I seem to remember hearing it's rather less starchy than other hotels, seeing as how it caters to the entertainment industries."

"Sounds like it might be the right kind of place. You know how to get to this Hotel Triton?"

"I bought another map on my shopping spree this afternoon, so we shouldn't have any trouble finding it."

With Jane's navigating, Noah wasn't surprised to find they drove right to it. But Noah was surprised when he walked into a lobby of royal blue carpeting spotted with golden stars upon which sat bright yellow, tufted dervish chairs, curling toward the ceiling in front of a pastel flowered mural like something out of an Alice-in-Wonderland scene.

He stepped up to the registration desk, receiving an exuberant greeting from the short, fortyish, smiling clerk with the premature gray-white hair.

"Noah Armstrong! How nice to have you with us!"

Noah had discovered long ago that when he couldn't hide who he was, the only thing left to do was to take advantage of his notoriety.

"Good evening. I'd like a suite with separate bedrooms and baths for myself and the lady."

"Certainly. A pleasure, yes, a pleasure."

Noah signed the registration card he was given as A. Strong in deliberate bold, dark script.

As he passed the form back, Noah watched the desk clerk's face as he stared at the signature in some momentary confusion, found the fifty-dollar bill beneath the registration form and then refound his smile as he quickly pocketed the money.

The little man winked conspiratorially, his neat, white mustache twitching at the edges, just as Alice's white rabbit might have done.

"I apologize for my mistake, Mr. Strong. It will not happen again, sir. You can rely on me. How long will you and the lady be staying with us?"

Noah laid five one-hundred-dollar bills on the top of the counter this time.

"Let's take it one day at a time, shall we?"

The desk clerk looked at the money, scooped it up and then quickly handed over the key to the Triton suite, number 221.

"I sincerely hope you enjoy your stay with us, Mr. Strong. If I may be of any assistance whatsoever, my name is Bobbit. Please do not hesitate to ask for me. Do you need a bellhop to take yours and the lady's luggage?"

"No. I can handle it. Thanks."

As he turned to pick up their luggage, he caught Jane's admiring eye.

"I never realized that being a globe-trotting tennis star could equip someone with such enviable skills for handling hotel desk clerks."

He grinned, pleased at her obvious approval.

"Actually, we globe-trotting tennis stars develop lots of enviable skills. You might be surprised at some of them."

Her return smile just lifted the ends of her mouth. "It takes a lot to surprise me, Noah Armstrong."

But Jane was pleasantly surprised by the playful ambience of the hotel suite. Its silk taffeta furniture and iridescent pink-and-gold decorations had a lighthearted feel to them. The patches of cream and gold rectangles papering the walls above the main room of the suite complemented the yellow and turquoise rectangles in the connecting bed-room. The original artwork set over the dervish chairs was just offbeat enough to look like an inspired afterthought.

She headed directly for the connecting bedroom, hung up her two new outfits in a unique-looking armoire with a golden crown and dumped her new suitcase with her other clothes into a corner to unpack later. She swung her new purse onto the nightstand and from the pocket of her Windbreaker drew out the paper on which she had copied the list of names they had been unable to reach earlier.

Time to get to work.

She plopped onto the soft cream comforter of the queen-size bed and leaned back against a white-and-blue-striped throw pillow and a navy one with magenta buttons.

She could hear Noah busying himself with hanging up his clothes and putting things away in the even larger armoire in the suite's main room near the king-size bed.

She picked up the receiver and punched in the first num-ber.

One by one she called the Williamses. She got answers on all but two this time. She spoke with a Jeremiah Williams, a Jeffrey, a Joan and a Janella—but no Jane Anne. She consoled herself with the fact that she could cross four more names off the list.

Noah gave a perfunctory knock on the open door and came to sit on the bed beside her. He rested his arm against the upholstered blue-and-gold backboard and leaned over her shoulder to look at the names on her list.

"Who's left?"

His question brushed against her ear and swept away every thought in her head. He was a collage of warm male smells and fomenting sensuality that felt far too good and far too close.

"Jane?"

She gripped the paper in her hand. Earlier he had made her feel special and strong by showing his respect for her success in overcoming the fears of her childhood. She focused on that strength now as she raised her eyes. . . .

And realized her mistake too late. His eyes were, as always, open and readable. The desire for her in them—a desire firmly held in check—was so blatant and honest it jolted her. She saw herself in his eyes, caught like some butterfly in the bright, beautiful amber of a sturdy tree.

This is what it would be like to make love to this man, a warning voice blared. *He would capture you in those eyes, in his arms, in that all-encompassing desire. And you would never again be free.*

She dropped her head and closed her eyes. How could she think with him so close? How could she function?

Because she had to, that's how. There was too much at stake for her to let herself get caught up in forbidden feelings for this sensuous man. Everything depended on her keeping her emotions in check. She silently browbeat her brain back to the task at hand. But she hardly recognized the husky croak that had become her voice.

"The one Dusart that I got an answering machine on earlier is the only one I haven't called back. There's no address listed with the number. Just the initial *I* and the last name Dusart."

He leaned across her, picked up the receiver and handed it to her. The brush of his body was like that of an artist's across a canvas, sweeping away whatever image had existed on it before.

She took the receiver from his hand, her mind a complete blank as to why she would want it.

"You have the number?"

The number. . . of course. Written on the paper she was clutching so tightly.

She consulted the paper, punched in the digits with shaking fingers and listened as the answering machine again clicked on. She waited patiently for the sound of the beep.

"Hello, I called earlier. I'm trying to reach Katya Jane Dusart. My name is Jane Williams. I don't know if I have the right number, but if—"

A high, excited voice broke in on her message, bringing with it a whole new set of images and emotions.

"Jane? Jane, is that really you?"

Chapter Eight

Jane started at the woman's voice that had so unexpectedly broken through her message. Her eyes darted to Noah's and after reading the look on her face he leaned closer to listen in on the telephone receiver.

She could actually feel the heat from his skin, smell the warm, musky male scent of him. She clutched the telephone as though it was the last thread of the slim lifeline leading back to her brain. Her answer spilled into the receiver in a desperate croak.

"I . . . yes, this is Jane Williams. Who is this?"

Something that sounded like a sob exploded in her ear.

"Jane, my sweet little Jane! I can barely believe I'm talking to you after all these years! Finally, my prayers have been answered!"

She sat up straighter on the bed, her brain rallying to make sense of what she was hearing. "Excuse me, are you Katya Jane Dusart?"

"No, no, child, this isn't your mother. This is your grandmother."

"You're Katya Dusart's mother?"

"Yes, dear. Your grandmother Ina. Of course, I don't expect you to remember me. You were just a toddler when last I saw you. Oh, how exciting this is! Where are you?"

"I'm here in San Francisco. At a hotel."

"Wonderful! Are you far from the house?"

"I don't know. Where do you live?"

"Didn't your mother give you the address, dear?"

"No, Mrs. Dusart. My...mother...never mentioned you."

An uncomfortable silence met Jane's admission. When Ina's voice resumed, its tone carried a tentative note.

"I don't understand."

"It's a long story. Look, it's awkward talking over the phone like this. I have so many questions, Mrs. Dusart. And it appears you do, too. I think maybe they'd best be asked and answered in person, if you don't mind."

"Mind? My dearest child, nothing would please me more. Come this very moment if you can."

"There's a friend I'd like to bring with me."

"Of course, dear. Your friend is welcome, too. What hotel are you at?"

"The Triton, right across from Chinatown."

"Yes, I know exactly how to direct you from there. Don't worry if it sounds complicated, it won't be once you're in the car. Do you have something to write with?"

Noah whipped out a pen and paper and as he listened in, jotted down the address and the directions provided. Jane thanked the excited woman on the other end of the line and hung up the phone.

Jane immediately moved away from Noah.

"You look absolutely flabbergasted. Didn't you expect your efforts to be successful?"

"Intellectually, I suppose I did, Noah. But emotionally this is hitting me on a whole different level."

He took her hand with his, gave it a reassuring squeeze. "Because the woman you just spoke to might very well be your grandmother?"

His gentle touch charged through her. She extricated her hand from his reluctantly, a small sigh of regret escaping her lungs.

"Something like that."

"Are you excited about meeting her?"

"Uncomfortable. I've gotten her expectations up. She seemed so warm and nurturing. I hadn't thought about how unfair this could be to her."

"You mean, if you prove not to be her grandchild."

"Yes. Well, it's done now."

She slid off the bed and turned back to face him.

"Let's go see what Ina Dusart has to say. If I really am her grandchild, she's the one to tell us about any nasty skeleton that's hidden in the family closet."

INA DUSART CERTAINLY HAD plenty of closets in which to house skeletons in her nineteenth-century rendition of a Queen-Anne-style home. It was the characteristic asymmetrical construction with irregular roof lines, lots of nooks and crannies and the kind of spindlework friezes and gingerbread ornamentation that broadcast its abhorrence of anything that could be interpreted as a smooth-wall appearance.

Ina looked like a moving nineteenth-century rendition herself, with her elaborate lace collar and cuffs, and pleats in nearly every direction on her soft peach flowered dress that hugged her angular frame. Her hair was short, tight pepper curls above her thin parchment-crinkled face and faded brown eyes. Noah guessed her to be around his grandparents' age, which would put her in her early seventies.

But her face shed ten years when she caught sight of Jane on her porch.

"Jane! My dear, I would know you anywhere! You have your grandfather's coloring and his square chin."

Jane let herself be gathered in a hug, looking decidedly uncomfortable. Noah could almost see her sigh of relief when Ina finally released her.

"Come in. Come in."

As Ina Dusart stepped back, Jane obligingly followed her into a dimly lit living room of lemon furniture polish smells, darkened butterfly-on-buttercups wallpaper and heavy,

rolled-arm furniture carefully covered with sunflower doi-
lies.

"This is Noah Armstrong. He's the friend I mentioned I
was bringing."

Ina barely glanced in Noah's direction as she captured
Jane's hand in hers.

"Come, sit down. There is so much I wish to ask."

Jane let herself be led to a slightly lumpy love seat covered in a faded floral pattern. She sat on its edge, resting her
elbows on her knees, as she watched the excited Ina Dusart
pour them each a cup of tea from a lovely silver service that
was obviously reserved only for special company. Their
hostess next passed them a plate of lemon cookies. Jane and
Noah took one.

Ina Dusart hummed a happy little tune to herself. When
she had served her guests, she sat across from them on a
matching love seat, her faded brown eyes made young with
excitement.

"Now, dear, tell me all about yourself."

Jane sipped her tea and bit into a lemon cookie, chewing
and swallowing it with slow, deliberate moves. Noah had the
distinct feeling that she was unsure of how to begin. He'd
never seen her look more ill at ease.

"This is unforgivable barging in on you this way."

"Don't be silly. I'm so happy to see you I could burst. If
you only knew the years I have prayed for just a glimpse of
my darling grandchild—"

"But that's just it, Mrs. Dusart. You see, I don't know if
I am your grandchild."

"Not my grandchild? But your name is Jane Williams.
You knew my number. You asked for your mother."

Jane set her teacup and unfinished lemon cookie on the
dark oak coffee table.

"I asked for Katya Jane Dusart because her name is listed
on a birth certificate for a Jane Williams born in San Francisco around the time I was. Mrs. Dusart, my name, where

I was born and the approximate date I was born are all I
know about my beginnings.''

"Are you saying you don't know who your own mother
was?''

"That's exactly what I'm saying.''

"Then who reared you, child?''

"I was adopted when I was two years old by a couple in
New Jersey after my parents were killed in a bus accident.''

Ina Dusart stiffened.

"Killed? Katya is dead?''

"Please, Mrs. Dusart. We need to take this one step at a
time. My mother is dead, yes. I don't know if she was your
daughter.''

But Ina Dusart wasn't listening. She seemed to have been
transformed into a stiff, lifeless doll—her faded eyes, salt-
and-pepper hair and peach-colored dress became absolutely still.

"Mrs. Dusart? Ina? Are you all right?''

At the concern in Jane's voice, the lost expression in the
elderly woman's eyes disappeared, and she focused once
again on Jane's face.

"I always thought she never returned because she couldn't
forgive me. I never for a moment imagined she could be...''

Weak, watery tears leaked out of the corners of Ina's eyes,
wetting her wrinkled, parchmentlike skin. Jane got up and
went over to the distraught woman. She knelt beside her
chair and took the aged, spotted hands inside her own.

"Ina, please listen to me. I don't know that Katya was my
mother. I don't know that she's dead. I may be another Jane
Williams. I need your help to find out the truth.''

Ina reached into her pocket and drew out a cotton handkerchief. She dabbed at her cheeks and eyes.

"But you look so like your grandfather, Jane! How can
you not be our grandchild?''

Jane smiled at her.

"Having a similar feature or two isn't enough to be certain, Ina. What I need are facts. And I believe you're the one who can supply those facts. Will you help me?"

Ina's eyes warmed to Jane's smile. "I'll tell you whatever I can. What is it you want to know?"

"When was the last time you saw your Katya?"

"Twenty-eight years ago."

"Why did she leave? What went wrong between you?"

Ina sighed heavily as though she were still carrying a burden from those times.

"I don't know what went wrong. Her father and I brought up Katya with the same values we held dear. Everything was fine through high school. Then she went off to college and met that ... man."

"What man?"

"His name was Rusty. He was an older student and he used his age to dominate and indoctrinate her with his crazy ideas. I knew the first time she brought him home to meet her father and me that he was trouble. She introduced him to us as a man of principle. You wouldn't believe what he called principles!"

"What were they?"

"He didn't believe in marriage, he said. Came right out with it as though it was a badge he was proud to wear. When we asked him about school, he happily announced he was flunking out of college. Said he'd only enrolled to avoid the draft, anyway. 'Make love not war,' he said. Those were his *principles.*"

"Did you openly disapprove of him to your daughter?"

"Naturally. Her father and I told Katya not to see him anymore."

She stopped to wipe a new set of tears from her cheeks.

"She didn't listen, did she?"

"She told us we didn't understand a 'man' like Rusty and that the times were chánging, leaving us behind. 'Make love not war,' she parroted the day she left home to move in with him."

"What happened then, Ina?"

"They made love, all right. Eight months later she came back to us seven months pregnant. That was just after they'd begun to make their war."

"Make their war?"

"After selling her on the doctrine of marriage being such an abhorrent institution, suddenly Rusty decided it might not be so bad when the military rules changed and he learned a wife and child could keep him from getting drafted. He told Katya he wanted them to get married. Katya fled back to us, confused and feeling rather foolish and betrayed for buying so strongly into a principle that Rusty had found so easy to discard in the face of expediency."

"So they didn't marry?"

"No. And despite the fact that having a child out of wedlock was still quite unacceptable at that time, Jane, I must confess to you that both her father and I were relieved when Katya refused to take Rusty's calls over the next several weeks. She had her baby girl, our lovely little Jane, with just her dad and me by her side."

"The birth certificate shows the father as Stanley Russell Williams, a cartographer. Was that Rusty?"

"Yes. It was at Katya's insistence that we described him as a cartographer, because in the months when they'd both dropped out of school and had been living together in this sort of communal apartment house, she said Rusty spent most of his time meeting in a backroom of the house with a group of guys drawing maps on how to get to different buildings and such around the city."

"Sounds like an odd thing to do."

"Odd is a kind word to describe that man and his doings. Anyway, a few months after Jane was born, Katya reenrolled in college, and I took over the care of the baby."

"What happened to Rusty?"

"He sent word just after the baby was born that he'd gotten a draft notice and had left for Canada to avoid being conscripted. Then we didn't hear from him for a long time, and I began to think that things had returned to some semblance of normalcy. Until one day he just popped up, like a nasty virus, infecting our healthy little family all over again."

"What year was that?"

"It was 1966. He told Katya he'd come for his woman and his child. He apologized for asking her to marry him before. Explained it had been a moment of weakness. He said he had a nice place for them in Canada, and he'd made lots of friends. They were supposedly involved in some important work, and he wanted Katya to be a part of it all."

"And she went with him?"

"I couldn't believe it. I would have sworn she'd gotten over him and those crazy ideas. It had been more than eighteen months! She'd been doing so well back in college. But she packed her things and little Jane's, and in less than an hour she was gone."

"What did she say?"

"She said Rusty was her future. She said that her father and I were her past. I begged her to wait until her father got home from his rounds as a postman so he could talk to her. She said she didn't have time. That Rusty needed her right then. That he'd proved his love for her and their child by putting himself in terrible danger of being arrested just to come back for them."

"She must have still been in love with him."

"So she said. She told me then that it had been awful for her without him, but she hadn't wanted to complain. I told her I was afraid for her, going off to a foreign country with a wanted man, her little Jane still so young. But she wasn't thinking what was best for her or her baby—just what that man wanted. I was so angry that I told her that if she left the house then, she had better never come back again because she wouldn't be welcome. And, heaven help me, she never did."

The tears once again leaked out of the faded eyes and wet the wrinkled cheeks.

"I didn't mean it, Jane. Please believe me. They were words said in frustration and anger. I've regretted them every day since."

Jane grasped Ina's hands more firmly.

"I know. Did Rusty say where they were going?"

"To Canada, I assumed."

"So he mentioned nothing about the route they would take or where they would stop along the way?"

"I didn't talk to him, Jane. He remained on the porch the whole time, pacing, impatiently calling out to Katya to hurry up."

"Did you ever meet Rusty's parents?"

"No. When I first met him, I asked about them. He said something to the effect that they were the pitiful examples of the decadence to which American society could climb and then refused to discuss them further. Katya mentioned once that they lived back East, and that Rusty got monthly checks from them."

"Is it possible that Rusty took Katya and Jane back East to meet his family before crossing the border into Canada?"

"He never struck me as the considerate kind of son who would give a moment's thought to his parents' feelings. He certainly never gave a moment's thought to ours. I'll never forget my dear Henry's face when he came home that evening to find his daughter and granddaughter gone. Without a word to him. Without so much as a goodbye."

Ina dabbed her handkerchief over the now-swollen lids of her eyes.

Jane gave her a moment before asking her next question.

"Ina, have there ever been any unusual childhood illnesses in the family?"

"Oh, no, child. You don't have to worry. You come from healthy stock. Your grandfather was an only child, but a healthy one."

"Do you have brothers or sisters?"

"I had a sister, but she died in a boating accident when we were young."

"Any aunts or uncles?"

"One uncle. Marcus. Wonderful family man. Had six sons and six daughters. Lived to be eighty. I remember his eightieth birthday party well. All his children and grandchildren turned up, and they made a houseful, I can tell you. Made me wish Henry and I had been blessed with more than our Katya."

"Do you know the names of any of your daughter's friends from that time? Or Rusty's?"

Ina shook her head. "I didn't want to know about them."

"What month did your daughter and her baby leave?"

"In May of 1966. That's when that Rusty stole them from us."

"Do you remember hearing about a San Francisco family involved in a bus accident in Vermont in September of that year, where the only survivor was a two-year-old girl?"

Ina drew up at Jane's question and blinked at her.

"No, I'm certain I didn't hear about any such accident."

"I guess it's too much to ask you about such a news report twenty-eight years later."

"No, it isn't, Jane. I have always read the daily newspaper and watched the television news every night. I assure you, I would have taken notice of the report of such an accident involving a San Francisco family."

"Your husband is dead now?"

"Eight years ago. Heart attack. He never saw his daughter again, or heard from her. She just dropped off the face of this earth. Broke his heart and mine, I can tell you. It was the not knowing what happened to her and our grandchild that was the worst."

Ina's eyes focused on Jane's face then, and she smiled.

"Oh, child, your grandfather would have been so happy to see you grown into such a lovely woman. Let me show you the pictures of you as a baby. And Katya, too. I'll be right back."

She was up and out of her seat in a flash.

Jane raised her voice to call after the fast-disappearing woman. "Ina, I still don't know if I am—"

It was too late. Ina Dusart had already vanished into the backroom, out of earshot.

"WELL, INA'S CONVINCED. And she was right about there being some resemblance in coloring and features between you and Henry Dusart in those family pictures. What do you think, Jane? Does it fit?"

She twisted toward him from her position in the passenger seat. "Some of it seems to. Katya, Rusty and the baby disappeared around the right time. They were never heard from again."

He detected the reservation in her voice. "But?"

"But if Katya left home with her little girl in May of 1966 for Canada with this Rusty, who was in danger of being arrested every moment he stayed in the States, would it be likely that the three of them would still be traveling in Vermont in late September of that year when the bus accident occurred?"

"Maybe they went to Canada and then traveled to the New England states later to visit Rusty's relatives."

"You think Rusty might have turned over a considerate leaf?"

"Actually, I was thinking about those monthly checks Katya said came from his parents. They might have dried up when he became a draft dodger and took up residence in Canada. Perhaps he decided to bend another one of his principles and appear on their doorstep with a grandchild, hoping for a handout."

She stared out the windshield, her tongue licking the side of her mouth. Noah could see she was grappling with something disturbing.

"Jane, I'm sorry if that sounded disparaging of the person who could very well be your father."

She looked over at him and the frown faded.

"Well, considering that earlier you had him pegged as a possible bank robber, finding out this guy might have bent a few principles to get a handout for his family would be a welcome discovery, I assure you."

"Then is it that you're bothered by the fact that there're no unusual childhood diseases in the Dusart line?"

"There could still be something back in the family history that Ina isn't aware of. Uncle Marcus might have been from an uninfected part of the family gene pool. Ina or even her husband's side could have carried something."

"Which finally showed up in your child. I see what you mean. Then what *is* troubling you?"

"Couple of things. Number one is that if Ina really does read the newspaper and watch the TV news every day, why didn't she see the news report on the bus accident?"

"Even people of habit sometimes deviate from their routine. She just might not have read the paper or watched the television that day. Could be just as simple as that, couldn't it?"

"I guess it could."

"But there's something else, isn't there?"

"Yes. Not having one's parents officially married might have been a problem thirty years ago. But it's hardly the kind of skeleton that could rattle even the Tremont name in this day and age."

"So you don't think we've opened the right closet door and found the right skeleton yet, is that it?"

"That's it. There's got to be another door somewhere. There's just got to be."

"Maybe we might learn something if we talk to the child welfare people."

"I doubt it. They sent everything they had to my adoptive parents through the San Francisco attorney in response to that court order I told you about that got issued when I was a teenager."

"What do you remember from those documents?"

"That they were hardly worth the time and effort."

Noah pulled up to the entrance of the Hotel Triton. But when Jane got out, he didn't follow.

"You're not coming up?"

"Not right away. I left some running clothes and shoes in the back seat after our shopping trip this afternoon. I thought I'd go for a therapeutic jog while there's still some light left."

"I hope you're not planning on going back to the Fort Point area. They might be watching it."

"We passed a park just a few blocks back. I'll retrace my path to it."

"How long do you think you'll be?"

"It may be a long jog, Jane. Don't wait up."

She paused, her hand still resting on the open passenger-door window.

"Noah, is everything all right?"

He flashed her a smile. "Fine. Just part of the prescribed regimen I promised my doctor I would adhere to."

She watched him drive away, knowing that he wasn't telling her the half of it, but that he didn't have to because she was already all too aware of that other half. Separate bedrooms and bathrooms notwithstanding, sharing a suite together was difficult on both of them. He was giving her some breathing room. And she needed it.

She turned toward the entrance to the hotel, carefully checking out who was loitering around this downtown gallery district across from the Chinatown gates.

She saw a rugged-featured, sandy-haired man gazing into a gallery window. He ignored her. A young man and woman spoke to each other in the soft, musical sounds of a foreign language as they headed down the alley on the right. She watched them punch in some code to the employees' entrance and then disappear inside the hotel.

After one last quick look behind her, she entered the hotel, made her way up to their suite and locked the door behind her.

She had something she must do.

She headed for her adjoining bedroom and plopped down on the queen-size bed next to the phone as she had earlier that evening. The impression of his body was still there beside her in the soft comforter. Almost of its own volition, her hand traced the indentation. She could almost feel his warmth.

She caught her reflection in the mirror on the wall, the flush in her cheeks, the shine in her eyes.

She snatched her hand away, shaking her head. She was being very foolish. And she was wasting time.

She reached for the phone, resolutely punching in the number. It rang twice before it was picked up on the other end.

"Hi. I'm glad to find you in. I've got a lot to tell you."

"And I've been waiting for your call. I've got a lot to tell you, too."

IT WAS NEARLY MIDNIGHT when Noah finally inserted his key in the lock. The door to her adjoining bedroom was closed. No light shone beneath it. He expected her to be asleep. He'd stayed out this late precisely so she would be asleep when he came in. But still, a part of him registered disappointment.

He walked into the master bath, flipped on the light and began to fill the Jacuzzi. He tore off his jogging suit and shoes and placed the tennis ball he used to strengthen his hand and arm muscles on the side of the tub. He'd run himself ragged, to the very point of exhaustion, and he'd done it purposely. He knew he had to if he was to live up to his word and stay out of her bedroom tonight.

It was where he wanted to be, despite all his aching muscles and all the logical reasons against it. And he knew that with the least bit of encouragement from the lady, it's where he would be.

She hadn't offered encouragement, but he'd sensed her attraction to him with every male cell of his body. He felt her quiver every time he brushed against her, something he'd begun doing purposely and far too often. He wasn't a saint, but he'd always considered himself the kind of man who could control himself. He was beginning to wonder if he'd ever known what control was.

He turned on the TV that was set into the mirrors above the Jacuzzi, and settled himself in the hot, churning water.

The news was on. Noah only half listened to it. He watched the spirals forming on the surface of the water in response to the agitation beneath. He closed his eyes, willing the Jacuzzi's heat and therapeutic agitation to ease the tension from both his thoughts and muscles.

It might have worked if a familiar name hadn't come blasting out of the TV right about then.

"Since Judge Loren Tremont's nomination to the Supreme Court, White House sources have been confident that the respected judge's confirmation would be merely perfunctory."

Noah bolted upright, his eyes flying open. On the screen was a full-face picture of Loren Tremont, one of those professional pictures that accentuated all the positive features of a face and none of the negative. Loren Tremont looked wise, trustworthy and strong.

"However, the panel of senators told reporters today that despite the formidable reputation and wealth of Judge Tremont, they promise to wage as aggressive an investigation into his financial holdings and moral character as they would of any other nominee."

Noah watched and listened to the two senators being interviewed. They didn't look or sound to Noah as if they were at all eager to be launching an aggressive investigation into the powerful Judge Loren Tremont's personal life. But then,

Noah admitted, he probably wasn't seeing things with a very objective eye at the moment.

"In other news—"

Noah grabbed the remote control and switched off the set.

He snatched at the tennis ball with his left hand and squeezed it until his muscles hurt from the strain. Then he threw it against the wall.

How could a man whose own daughter-in-law couldn't trust him be trusted to sit on the Supreme Court of the land?

Noah took a deep breath and ducked under the water of the Jacuzzi, finding it cool in comparison to the heat of his anger.

The rest of Jane's family didn't sound any better. The ineffectual Charles, the money-grubbing Gerard, the emotionally impaired Victoria.

Noah surfaced, remembering all too vividly his first glimpse of Jane, fighting desperately for her life in the crashing waves of the icy bay. Then he saw her resolute face as she explained to him the real reason she couldn't call her family. Here Jane was in deadly danger, and she couldn't turn to any of them.

His anger was agitating inside him as fast and furiously as the pumping Jacuzzi. Of all the Tremonts, the only one who seemed to be worth the proverbial plugged nickel was Great-Aunt Melissa.

"MELISSA, I THOUGHT you were going to talk Jane out of this foolhardy venture!"

Melissa Tremont ambled down the deep persimmon-colored carpet leading from her dark entrance hallway to the light natural wooden floors and apricot-colored walls of her sunny sitting room. She plopped her large frame onto a bright blue-and-yellow flowered couch, lifting her swollen ankles up to its edge with an audible sigh of relief.

Only then did she turn an eye to the far-too-thin fortyish woman with the stringy, shoulder-length auburn hair framing a remarkably bad complexion, who had followed her with anxious, angry steps from the door.

"If you came over here just to rail at me, Judith Fitch, you're going to find yourself personally heaved out that door you just came in. I get enough such bad manners from my relatives, and I'm certainly not going to put up with them from you."

Judith Fitch didn't look particularly concerned over the threat of being tossed out. She didn't wait to be asked to be seated by her large, less-than-gracious hostess. She picked out a crisp blue-and-white-striped chair across from Melissa Tremont's brightly flowered couch and fell into it.

"Melissa, I don't understand you. How can you just sit there, knowing where Jane is and what she's doing?"

Melissa rubbed at the ache in her swollen, misshapen knuckles. "What do you propose I do about it, Judith? Rant and rave? Scream and shout? I did my best to discourage her. And you know I did."

Judith's short, jagged fingernails scratched nervously at the fabric of the chair arm.

"Jane's always been stubborn and wild and never one to listen to reason. Oh, hell. I need a drink."

Melissa raised her eyebrows. "At nine o'clock in the morning?"

Judith threw Melissa an irritated look as she pushed herself out of the chair and made her way over to the mandarin-colored, freestanding bar on the other side of the room. Melissa watched her bony, nervous hands grab for the Vodka bottle and pour three fingers into a waiting glass. She downed half of it in one gulp.

Judith stared into the remaining clear liquid, her tone dripping with melancholy.

"Dad was an alcoholic."

Melissa didn't need to hear the reminder of the woman's words. She'd watched Walton Fitch slowly drink himself to death over the years, a sensitive man who unfortunately felt the burden of every secret he kept. She didn't want to watch it all over again with this, his only child.

Judith held the glass of clear liquid up to catch a beam of sunlight pouring through an open skylight.

"It was the pain of the liver cancer that finally got him, you know."

Melissa stared at the thin, shaky woman with the bad complexion and wondered if this maudlin mood had been precipitated by one too many of the Fitch family's preferred painkillers.

"Is that what you've decided to do, Judith? Emulate your father by becoming an alcoholic and dying of liver cancer?"

Judith turned on Melissa, anger suddenly bringing her dull, muddy eyes to unaccustomed clarity.

"How can you say such a thing to me? Who do you think you are?"

"Could be I'm your friend, Judith. Maybe your only one. Put the glass down. You don't need alcohol to get you through this. Come sit over here. There's coffee in that pot. Help yourself."

Judith held on to the glass but repositioned herself in the blue-and-white-striped chair opposite Melissa. She leaned forward, resting her bony elbows on her bony knees, eyeing the older woman like a rebellious teenager who'd been temporarily suppressed but not completely cowed.

"What happens if Jane goes looking into the San Francisco child welfare files, Melissa? Are you prepared for the questions that would bring?"

"She already tried that when she was eighteen, and Walton handled it. Wouldn't make any sense for her to try it again. And even if she did, she'd get nowhere without a court order."

"What about the San Francisco attorney who worked with Dad? If she talks to him and—"

"That San Francisco attorney was Desmond Edelson. He died six months ago."

"Then it's all right. The journey will prove futile. She won't learn anything."

Melissa exhaled in weariness from the pain in both her swollen joints and her thoughts.

"Nothing is for certain, Judith. The trouble is that while old secrets represent buried garbage to the hider, to the seeker they can be as alluring as buried treasure."

Judith ignored the pot of coffee and downed the rest of her vodka in an enormous, nervous gulp.

"What's that supposed to mean?"

"It means that the urge to dig them up is strong. Jane may search until she finds a shovel out there we didn't even know existed."

Judith looked at the bottom of her empty glass, a forlorn expression on her long, thin face. "What can you do?"

"Stop her now, before she can get too close for a whiff of that garbage."

Judith tilted up her face. "You can do that?"

"I've already done it."

"You have? How?"

"You don't need to know how."

Judith eyed Melissa with growing speculation and a hint of malicious curiosity. She twirled the empty glass between her palms.

"You know, Jane spoke again, only last week, about her memories of the red bridge and how her mother called it golden. Amazing how youngsters can remember things from so far back. I can't tell you how often I wanted to tell her the truth, just to see her face."

Melissa forgot the pain in her hands and the pain in her ankles. She swung off her seat on the couch and landed squarely on her feet. She rose to every centimeter of her five-foot-eight-inch height and stared down with angry green eyes at the stick of a woman sitting across from her.

"But you never would, would you, Judith."

Melissa's firm tone had not asked a question. She had issued a warning.

On the receiving end of that warning from the formidable and suddenly hostile lady before her, Judith Fitch's eyes darkened to ink stains against her pale face, her thin frame shaking like a tightly strung guitar string.

"No, no, Melissa! I promise you, no!"

Chapter Nine

"I need a walk, Noah. Several brisk times around the block should do it."

She led the way out of the Hotel Triton's Café de la Presse and through the colorful, undulating angles of the whimsical lobby.

"You feeling all right, Jane?"

"Just a little full after that breakfast. And a little stiff. I'm used to a more physically active life-style."

"You mean getting thrown into the bay and having to swim for your life isn't enough of a workout?"

A small smile lifted her lips. "That was over twenty-four hours ago. Except for a certain…ah…soreness in my jaw, I don't feel any residual effects from that unscheduled dunk in the bay."

Noah heard the good-natured recrimination in her tone. He glanced at her profile and was surprised not to see the deep blue bruise that had been there the night before.

"You're certainly a fast healer."

"Actually, that's the wonder of makeup you're admiring."

Yes, he could see it now, some kind of covering cream. And there was a subtle darkening around her eyes and on her cheeks and lips this morning that he hadn't noticed before, either. It was very artfully done. She looked even more beautiful, if that was possible.

"It's not the makeup I'm admiring."

Her eyes flashed to his, and he read both excitement and dismay in them both before she looked away.

He shouldn't have said it, of course. He had no right to make love to her with his words any more than he did with his body. But his tongue seemed to have taken a detour around his brain this morning, perhaps in part because he'd just spent a night tossing and turning while thinking about her being in the next room—in the next bed.

She set a brisk pace once they exited the hotel. After a couple of times around the block, they crossed the street to pass through the Chinatown gates.

Warm, exotic smells filled the air. The clatter of opening shops filled the streets with an energetic beat. The morning sunlight felt good. As physically exhausting as his past couple of days had been, Noah felt stronger for them this morning. It wasn't exactly the slow, careful regimen the doctor had prescribed, but then maybe the return of his strength was due more to the woman at his side than the laps in the sea or around the track.

Jane was licking the corner of her mouth in that characteristic, worried way. She seemed as preoccupied with her thoughts as she had been when he awoke to find her freshly showered and fully clothed at the foot of his bed, asking him if he was hungry for breakfast.

Breakfast wasn't what he'd been hungry for. But he'd settled for it.

He'd tried to give her time to share her thoughts with him without openly asking. But the more he was with her, the more he realized she wasn't the kind of woman to be forthcoming with her innermost thoughts. It looked as if there was nothing he could do but get out the old verbal pliers and start pulling.

"Something's happened, hasn't it? Something you haven't told me about?"

She came out of her preoccupation and glanced up at him. Her brisk pace slowed.

"You returned to the suite so late last night, I didn't have an opportunity to tell you."

He didn't remind her that he'd just given her over an hour of opportunity. "What is it?"

"I called the Boston hospital when I got back to the room last night."

The words had an ominous sound to them Noah didn't like. He stopped and turned to face her. She stopped, too, and tilted up her face to his. He moved closer and reached for her hands. Slowly he entwined his fingers through hers to let her know he was there to cushion any blow.

"It's not your son?"

"No, he's fine. But something else is going on."

He wanted to know, of course. But right now his thoughts were getting fuzzy as his whole body responded to her closeness and the fact that not only had she not immediately withdrawn from his touch but that her azure eyes were without their normal guard, touching him with a warmth and openness that drained the breath from his body.

He fought for sanity... and lost, as his name formed on her lips.

"Noah."

He wrapped his arms around her and drew her to him. Whatever thoughts he had left—dissolved amid the incredible jolt of desire that shot through him when her breasts rubbed against his chest, her hips against his. His mouth found the heat of her lips, his hands the dark, silky coolness of her hair.

Shock waves reverberated through him as she returned his kiss. She was so incredibly soft, yet firm; sweet, yet hot; yielding, yet advancing; following, yet leading.

An avalanche of sensations—too fast, furious and incredibly complicated to recognize—swept through his body and carried him far away.

He didn't know where he was or who he was. All he knew was that she was there with him. No one and nothing else existed or mattered. Her response told him that this was true for her, too.

For one glorious, incredible moment....

Only, then it was over.

He felt it first in her sad sigh escaping into his lips. Then in her hands that pushed against his chest as she drew out of the kiss.

"Noah. No. Please."

The distress in her words brought him spiraling down from the high cloud of ecstasy, crashing onto the terra firma of reality. He landed hard.

It wasn't where he wanted to be. Getting his arms to release her from that tight hold that kept her so splendidly close took several deep breaths and all the discipline he had ever possessed.

When he finally drew back he was shaking—both inside and out. And it didn't help at all when he looked into her face and found it flushed with forbidden heat, her eyes filled with the same desire and despair that raged within him.

She stepped back, then turned away and stood absolutely still. The sun kissed and caressed her skin, streaked her long, thick hair with dark fire. She was so close ... yet so far.

What had ever made him think he could be with her day and night, sharing the excitement and danger of this search, and still be able to keep his distance?

Because she's married, you fool. And she's so damn vulnerable, for all that brave strength she displays. You're the only one left to help her. And if you take advantage of your position and press this physical attraction between you, you'll be the biggest louse who ever lived.

Noah's emotions reeled with the blow of that mental reminder. It ate at the very heart of the man he always considered himself to be. He had to stay away from her, because he knew if he didn't, even if she could forgive him, he'd never forgive himself.

He took a deep breath and then another. "Jane, I'm sorry. That . . . won't happen again."

She said nothing, just began to walk again. But this time her pace was slow and deliberate. He fell into step beside her. He heard the voices of the shopkeepers and shoppers, but they were vague background noise to the beat of the blood in his ears.

The minutes collected slowly, as though each was being carefully chosen and strung between them, matching beads in time to help provide what they both needed most—distance.

By the time they had walked the length and breadth of Chinatown and had returned to the gate, he had his self-control back once more—and the firm resolve never to lose it again.

"You were about to tell me something you learned, Jane. What was it?"

For a moment he didn't know if she would answer. But her hesitation was brief.

"A message was left at the hospital for me. It said to come to Boston immediately because the results of one of my son's tests had revealed something exciting."

"This is good news, then?"

"No, I talked with my son's doctor. He said the tests are going well, but they won't have the results back on them for several days. Someone else left that message for me."

"Did this same message get sent to that friend impersonating you at the hospital?"

"No. If I had just called for a status report on my son's tests and hadn't talked directly to my friend and then the doctor, I might have been taken in."

"Who took this bogus message?"

"Someone at the nurses' station. They can't find out who. But the message apparently came in by telephone with instructions that if Mrs. Charles Tremont called to inquire about her son, it should be read to her."

"Is your son's doctor a man?"

"Yes."

"Then that means whoever is behind this is a man."

"Not necessarily. A woman could have left that message pretending to be from the doctor's office."

"So whoever planted this bogus message expected you would call. That, coupled with the 'come to Boston immediately' message, clearly means they know you aren't really there. I'm sure I don't have to tell you the same person who hired these two goons must be the one who left that message."

"So it would seem. Since we appear to have lost the two here, whoever this person is must be trying to lure me back there in order to have another shot at me."

"Will your friend in Boston be safe?"

"She should be, since whoever is after me obviously knows I'm out here. But you, Noah, are another matter. If they find us again—"

"Jane, don't."

"I'd feel a lot better if you—"

"But I wouldn't feel better, so the matter is closed."

He stopped and faced her, struggling not to take her hands. He knew he couldn't trust himself to touch her again. "I told you yesterday, we're in this together. To the end. I meant what I said."

Her body had tensed the moment he'd faced her again. Color rose to her cheeks. The blue of her eyes swam liquid and warm at the edges of her softening guard.

God, how he wanted that guard totally down when she looked at him! He wanted to see again what her eyes had said to him before. He wanted her back in his arms. He wanted—

She turned away again, and rightfully so. She must have read all those thoughts in his eyes.

He tried for as much casualness in his voice as he could manage. He didn't manage a whole lot. "This attempt to get you away from San Francisco may be a good sign. It may mean we're getting close. Any idea what we should try next?''

He heard her take a deep breath and let it out with a small sigh.

"I thought maybe the library."

"The library? Why?"

"The fact that Ina Dusart never heard about or read about the bus accident continues to bother me. I'd like to go through the newspaper archives at the library to see what kind of coverage the story received."

THE LIBRARY WAS BUSY. They found a corner cubbyhole in the back with two viewers, side by side, just vacated. Noah stood proprietary guard while Jane approached the reference librarian to get microfilm of the 1966 newspapers. When she returned, she had two reels in her hand.

"There were two major newspapers then, the *Chronicle* and the *Examiner*. Which do you want?"

"I'll take the *Chronicle*. What date are we looking for?"

Jane handed over one of the reels and sat beside him. "September 24."

Noah set his reel into the machine and turned quickly through the dates.

"Got it. A Saturday—we're in luck. Saturday papers are always the thinnest."

Slowly they turned the knobs of their respective viewers, each carefully reading the headlines of the microfilmed newspapers. As Noah predicted, it didn't take long. But it wasn't a productive search.

Jane's tongue played at the side of her mouth. "This doesn't make any sense. Why can't we find the story?"

"Maybe it didn't get into the newspaper until the next day. Let's look at the Sunday edition."

Jane nodded as she joined Noah in advancing the screens. Once again they each began on page one, carefully reading each headline. The thicker Sunday newspaper took a lot more time. Noah was just about ready to give up when he heard Jane call out excitedly. "Look!"

Noah abandoned his screen and slid his chair closer to Jane's so he could read over her shoulder.

But she smelled so sweet and warm and near that for a moment his eyes just refused to focus.

"You see it?"

"See what?"

"There," she said, pointing to a corner of the screen.

He followed her pointing finger to the small headline that appeared three-fourths of the way down on the right-hand side.

Bus Accident Kills 45

Northrock, Vermont. (AP)—Forty-five people died yesterday when their bus skidded on freakishly icy roads and crashed into a ravine, bursting into flames. Four survivors, two men, a woman and a child were rushed by ambulance to the nearest hospital. Authorities say that it will take time to identify the victims because of the badly charred remains. The survivors' names have not been released.

Jane leaned back. Her tone sounded slightly deflated. "Not much of a story. It doesn't say anything about the child or anyone else on the bus being from the San Francisco area, does it?"

"Maybe a follow-up story might. Let's look at Monday's paper."

They found a follow-up story in the *Chronicle*'s Monday paper, but nothing in the *Examiner*. The follow-up story reiterated what was in the *Examiner*'s Sunday article, with the only new information being that one of the initial male survivors had died in the hospital.

"Still nothing about the child being from San Francisco or any of the names of the victims. Could it be that information was never released to the press?"

"Only one way to find out. We've got to look for more follow-up stories."

Noah and Jane diligently checked through the headlines on the papers for the next two weeks, but found no further mention of the bus crash.

"Strange, the story just dying like that. At least now we know why Ina didn't remember hearing about a bus accident involving a child from San Francisco. There's nothing in either of those stories we found that connects the people on that bus to San Francisco. I wonder why?" said Jane with a frown.

"Were you hurt in the crash?"

"Surely I would have been told if I had been."

"When were you adopted?"

"October 24, 1966."

"A month to the day after the accident. If you'd been hurt in anything but a superficial way, I very much doubt they would have allowed you to be placed so soon. You know what this means, Jane?"

She looked up at him, only to quickly look away to fiddle with the knobs on the viewer. She'd been avoiding prolonged eye contact ever since Chinatown. Considering what his eyes were broadcasting, he could hardly blame her.

"What?"

"That no one in San Francisco, other than child welfare and that attorney Edelson, ever knew you claimed to be from here. Could that have been deliberate, do you suppose?"

"If so, it brings up some intriguing possibilities. I may have been wrong to think that there was nothing unusual about my adoption. I'm going to call child welfare and see what happens when I throw a few accusations around."

While Jane went off looking for a phone and telephone directory, Noah spent his time printing the two articles they had found on the bus accident. He had just finished returning the microfilm rolls to the reference librarian and paying for his copies when Jane came back, with a curious look on her face.

"You found out something from child welfare?"

"I talked to three different people. They were pleasant, but firm. One, they told me they would discuss nothing over the phone. Two, they would release no information without the properly signed legal document that authorized them to."

"You knew it was a long shot, Jane."

"So was finding Desmond Edelson's name still in the yellow pages. But I did."

"What?"

"He's still practicing, Noah. Amazing, isn't it? His address is in a building off Market, which is the financial district. He must have done well over these years. That's expensive real estate. Lease has to be hefty."

"You've been studying that map again when I wasn't looking," he said, teasingly.

She smiled. "We can probably be there in under twenty minutes."

"You mean go now? Without calling first?"

"I've just learned my lesson with child welfare. If we call, we'll probably get a secretary who's been trained to put off anybody who doesn't have an appointment. I vote for just showing up and worming our way in."

"You've got guts, Jane."

"You're not without a few of those yourself."

She lightly flipped the words over her shoulder as she headed out of the library at a fast clip. Noah scurried to get to her side, relieved the tension had eased between them and determined to keep his emotions strictly in control from now on.

He'd given her a promise, and he was going to keep it—somehow.

DESMOND EDELSON'S secretary was a young male, who wore a stiff suit and sported a formidable face. Noah had never needed to get past a secretary before. He'd always been expected by the person behind the closed door. He approached hesitantly.

But not Jane. She strode up to the formally clad young man with her husky voice broadcasting full confidence.

"My name's Williams. I'd like to see Desmond Edelson immediately. It's very important."

Her forceful charge and words made not one dent in the fixed expression on the secretary's face.

"I'm sorry, Ms. Williams. Mr. Edelson only sees people by appointment."

"You mean he's with someone now?"

"He is reviewing his brief for an upcoming court case. If you would like to tell me the nature of your business, I'll see if I can find a free hour sometime next week."

"Oh, an appointment won't be necessary. Just tell him our department did everything we could to save his home, but the fire was quite difficult to control."

Jane turned and was halfway to the door before the secretary had time to respond. He shot out of his chair, formality fleeing as his voice ascended two octaves.

"Fire? Did you say fire?"

Jane came to a gradual halt and took her time in pivoting on the thick carpet to face the secretary.

"You heard me correctly."

"One moment, Ms. Williams. I think you'd best see Mr. Edelson immediately."

The secretary picked up the phone and punched in the intercom. He tried to keep his conversation confidential, even cupping the mouthpiece with his hand. But the impact of Jane's words had definitely caused him to lose his composure and raise his voice. His side of the conversation could be heard quite distinctly.

"Yes, I know you didn't want to be disturbed, but you'll want to see these people. It's about a fire at your home."

The secretary listened for a moment more, then replaced the receiver on its base and nodded toward the closed door beside him. "Go right in."

Noah treated himself to a private smile at Jane's ingenuity. She had successfully stormed the citadel. But now the real test came. How was she going to handle the attorney once the deception was exposed?

At full speed, it seemed. Her step never faltered as she charged the closed door, twisted the knob and went barreling inside.

Jane heard Noah behind her, closing the door to the inner office. It was a large room, nicely appointed in dark walnut, sailing ships floating in the pictures and some really spectacular ones suspended in bottles filling an entire display case.

But Jane took them all in with a very quick glance. Most of her attention centered on the small man behind the large desk. He'd risen to a height no greater than her own. He reminded her of a Chihuahua. Thin, neat and shaky, he was attired in a camel-colored suit and had large brown eyes.

But what surprised Jane most was his age. The man before her was barely forty.

His voice was high, uneven. "This is something about a fire? At my home?"

She boldly walked up to the desk.

"You're not Desmond Edelson."

He seemed disconcerted by her proclamation, then hesitant. "No. I'm Dorsey Edelson."

She extended her hand for a shake. "I'm looking for your father. My name is Jane Williams."

Edelson froze in the act of holding out his hand. He stiffened visibly, his large eyes stunned and staring.

"My father?"

"Desmond Edelson. He handled my adoption twenty-eight years ago."

Edelson's hand came back to life and resumed its reach for hers. His shake was perfunctory and brief.

"You're mistaken, Ms. Williams. My father wasn't Desmond Edelson. Desmond was my uncle."

"Was?"

"Yes. He died. Six months ago."

"I'm sorry. My condolences, Mr. Edelson. I presume you've taken over your uncle's practice?"

"That's correct. But I believe you are in my office under false pretenses, Ms. Williams. Your visit has nothing to do with a fire at my home, does it?"

He'd recovered from her initial onslaught. She knew she had to throw him a new curve.

"No, but I didn't wish to alarm your secretary by mentioning the irregularities surrounding my adoption. I'm sure you can appreciate why."

"Irregularities?"

"Mr. Edelson, this is my colleague, Mr. Armstrong. Shall we sit down and discuss this very serious matter?"

Dorsey Edelson nodded at the two chairs in front of his desk. He resumed his chair, leaning over his desk as though for support. His hands found a pen and he held on to it firmly.

Jane and Noah took the indicated chairs. The man before them said nothing, just watched her with nervous hands and nervous eyes.

"Did your uncle discuss my adoption with you?"

"No."

A quick, sharp answer.

"You've never heard my name before?"

"No."

Too quick? Too sharp?

"Then you must not be aware that Desmond Edelson contacted me about the . . . questionable part he played in that adoption."

Something like panic flashed through Dorsey Edelson's eyes. "When was this?"

"About a year ago."

"My uncle became . . . very ill a year ago."

"Then he must have mailed the letter just before his illness."

"Letter?" Some of the panic dissipated. "Where is this letter? Show it to me."

"I don't have it on me, Mr. Edelson. But I'll be happy to give you the gist of its contents. Your uncle said he wanted to see me. He said there were some irregularities about my adoption that he needed to tell me about. Something about his conscience bothering him all these years. He said he needed to discuss the matter in person."

"I don't believe it. He never would have written you."

"If you don't know anything about the circumstances surrounding my adoption, how could you possibly be so certain that your uncle didn't write to me about it?"

"Because he never wrote anything. He hated to write. He dictated all his correspondence."

"Well, no doubt the secrecy surrounding my case prompted him to act uncharacteristically. Besides, if your uncle didn't send such a letter, why would I be here?"

His large eyes narrowed. He'd half bought her bluff, but only half.

"If you say my uncle sent you this letter a year ago, why did it take you so long to fly out here to see him?"

Jane shot forward eagerly in her chair.

"*Fly out here?* Mr. Edelson, if you don't know anything about me or my case, how can you possibly know I had to *fly out here?*"

A nervous twitch developed at the corner of Dorsey Edelson's left eye. His hands strangled the helpless pen within them. A long moment passed before he spoke again.

"Ms. Williams, I just naturally assumed that if you'd been from the immediate area, you would have managed to get here sooner. After all, you claimed you were notified a year ago. I repeat, what kept you from responding more promptly to this alleged letter hinting of alleged improprieties?"

It was a good save, if it was a save—and a smart tactic. Go back on the offensive, she thought, holding her position on the edge of her chair.

"Childbirth and a very sick little boy prevented me from coming sooner, Mr. Edelson. Tardy or not, I'm here now. And I'd like to see my records."

Dorsey Edelson pushed back his chair and rose to his feet. "I'm sorry, Ms. Williams, but I cannot help you."

Jane kept her seat. "You mean you won't help me."

"I mean I cannot help you. Even before the major illness that led to his incapacitation and death this past year, my uncle's mind had been slipping. If he did send you such a letter ranting about some impropriety, that was the reason. He was not himself."

"What do you mean, not himself?"

"I mean my aunt and I found him burning the records of all his past cases in the fireplace one night, babbling incoherently. We soon found he had also made a few... unfortunate calls to clients. A week later he suffered the full mental breakdown that reduced him to a virtual vegetable until his death six months ago. So you see, Ms. Williams, there is no file."

"And if I came back here with a lawyer, the police and a court order?"

"Go right ahead. Add a search warrant if you can convince a judge to issue one. Interview my aunt. My cousin witnessed the record burning, too. Speak to her. I can't produce what doesn't exist. Now, as my secretary no doubt explained, I have a brief to review. Perhaps you and Mr. Armstrong will let me get back to it."

NOAH WAITED UNTIL THEY were back in the car before commenting on their meeting with the attorney.

"It was a good try, Jane. You almost had me believing Desmond Edelson sent you a letter. That was a nervous little man for a while there."

"But why was he nervous? Because he thought I might represent a suit against the firm for alleged improprieties in a twenty-eight-year-old adoption? Or because he knows there were definite improprieties in that adoption and wants to keep me from learning about them?"

"I would have assumed the former, but something in your tone makes me think that you're considering the latter. Why?"

"At first I thought he acted sort of stunned because I mixed up his uncle and father. But now I'm wondering if his initial reaction to me was because when I gave him my name, it rang a bell."

"And you think that now because . . . ?"

"His phraseology, 'fly out here.' Remember? He explained that he assumed I came from out of the area. But even so, that doesn't quite explain that phraseology he used, does it?"

"I see what you mean. You could have been from the state of Washington, in which case he would have said 'fly down here.' Or from Los Angeles, in which case he would have said 'fly up here.' But he definitely did say 'fly out here,' which is something you say to someone from the East Coast."

"Exactly. And the only way he'd know that Jane Williams was from the East Coast is if he knew about my case."

"It's a small thing, but I agree it does bear consideration. Do you think he made up that business about the records in the fire?"

"No. He was too willing for us to talk to his aunt and cousin. Still, that doesn't mean he didn't see the file before it was burned or talk to his uncle about the adoption."

"But if your adoption was not the kind that required secrecy, why wouldn't Dorsey Edelson just come clean with what he knows?"

"I can only think of one reason, and what we learned at the library this morning bears it out. Maybe I've been lied to. Maybe there were things about my adoption that were kept secret."

"You mean because nothing was ever mentioned about your being from San Francisco in the news reports?"

"Yes. I always assumed that the extra money my adoptive parents paid to get me was because of the age requirements they were anxious for the authorities to overlook. But what if the extra money was paid out for another reason?"

"Like not making any attempt to look for any living relatives?"

"Exactly. If Ina Dusart is really my grandmother, nothing in the news reports gave her any clue that a child of my age saying she was from San Francisco had been orphaned in that bus crash. And because that information wasn't released, Ina had absolutely no opportunity to come forward to claim me."

"You think your adoptive parents were capable of going along with getting you that way?"

"No. I very much doubt they knew that what they were paying for was to squelch a search. When they spoke to me about it, they always said that the extras they paid were to help circumvent the requirement for the adopting couple to be within a certain age."

"That probably was the story they were given. Well, what now?"

"We're close to the Triton. I'd like to go back to the hotel room and make a call."

"To whom?"

"Ina Dusart. I realize now that I missed posing a couple of important questions to her."

"Such as?"

"What Katya's blood type was. And her baby's."

"Why? Do you have an unusual blood type?"

"No, but if Katya's child has a different blood type from mine, then that would reduce the chances of my being that child. I should have asked her that right away. I don't know why I didn't think of it."

"Give yourself a break, Jane. The shock of meeting someone who could very well be your grandmother is enough to shake anyone up."

As soon as they entered the suite Jane headed for her adjoining room. The maid hadn't made up the bed yet. She plopped onto it and reached for the phone. Noah had followed her, but she noticed that this time he refrained from sitting next to her. He stood on the other side of the nightstand.

She understood the physical distance he'd put between them since that moment in Chinatown when they'd both lost their heads. She could still feel that kiss and how tightly he'd held her—so tightly that even their heartbeats had pounded as one.

He'd never hidden his want of her. He was too honest for that. She had been counting on his self-control. She hadn't been prepared for his suddenly losing it or her reaction to that sudden loss. His want had completely overcome her, driving every logical thought out of her body, leaving only her desire for him.

In one quick instant she had been lost to the primitive, undeniable heat that poured from his body into hers, scorching her blood, melting her very bones. It was everything she had imagined and more.

Thank God his control was back now. She couldn't handle another embrace like that—not if she wanted to keep a semblance of propriety between them.

She tried Ina Dusart's number. After two rings the answering machine came on.

She waited until the beep to leave her message.

"Ina, this is Jane Williams. I came to see you last night. I have a couple of—"

"Who are you? Why are you doing this to me?"

She bolted upright. It wasn't just the fact that Ina had cut in on her message that surprised her. It was the tone and content of Ina's words.

"Ina, this is Jane Williams. What's wrong?"

"Jane Williams, ha! Don't pretend with me. The police left here fifteen minutes ago! They told me all about you and your nasty scheme."

"Police? Scheme? Ina, what are you talking about?"

"You're nothing but a con artist, you and that partner of yours. Preying on the emotions of older people who have lost track of their loved ones. Pretending to be those loved ones so you can extract money from us!"

"Ina, that's not true!"

"Save your breath. I'm not listening to any more of your lies. Those two policemen are going to catch up with you. And when they do, I hope they put you away forever!"

Jane started at the dial tone suddenly blaring in her ear. She dropped the receiver onto its cradle and jumped to her feet as the full implications of Ina's words made themselves felt.

"Noah, we've got to get out of here."

"What is it? What did she say?"

"Two 'policemen' left Ina Dusart's a while ago. They gave her some outrageous story about our being con artists out for her money. They must have been Marty and Vance."

"And you told Ina last night where we were staying. I get the picture. Let's get packed."

They threw everything into their suitcases and were heading out the door to the suite a mere minute later.

But it was a mere minute too late. Because stepping off the elevator at that very instant down the hallway, directly in their path, were Marty and Vance.

Chapter Ten

"Quick, Noah! The stairwell."

Noah slammed shoulder first through the stairwell door. They ran down the steps at top speed, neither wasting a fraction of forward movement to look back.

Seconds later the sound of the door crashing open above them reverberated through the stairwell. Then came the sound of stamped feet in quick pursuit.

When Noah and Jane barreled out the bottom stairwell exit, Jane whispered urgently, "They'll be expecting us to go through the lobby. There's an employees' side entrance that leads out to the alley. Follow me."

She darted ahead with Noah right behind her. They charged out the side door and sprinted down the alley, and then over one and a half blocks to where the car had been valet parked on Sutter. Noah snatched the keys from the attendant, flipping him a ten. It took just seconds to throw their luggage into the back and jump inside. Noah gunned the engine and they were off.

But not fast enough. As they sped out the entrance and turned onto the street, Marty and Vance came running down the sidewalk on a direct collision course with them.

"Jane, get down!"

Noah locked eyes with the dark, stocky Marty. He read anger and vengeance in that face. A small, nasty smile curled the man's lips. It was like a slow-motion film being unwound before Noah's eyes.

Marty halted, spread his feet, lifted his arm and pointed his gun directly at Noah. Noah could almost see his finger pulling back on the trigger.

Noah had already scrunched down as far as he could in his seat, and the pedal was to the metal. There wasn't a thing more he could do.

Then suddenly, from out of nowhere, another car came whipping around the corner and drove between them, blocking Marty's aim.

Noah passed safely out of range and it was over. Except for the loud cursing that echoed behind them from the angry men left on the sidewalk.

Noah let out a breath he didn't even know he'd been holding as he straightened and Jane's head rose above the dashboard.

For the next ten minutes he concentrated on his driving, darting right and left at top speed in so circuitous a route that he was certain any car trying to follow would be lost. Then he slowed to the speed limit and glanced at Jane.

"These guys can't really be San Francisco cops."

"I doubt it. But they obviously convinced Candy in birth records that they were. It's the only thing that would explain why she gave them the same birth certificates she gave to you. And when they found Ina, they fed her that line and tricked her into giving away our location. They're going to be hard to shake."

"If we stay in San Francisco."

In his peripheral vision he saw her turning more fully toward him. "*If* we stay in San Francisco? Noah, what are you suggesting?"

"Let's go to Vermont."

"Just like that?"

"It's the next logical step. We've exhausted our leads here. Even if Dorsey Edelson knows anything, he's not about to say. The child welfare people won't help us. Ina Dusart won't answer any more questions thinking what she does about us. And it's the fastest way I can think of to lose two bogus San Francisco cops."

She said nothing for a moment, but he could almost feel her mental scales weighing the suggestion.

"You're right, of course," she finally said. "The only real firsthand information we can get about that bus crash and its victims is where it happened. Let's head for the airport."

"Any idea what direction that would be?"

"Another mile down this street and there should be an on-ramp for the freeway going south."

"You have to have a built-in compass. It's the only explanation."

She laughed then, a happy, husky sound. He was amazed how she could find a laugh after the danger they'd just escaped . . . and still did face, for that matter. He was equally amazed to find himself joining in.

THEIR WAIT at the San Francisco airport proved a long one. The first flight they could get to Vermont didn't leave until one-fifteen the next morning. Noah booked two flights. His explanation was straight and to the point:

"No telling if their fake police ID's can get past airport personnel. Our red herring is a USAir flight to Los Angeles for Mr. and Mrs. Armstrong, paid for with a credit card. Since they know I have a place there, they just might fall for it."

The tickets he booked to Vermont were with Northwest, using the names of David and Alida Glowen. He paid for them with cash.

"How did you come up with those names?" Jane wanted to know.

"They're my maternal grandparents. Great couple. Well into their seventies and still as much in love as the day they married fifty-five years ago."

"Where do they live?"

"Alaska. Born and bred there, same as me. Met in an Alaskan snowstorm. My grandfather was only seventeen. His sled team fell through the ice, and he alone survived. He walked for four days without food or water, trying to find help. He was snow-blind by the second day."

He read her changing expression, but resisted his desire to take her hand in reassurance.

"Not to worry. Story has a happy ending. My grandmother and her brothers found him half-frozen on the ice. She was sixteen. She stayed by his side night and day, nursing him back to health. He proposed to her even before he regained his sight. He'd fallen in love with her voice the first time he heard it. Then when he saw her face, he fell in love with her all over again."

Jane didn't know why the story left a lump in her throat. Maybe it was the image of that young love still so much alive after fifty-five years. Or maybe it was the smile that rested in Noah's eyes as he spoke about these people who belonged so strongly to each other—and to him.

They took their time over a leisurely meal, then walked around the airport, always keeping an eye out for the men they knew could appear at any moment. The quiet between them now had an intimate feel.

"What is your place in North Hollywood like?"

"Small and unexciting. I bought it because it has a great tennis court in the backyard."

"The accident happened in Southern California, didn't it?"

"Yes."

"Why didn't you just go to your own place?"

"Because it has a great tennis court in the backyard."

He'd said it easily, but she knew it hadn't been easy for him at all.

"Besides, I knew that was where everyone would try to find me. I needed some quiet time to myself."

"And instead you got mixed up in this madness." Her words gushed with self-recrimination.

His hand brushed hers, ever so slightly. "I'm not sorry, Jane. No matter what happens, I'll never be sorry for a moment of it."

He fell silent, but his eyes said much more to her. As always, their honesty prevented any subterfuge. She looked away from their message—for many reasons. But the primary reason had shifted over this past eventful day and that knowledge sent both a thrill and a sense of dread up her spine. So much stood between them. And when he knew the truth of her past, would this man still look at her like that?

"I imagine being a part of one of the most prominent families in America has its share of good and happy times?"

He was making a valiant effort, but she knew it was a halfhearted one. The last thing she wanted to do was to cause him any further pain.

"I'd rather talk about you. What were the good and happy times that preceded your becoming a tennis star?"

He smiled, with his eyes as well as his lips.

"A woman who's willing to listen to a man talk about himself. You're a rare lady. Ah, where do I start? My misspent youth, I suppose."

It didn't sound misspent at all to Jane, just spirited and free, and full of the ability to laugh at his own mistakes. She smiled as he regaled her with images of sailing across frozen lakes propelled by an arctic wind with one of his mother's best sheets tied to a broom mast. He confessed that the resultant collision with a tree wasn't nearly as painful as the later penalties his mom had imposed when she got that sheet back in tatters.

Then there was the day he rescued a doe caught on the frozen lake by wrapping his coat around her neck and pulling her to a firm foothold in the adjoining forest. He talked about how good it felt when she scampered off. And how bad it felt when he watched neighbors cleaning their rifles for the deer-hunting season after that. Many more youthful adventures followed, and she was sorry when the stories came to an end.

"You mentioned a sister once and a two-year-old nephew. What other family do you have?"

"Actually, I've got quite an assortment. My parents and grandparents on both sides are still alive and active. My sister, Noel, is a couple of years older. My brothers, Nathaniel and Nelson, are younger by one and three years respectively."

"Your first names all start with *n?*"

"My father's name is Norman and my mother's is Nancy. As I see it, they couldn't resist perpetuating the big *N* dynasty."

He got another small smile out of her. "Are they all as tall as you?"

"I'm the runt of the male litter. Dad's six-four. Nathaniel and Nelson both passed six-five by the time they were eighteen.

"Even Noel is six feet tall. She almost qualified for the Olympics as an ice skater a dozen years ago. Now she makes porcelain dolls that wear buckskin and sing opera when you squeeze their arms. My younger brothers are partners in a fledgling fishing fleet, an unlikely enterprise, since Nathaniel holds a doctorate in metallurgy, Nelson has a masters in Latin and neither of them know anything about fishing.

"Then there's my dad, who after getting his pension as a government geologist has determinedly opened a pizza delivery place with twelve exotic toppings and the proud motto that it will be delivered no matter what the weather, although no guarantee is given that it won't be frozen when it gets there."

She chuckled as she pictured frozen pizza being delivered.

"And last, but not least, there's my mom, who breeds prize huskies and who knows how not to be too impressed by her eldest son's fame. She recently relegated my Wimbledon trophy to the far end of the mantel in order to proudly display her two-year-old grandson's handmade Mother's Day card."

He spoke easily, humorously, warmly, honestly. He was a man who knew about family love—the real kind. The kind that made children feel secure and encouraged them to blossom forth in whatever direction they chose, as long as they did so with modesty and maintained a strong sense of right and wrong.

Noah suddenly stopped and turned toward her.

"What's wrong?"

"Nothing. That was our call. Time to board the plane." She looked at her watch.

"Ten to one. The time went so fast."

"Never, never turn a man's head that way. If you leave him with the impression that he's a stimulating conversationalist, you'll never get rid of him."

He said it with good humor and punctuated it with a laugh. She preceded him to the line waiting to board, wishing for many things that she knew were impossible.

Jane wasn't someone who could sleep on planes, even in the comfortable first-class seats Noah had purchased for them. She was rather surprised to find that less than twenty minutes into the air he was dead to the world. Another one of the learned talents of an international tennis star, apparently.

Of course, he must need the rest. His energy and sparkling vitality for life made her forget sometimes the kind of injuries his body had so recently sustained. She got a blanket out of the overhead compartment and draped it over him. The light brush of freckles over his nose twitched in time to his low, gentle snore.

She smiled. He never spoke of the pain, never complained. He'd showed her a lot of different strengths over the past few days. Damn, she'd been with strong men before. How was it that this man's strength could make her feel so weak?

Her eyes clouded with a welling frustration and forbidden need. She turned away from them. She passed the next long hours watching an in-flight movie she'd already seen and flipping through magazines she'd already read. She hated plane trips, and she'd had far too many recently.

By the time they finally landed in Minneapolis for a plane change, her body ached from inactivity. Their connecting flight was delayed several hours. It was nearly seven in the evening, Vermont time, when their propeller aircraft touched down at Vermont's Burlington Airport, ending the final leg of their trip.

"You look beat, Jane. I say we rent a car and head for the nearest hotel."

She straightened her sagging shoulders, shoving a forced energy into her tone. "Not on my account, Noah. We should really start investigating right away. I'll be fine."

Of course she chose that precise moment to stumble and would have gone down face first if his steadying hand hadn't grabbed hold of her arm at the last second.

"Yeah. You'll be fine, all right."

All the way through the car rental process and the subsequent search for a motel room, he listened indulgently to her continuous ramblings about why they needed to get right to work. Renting a car wasn't so easy and he was forced to settle for all that was left—a green Gremlin. And finding a motel proved even more difficult.

Burlington, which rested on the terraced slopes of sparkling Lake Champlain, was a fairyland of vibrant, spectacular fall color, and was consequently, beginning to fill up with visiting foliage enthusiasts.

When Noah finally found an available room and bath, it was a private rental by a resident with a summer home on the lake. Noah grabbed it, despite the fact that he was told they could have it for only one night.

Noah led Jane inside the private side entrance, found the room small and the furnishings utilitarian, but was thankful that at least it possessed two beds and a small balcony overlooking the lake.

He set her on the closest bed, continuing to ignore her protests that she wasn't tired and that they should get on with their search, as he helped her off with her Windbreaker and unlaced her shoes. The moment her head hit the pillow, she was out.

The sun was setting on Lake Champlain, a vibrant persimmon ribbon shimmering on the purple-blue water.

He sat on the other bed and watched her. A small smile played across his mouth. He'd begun to think she could outlast the Energizer Bunny. She obviously thought she could, too.

He'd learned a lot about her in their airport conversation the night before, despite the fact—or maybe because of the fact—that he'd done most of the talking.

He'd watched her face as he spoke of his growing up in the wilds of Alaska, learning about survival, learning to rely on others and be relied on. Her adoptive parents must have been able to provide her with monetary things. But when it came to other things, she clearly felt she'd missed out. That much had been quite plain in the wistful longing in her eyes. He wasn't sure exactly what those other things were, but he thought he'd caught a glimpse of them when she talked about being made afraid as a child. He sensed that she still felt under the cloud of that conditioning and fought as strongly against it as she fought to find this secret surrounding her birth.

She slept on her side on top of the bedspread, her left arm beneath the pillow at her head, her right arm curled at her waist. The soft colors of the setting sun streamed through the balcony window to bathe her in their warm, rosy glow. His eyes traced her lithe frame from the gentle arc of her hip to the curve of her shoulder to the rich creaminess of her skin and thick dark silkiness of her hair.

A mere scrap of a woman. Stubborn. Infuriating. So incredibly exciting.

For a moment he allowed the forbidden images of undressing and making love to her to cloud his mind. Then, before they could get out of hand, he forcibly swept them away.

These were dangerous thoughts to indulge. But he knew he could not think about the fact that he could never have this woman. That thought would drive him insane.

When he thought again of all she had faced and the difficult and dangerous task she'd set for herself, a protective wave swept through him so powerful that it left him shaking.

He'd told her he'd be beside her to the end of her search, and he knew he would be. But Noah also knew the doubt that lay around the edges of that promise. A successful end to her search did not mean success in other ways.

Unless it was Charles Tremont behind these attempts on his wife's life. Was that too much to hope for?

Listen to me, he thought. *How could I be hoping that Jane's husband is trying to kill her?*

Because he wanted all vestiges of feeling she had for Charles to be wiped away. Because he wanted to claim the feelings that lay between them.

Because he was afraid that unless Charles was guilty, Jane would be going back to him. He didn't want to think of her with another man. He was far more selfish and possessive than he'd ever realized.

And shouldn't he be? After all, he was the one by her side. He was the one she'd given her trust to. He was the one she would share her secret with. He was the one protecting her. And he was the one who would be with her to the end.

He draped the spread over her body and leaned down to kiss the smooth warmth of her cheek. Then he lay on the other twin bed and, knowing she was safe and sound and with him, he fell asleep.

"WHERE IN THE HELL IS JANE?"

"Loren! Your language!"

Loren Tremont pounded across the hardwood floor of his study and charged through the eggshell-white French doors leading to the inner courtyard of his estate. There he spewed obscenities under his breath as he walked through his perfectly pruned gardens.

Victoria dutifully followed her husband, recognizing the exercise as his attempt to reclaim his control. She had witnessed only two things in her married life to the Honorable Judge Loren Tremont that had made him so thoroughly lose his temper: the severe stock market dip that black October day in '87 and his daughter-in-law. He'd recovered from the financial shock of that market dip, but his daughter-in-law was another matter altogether.

Victoria caught up with Loren near the rosebushes. She stood behind him and spoke in a loud voice in order to get his attention. She knew he was a man who did not like to be touched.

"Dear, we've left an urgent message with instructions. That's all we can do."

He said nothing for a moment, but she saw the telltale sag in those stalwart shoulders during this private moment. It sent an uncomfortable twinge through her already-taut body.

"He's so sick, Victoria. Just like... I didn't want to believe this genetic thing, but if it's true that they are..."

Victoria reminded herself she must keep calm. Absolutely, positively calm.

"Do not worry, Loren. You have so much else on your mind. I will see to it. You can rely on me to do what is necessary."

Loren turned partially to her, and she saw the slight sagging of his jowls and the lines about his eyes. Victoria's heart jolted.

"Noah, I swear if I saw this landscape reproduced on a canvas, I would never believe the colors had come from nature. Look at it!"

He smiled, rather touched at the exuberance in her voice, and surprised, too, that a person who lived on the East

Coast could be so completely impressed by the change of season, something she witnessed every year.

"I'm looking, Jane. It's nice, very picturesque. But at the moment I'm more concerned with where we are."

Reluctantly her eyes dipped back to the map laid out on her lap in the passenger seat.

"We should be there soon. The road leads off to the left after this covered bridge coming up."

"Didn't you tell me the same thing just before we went over the last two covered bridges?"

She had the grace to smile. "This next one has to have a sign that says Northrock following it."

"It has to, huh?"

Fortunately for Noah's growing unease, it did. An arrow beneath it pointed left and headed down another fairy-tale lane of glorious fall color. A half mile later the road rose and dipped once more.

They saw the sign first: *Entering Northrock. Settled 1761. Population 501.* And then the road dipped and there it was, small and beautiful, a sudden little crowd of buildings on either side of the country lane after miles of nothing but the impossibly glorious colors of a northern Vermont fall.

There was a redbrick church with round windows and a square bell tower with a Romanesque arch above it and a large town clock built into the face. Across the street was a two-story stone structure that looked like an old courthouse, sturdy and unadorned, except for a whitewash that left it glistening in the sun.

On either side of these two dominant structures were no more than half a dozen small, white, single-story houses with deeply pitched roofs, their green lawns displaying a light mosaic of bright fall leaves.

"Blink twice and you'd miss it. But it's lovely."

"At least at this time of the year," Noah added.

"During winter it must be a wonderland."

"Jane, the words *winter* and *wonderland* up here are an oxymoron."

"That's an unusual attitude for a man brought up in Alaska."

"I'm an unusual man. Hadn't you noticed?"

She looked away, their easy banter suddenly not so easy. "There's a sign in front of that stone building."

They pulled up to it and read the beautiful, carved wood directory in front.

"According to this directory, this building houses not only *The Northrock News,* but the post office, library and a small grocery store, as well.

A narrow parking lot, nearly obliterated by leaves, sat just on the other side. Noah pulled into it, and they got out of the car to go inside. The heavy, wooded double-door entry opened into a hallway with four separate inner doors. All were open. The far right door sported a brass plate with The Northrock News engraved on it, and that's where they headed. Noah rapped his knuckles on the open door as they entered.

The little round man inside had his back to the open doorway. He was leaning over a metal type-case tray, which contained special divisions for each alphabetical letter and punctuation mark. His hair was a white, fuzzy monk's tonsure. He wore a black leather apron and a long-sleeved white shirt rolled up to the elbows. He and the old-fashioned press behind him could have come out of a 1940s black-and-white movie.

Jane called from the doorway. "Excuse me."

He ignored her as he continued to assemble lines of type with his right hand, positioning them in the metal stick held across his left palm.

Jane stepped up to the worn wooden table he bent over and touched him gently on the arm.

He turned with a start toward her. His face was quite full, made up of puffy red cheeks and a bulbous nose. Surprise sparked out of dark, intelligent eyes, underlined by half-moon reading glasses. He hastily put down the metal stick in his left hand and reached for his hearing aid at the other edge of the wooden bench, which he promptly affixed to his ear. His voice was as warm as his cheeks.

"Sorry, don't like to wear this contraption unless I have to. Makes my ear sore. Name's Ichabod Hayes, folks. Everybody just calls me Ichy."

He gave them a small smile and held out a slightly smudged pudgy hand. Jane liked the warm, solid shake behind it.

"I'm Jane Williams and this is Noah Armstrong. Are you the editor of *The Northrock News?*"

"Yup. Owner, editor, chief reporter, typesetter, printer and everything else you can name. I also own the grocery store and serve as postmaster and librarian. Something I can do for you folks?"

"Matter of fact, there is. How long has *The Northrock News* been around?"

Ichy looked them both over well for one long, full moment, curiosity clearly building in his dark eyes.

"More 'n a hundred years."

"Do you have all the back issues?"

"Yup."

Jane fought down the anticipation percolating inside her. "Mr. Hayes—"

"Ichy."

"Of course, Ichy," Jane amended, finding it not so difficult to say to that round, smiling face, after all. "Do you suppose we could see some of the back issues?"

Jane felt a keen stab of curiosity from the little man's eyes.

"Don't see why not. Archives are upstairs."

He walked with a pronounced limp as he led them out of the room, through a passageway at the end of the hall and up some wooden steps leading to the second floor. It was an old, dark stairwell. Jane and Noah followed Ichy carefully over the worn wooden steps, holding on to the sturdy banister.

Ichy called to them over his shoulder. "Don't get many strangers up here in Northrock, especially not ones interested in local history. You writing a book?"

"No. Just following a personal inquiry."

"Interested in any particular year?"

"Yes—1966."

Ichy stopped abruptly on the top step and turned to look down at them. Jane noticed that the red puff of warmth in his cheeks seemed to suddenly recede. The warmth had also gone from his voice.

"The bus accident. You're interested in the bus accident."

Surprise raised Jane's voice. "How did you know?"

"I always knew someday someone would come. And here you are. Well, well. Maybe now I'll get some answers to the mystery that has haunted me for twenty-eight years."

Chapter Eleven

Jane and Noah couldn't get any more out of Ichy as to what his cryptic statement meant. He kept insisting that he'd talk to them only after they read the stories.

The upstairs room he led them to was long and dark and full of the paraphernalia of broken down printing presses, some of which looked as if they dated back to Gutenberg's day.

Ichy studied the contents of several metal cabinets before he pulled out a carefully bound but incredibly dusty book containing the fifty-two editions of *The Northrock News* for the year 1966. He struggled with his burden, finally dropping it on an equally dusty old wooden table, the twin of the one he had downstairs.

Then he left them in silence. Noah and Jane settled themselves on two hard wooden chairs and began to flip through the age-yellowed pages of the weekly newspaper, which ran four pages and was dated every Monday.

They came to an abrupt halt when they reached the only special edition that had a Sunday date, September 25. It was printed on one side of one page and sported a banner headline. A short story was punctuated by a large black-and-white picture, which took nearly half the page. It depicted a twisted piece of blackened metal, the caption below identifying it as a smashed bus.

Tragic Bus Accident Kills 45

A bus filled with fall tourists crashed yesterday when the driver lost control on the freakishly icy roads at Devil's Turn, a Northrock hazard that has caused many a previous tragedy. The bus tumbled down Devil's Ravine, bursting into flames, killing all but four of its forty-five passengers.

The survivors, two men, a woman and a child, were rushed to St. John's Hospital in St. Johnsburg. The condition of the survivors is unknown.

None of the identities of the victims or survivors has been released by the authorities. However, since the bus is owned by Sea-and-Scene, a New Hampshire company, it is unlikely any of its passengers were local residents.

According to authorities, the crash was apparently witnessed by a vacationing Canadian family, who stopped to give first aid to the victims, called an ambulance, but then mysteriously disappeared before the ambulance arrived.

Any residents of Northrock who have any further information about the crash should contact Sheriff Wright immediately.

"Did you notice whose byline this story carries, Noah?"

"Yes. Ichabod Hayes. No wonder he knew about the accident. He covered it."

"Is there a regular Monday paper following this special edition?"

"Let's see."

He turned the page. The picture of a child's stuffed bunny, which had unusual black-rimmed rhinestone buttons for eyes, sat on what looked like a pile of charred rubble. Its floppy ears had been burned. Its message sent a chill down her spine. Noah read aloud the story that went with the picture.

"Baby Girl Miraculously Escapes Injury In Bus Crash

The baby survivor of Saturday's tragic bus crash at Devil's Turn has been reported to be without injury by the staff at St. John's Hospital in St. Johnsburg.

The child, who told hospital personnel she's two, was apparently thrown clear of the rolling tour bus that exploded into flames at the bottom of Devil's Ravine. Although the girl has been unable to give authorities any other useful information, it is believed that she was traveling with her parents and that they are among the dead from the crash.

One of the two men who originally survived the crash died of smoke inhalation soon after reaching the hospital. The remaining man and woman are still considered in serious condition but expected to recover.

The identities of the survivors and victims are still not known."

"And no mention of your being from San Francisco, Jane."

"Maybe the doctors didn't understand what I was saying about a big red bridge that my parents called golden until later."

"Or maybe the information just hadn't come out in the newspaper yet. Let's continue reading on."

They did—through the next three weeks of papers. But, amazingly, they found no other mention of the bus accident, its survivors or its victims. *The Northrock News* had gone back to reporting the local events, chiefly centered around the impact of Washington legislation on a small, local, finished-wood industry struggling to survive against much larger manufacturing giants.

"That's odd, don't you think? I realize news that impacts a floundering wood-finishing industry is important, but that bus crash had to have been one of the biggest stories in years. And there's not another word about the fate of the survivors or the identity of its victims."

Noah nodded. "I think it's time we had that talk with Ichabod Hayes."

They found him downstairs in the small country store, waiting on two girls about eight, who both gave Jane and Noah a smile and a friendly hello. When the girls had left, Ichy beckoned Jane and Noah to a small wooden table with three chairs next to an unlit wood stove in the corner.

He picked up an enormous Sherlock-Holmes-type pipe from the center of the table and rested it, unlit, just inside his mouth. His puffy cheeks were now quite pale.

"Ichy, your story about that bus accident just faded away. Surely it shouldn't have, not after only two short reports, with so many questions still to be answered. What happened?"

He sucked on his pipe, his scrutiny internal and intense. "I remember it all, just like it was yesterday. I was fishing in the mountains when I heard the explosion. I thought it was a sonic boom at first. The air force frequently flew their jets over us in those days. Then sometime later I saw the flashing ambulance lights up on the road. I followed them to see what was going on."

He stopped and sucked on his unlit pipe some more.

"I was in Korea." He slapped his stiff right leg. "That's where I picked up this memento. I'd witnessed death as no one should. But that . . . that was a pretty gruesome scene, I can tell you. Even the ambulance attendants were shaken as they attended to the injured and counted the dead. I helped them with the latter. But after a while there wasn't anything more I could do."

"And so you thought of reporting the story?"

"Shooting it, first. I was a photojournalist in the service. That got me into the habit of carrying my old Leica camera slung around my neck. I had it with me that day. I snapped close-up pictures of the ambulance men as they worked on the survivors, trying to find the humanity in that scene. I remember tears coming to my eyes when I took a picture of a little pink bunny sitting on the rubble, its floppy ears charred but the rest of it whole—somehow having escaped the fire.''

"That was the one that got printed in the paper."

"Yup. That picture and the one of the burned bus. You could barely read the charred sign that said Sea-and-Scene, Portsmouth, New Hampshire, on its side. I had to climb up to the road to get that shot. Slipped hard a couple of times on the black ice that had slicked the surface. No wonder the driver had lost control on that turn. Miracle any of them survived. None probably would have if that Canadian family hadn't stopped."

"Did you ever learn any more about that family?"

"Nope. I arrived just after the ambulance. They were already long gone. The ambulance attendants showed me the evidence of the first aid they had performed. Apparently, after seeing to the survivors, they'd driven to a phone and called the hospital directly to report the accident. They didn't leave their names. The sheriff, Christian Wright, didn't even know about the accident until I got back and phoned him. While he went out to investigate, I began writing my story and convincing the editor to run it."

"You didn't own the newspaper then?"

"Oly Snowe owned *The Northrock News* then. Had for forty years. I was trying to talk him into selling it to me. But the old buzzard had printer's ink in his veins. Said he'd run it for another forty years. He might have, too, if that bus accident hadn't happened."

"Your story changed his mind?"

"More like the repercussions from it did. At first he was happy to run my piece. He looked through my photos, bought the prints and negatives, picked out the shot of the bus and kept the rest for follow-up stories. Offered me a byline and expenses. The 'expenses' part was what encouraged me to drive down to St. John's Hospital on Sunday to see about the survivors."

"Yes, we read your follow-up piece."

"Oly had no sooner distributed it than he was visited by the sheriff and those two men."

"Two men?"

"He told me two men from the Department of Transportation had strongly advised him to let the story die down so as not to impede their investigation. But he knew as well as I did that there wasn't anything we were printing about the story that should have impeded a traffic investigation."

"Then why did the men want the story stopped?"

"That's the question I asked Oly while I tried to stop him from burning my prints and negatives from the crash. Neither of my efforts was to any avail. Oly told me the pictures and negatives were his to burn, and he'd printed all he was going to about the bus crash story."

"Do you know why he acted that way, Ichy?"

"I saw the men when they left his office. Despite their civilian suits, just by the way they walked I knew they were military. Although why the military was involved in a bus accident, supposedly just involving a bunch of tourists, set off a whole new set of questions for me."

"Did you get any answers?"

"Not from Oly. Nor from Sheriff Chris Wright. Both treated me like some foreigner just because I was from Down East."

"Down East?"

"I was born and raised in Portland, Maine. I only came to settle in Northrock after doing my hitch in the army. Far as the locals were concerned, seven years in Essex County and I was still just "that Down Easterner." Anyway, I could tell that whoever those men were, they had intimidated Chris as much as Oly."

"But they didn't intimidate you?"

Ichy shrugged. "Maybe being brought up in a bigger town like Portland had taught me to be a little more questioning of authority. Or maybe I was born with just too curious a nature to let it go at that. I knew something was happening and I wanted to know what it was."

"What did you do?"

"Several things. First, I went back out to the bus crash site to see if there was anything that would give me a clue as to who was on that bus. I found the site stripped clean. No wreckage. No charred earth. Nothing."

"But how could that be?"

"I saw some enormous tire tracks, evidence that someone had brought in heavy equipment to scoop everything away. Since the crash evidence was gone, I went back to the hospital to check on the survivors. Only, the nurse who'd been my informant suddenly wasn't there anymore. I was greeted by an officious, thin-lipped administrator. He told me that the man, woman and child from the bus accident had all succumbed to their injuries."

Jane sat forward. "They were dead?"

Noah's voice rose beside her. "I thought the child was reported without injury."

Ichy's dark eyes gleamed at them both. "And so she was. The nurse had shown her to me the day before. But this administrator tried to tell me that she had had previously undetected internal bleeding. Claimed she had passed in her sleep the night before."

"You didn't believe him."

"Nope. Not about the child or the man and woman. That nurse had assured me the day before that they were on the mend."

"Did you look for that missing nurse?"

"Everywhere. But even the ambulance crew I met on the crash site had disappeared. And the word was out around the hospital staff that anyone seen talking to me would be fired."

"They didn't want you to learn anything more."

"But I did. This heart patient told me that the night he was brought in for chest pains, he'd been kept awake nearly all night by bright lights through his window and a noisy circling helicopter that kept landing and taking off from the roof."

"A helicopter?"

"That's what he said. Finally he got up and looked out. The helicopter had just flown away. He saw a military ambulance pull up to the hospital from the street below. He witnessed a woman in a wheelchair and a nurse carrying a young child being quickly taken out a side entrance. The woman and the child were handed into the ambulance. Then the vehicle sped off, lights and sirens curiously shut off for all the haste."

"You think it was the woman and child from the accident?"

"I'm sure of it. I found out that except for two small stories in *The St. Johnsburg Times* that copied mine nearly word for word, nothing else had been reported in the Vermont newspapers. Associated Press had picked up the gist of those two stories and sent them out over their network, but no one followed up after my second story."

"Didn't that seem a bit strange to you, considering that none of the victims had been identified?"

"Not just a bit strange, very strange. I told the news editor at *The St. Johnsburg Times* about what had happened at the hospital. He seemed interested at first, but when he called the hospital, they told him the whole bus crash story had been a hoax and that I was a crackpot. He turned around and told me to get lost."

"They denied the whole thing? How could they? Families had to be missing those people who died on that bus."

"Don't know. That's why I went to Portsmouth, New Hampshire, looking for that Sea-and-Scene tour company. Only there wasn't any Sea-and-Scene tour company in Portsmouth or anywhere else in New Hampshire."

"You said the sign was charred. Could you have misread it?"

"Nope. I saw it clearly. I even took a photo of it. I know what I read."

"What did you do next?"

"I drove back to Northrock and confronted Oly Snowe. I told him that even if it meant I had to start a second newspaper, I was going to print what I had learned and dig until I found the rest. That was when Oly presented me with an offer I couldn't refuse."

"Which was?"

"He said that if I let the story die, he'd sell me *The Northrock News*. But I had to promise that nothing I knew or ever learned about that bus or the people on it would ever be printed in the newspaper. He told me it was a matter of national security and that if I loved my country, I would do this."

"He was willing to go that far to kill the story?"

"Yup."

"And you took the deal?"

"I liked and respected Oly. I knew that if he was willing to give up that damn newspaper he loved so much, it had to be because he was convinced that what those men told him that day was pretty important."

"So you bought the newspaper, became editor and never printed another word about the bus crash."

"That's about the size of it. Now you tell me, why is that bus accident of interest to you and Noah here?"

"I could be that child who survived the bus crash, Ichy."

Ichy sat back, obviously surprised. Whatever he had been expecting her to say, her explanation obviously wasn't it.

She quickly told Ichy the story of her adoption after the bus crash and how she and her family had been on vacation from San Francisco when it happened.

Ichy sucked on his unlit pipe so hard his lips puckered.

"This doesn't make any sense."

"Why do you say that, Ichy?"

"Because you're not that child."

"Not that child? But if you didn't pursue the story, how can you be so sure that I'm not—"

"I promised not to print anything I learned. I didn't promise not to pursue any leads I might have."

Ichy rose from his seat and limped over to the small grocery counter. He leaned in back of it and brought out an old manila folder.

"There's something in here you'd better see."

He returned to the table and opened the folder. Jane and Noah scooted their chairs closer and looked over his shoulder.

"As soon as the heart patient told me a military ambulance had been involved, I knew that meant the young woman and child had to belong to a military family. The tour bus had come from Portsmouth, right next to Pease Air Force Base. So that's where I went.

"I might never have found them if it hadn't been for the bunny with those special black-rimmed rhinestone button eyes."

"The bunny in the photo at the crash site?"

Ichy's pudgy hand flipped through the pages in the folder until he came to an old news clipping from a military newspaper tucked into the rest. There was no story, just a picture. In it a uniformed colonel and a woman descended the ramp of a military transport plane. In the woman's arms was an infant.

Jane pointed excitedly to the bunny with the black-rimmed, sparkling rhinestone eyes being held tightly in the colonel's hand. "That's it. The one from the bus crash. When was this picture taken?"

"In 1964."

Noah read the caption. "Pease welcomes Colonel Bolton Belford, just returned after an eighteen-month tour of Taiwan. With Colonel Belford is his wife, Nadine, and their new infant daughter, Abigail, born overseas."

Jane twisted to look at Ichy. "Are you telling us that Abigail Belford was the child on that bus that crashed two years later?"

Ichy nodded.

"Were the Belfords killed in the accident?"

"Nope."

"I don't understand. If the Belfords weren't on that tour bus, how did their two-year-old daughter and her bunny get on it?"

Ichy's eyes clouded.

"Ichy, I've got to know the facts. All my life I've been told I was the child who survived that bus accident. Now you're asking me to accept that I'm not, without any real evidence or explanation. Can you understand how impossible that is for me?"

Ichy let out a long, deep sigh.

"I can tell you no more. But there is someone else who might."

"Who?"

"Nadine Belford. I'll call her, if you wish."

"Yes, please. But before you go, Ichy, tell me this. If you knew about the child and the young woman who were in that bus crash, why did you think Noah and I could be of help to you in solving the twenty-eight-year-old puzzle?"

"I thought you were going to tell me who the other people were on that mystery bus and maybe even about the lone man who survived."

"The man who survived?"

"The one that somebody lifted off the roof of the hospital by helicopter that night the military ambulance came for the woman and child."

NADINE BELFORD greeted Jane and Noah at the front door of a lovely, well-kept, turn-of-the century Vermont farmhouse sitting beside a quick stream that circled through acres of green grazing land dotted with lazy black-and-white cows.

Jane recognized the short, slim Nadine Belford immediately, even after only having seen her in a photo taken twenty-eight years before. Her blond hair had turned to silver, but the high cheekbones and other finely chiseled features of her face had weathered the test of time quite well.

Nadine smiled as she stepped aside for them to come in, but Jane knew it was a nervous smile, and she could see that the woman's hands were quivering.

Nadine led them through a hallway over wide, random pine planks to a living room of honey-colored pine paneling and a large collection of copper kettles and brass candlesticks, all of which seemed to blend in a warm, muted palette.

It was a cozy room. Jane knew that no matter what the weather outside, this room would feel warm and protected all year round.

Nadine beckoned Jane and Noah to a faded gingham couch with small, sawdust-colored throw pillows. She sat across from them on a matching gingham rocking chair and automatically picked up her knitting from a basket beside it. Her nervous hands got right to work.

Jane decided to follow suit. "Mrs. Belford, we appreciate your seeing us on such a personal matter and on such short notice. Did Mr. Hayes tell you of my concern?"

"Ichy said you had been told that you were the child that survived that bus accident twenty-eight years ago. That is quite...surprising."

Jane leaned forward. "Please understand, Mrs. Belford. I have no desire to invade your privacy. But if I don't know the particulars about what happened, I'll never be sure. This is extremely important. Extremely."

Nadine let out a long breath. She stared at the knitting in her lap. Her voice sounded very far away. "It was all so long ago. All the shame. The pain. The secrecy. Afterward I used to dream I had done things differently. Sometimes I would awake from those dreams smiling. But other times..."

Her voice trailed off as a visible shiver rippled through her.

"Mrs. Belford?"

Nadine raised her head. She took a deep breath, as though trying to rid herself of whatever had caused that uncontrollable shudder.

"I was twenty-one when I married Bolton Belford—a very young, naive twenty-one. He was thirty-five, already a colonel and a highly respected, battle-tested leader. I soon found out he expected the same unquestioning adherence to his orders from his wife as he did from his men. And if he didn't get it, he meted out what he considered suitable punishment."

"He abused you?"

"Mentally, physically, emotionally."

"Did you leave him?"

"I tried to. I fled home to my parents the first month. But he came and took me away."

"Your parents didn't try to stop him?"

"They didn't understand. Treated it just like a newlywed spat. But it wasn't, of course. Bolton told me if I ever tried to leave him again, he'd kill me. He also said if I went back to my parents, he'd kill them."

Nadine Belford resumed knitting, as though needing to keep her hands busy in order to get out her words.

"You see these things on Oprah and Donahue all the time now. Today people recognize domestic violence for what it is. There are laws, support groups. But back in the sixties...well, its reality was just not acknowledged. It was between a man and a wife, people thought. No one else's business. Victims had to find their own way out."

"What was yours?"

"To try to adhere to every one of his rules and become the dutiful little slave he obviously was determined his wife would be. One of the other officer's wives asked about my bruises once. Foolishly, I told her. It got back to Bolton, who disciplined me for my breach. I learned to keep my mouth shut and not to make any friends. I might have gone on that way if Bolton hadn't struck Abby one night."

"He hit your little girl?"

"It was then I knew that he intended to mete out his punishments on my child, as well as me. I couldn't let that happen to her. I packed our things the next morning with some vague idea of sneaking off the base and hitching a ride while he was at work. On the way to the gate I saw this tour bus pulled up to a restricted hangar. The bus was empty, the engine running. I got on, and Abby and I hid in the back on the floor under a tarp.

"After a few minutes the bus started to shake as people stepped aboard. I stroked Abby's hair and whispered to her to stay as still and quiet as she could. Then I prayed they wouldn't come to the back of the bus and find us. My prayers were answered. Whoever they were, they sat in the forward section. I never saw any of them, but I heard their distant, muffled male voices.

"Then the bus started up and we were off. I didn't care where. After about thirty minutes the drone of the engine put Abby and me to sleep. When I woke up suddenly, we were being thrown back and forth against the metal seats with a terrific force. I curled myself around Abby, trying to protect her. I heard shouts, screams, and somewhere in it all, something crashed against my head and I lost consciousness.

"The next thing I knew, I awoke in a hospital room with tubes coming out of me. I asked the nurse bending over me about Abby. She told me she was fine. Then two men in suits literally barged into the room, pushed the nurse out and demanded to know who I was and what I was doing on that bus."

"Who were these men?"

"They never identified themselves."

"You told them about sneaking aboard the bus?"

"I was too frightened to hold anything back. I told them everything. The abuse, the threat to kill me. And every moment I could clearly see how much they despised me for describing to them why I had to run away from this man the air force so exalted."

"What did they do?"

"Nothing. They turned and left without another word. That night I was awakened, put into a military ambulance, and Abby and I were driven back to Pease Air Force Base. I was taken to the infirmary. But when Abby was to go home to her father, we both got hysterical and the doctor finally agreed she could stay with me.

"Bolton came to see me at the infirmary the next day. He was furious. He told me his superiors knew about my flight and the reason for it. He told me I had put a blot on his record that had ruined his career. He told me that he wouldn't kill me and Abby, but that I would wish he had when we came home. Then he left.

"I was frantic, terrified. I didn't know what to do. Then this nosy little newspaperman sneaked into my room the next night to get a story, and when he heard mine, sneaked my daughter and me away."

"You mean Ichy?"

A soft smile curved Nadine's lips as her hands stopped knitting. "Yes. Brave, brash little Ichy. He took a terrible chance, hiding Abby and me in his own home, doctoring my still-healing wounds himself. He contacted a lawyer and had him file for divorce on my behalf."

Nadine's smile retreated from her lips.

"When Bolton was served with the divorce papers, he went wild, forced his way into my parents' home, thinking Abby and I were there. My parents told him they didn't know where I was, which was the truth, but he didn't believe them. He tore their place apart. Then, in an uncontrollable rage, Bolton started beating my father, trying to make him tell where we were. My mother ran to a neighbor for help. The neighbor returned with a rifle, yelled at Bolton to stop, and when he didn't, the neighbor shot and killed him."

Nadine's voice had dropped on those final syllables, as if she had placed a heavy period after a sentence that had gone on too long. There had been no sadness in her voice. Had it been her, Jane knew there wouldn't have been any sadness in hers, either.

"What about your father?"

"He recovered, although his injuries resulted in the partial loss of sight in his right eye. The shooting was ruled justified, the neighbor released."

"And Abby?"

Nadine Belford rose and walked to the honey-colored pine mantel. She picked up a photograph, walked over to the gingham sofa and handed the photograph to Jane. Jane recognized Nadine. Beside her stood a woman of about thirty with soft blond hair, who resembled Nadine closely, and next to her was a blond boy about six.

"That is Abby, Ms. Williams. And her son, Ichy, named after his godfather. So you see, despite what anyone told you, you are definitely not that child who survived the bus accident."

"NOAH, IT'S ALL BEEN a lie. From the time I was adopted, I was told I was this child who survived a Vermont bus crash, and now I find out that I'm not. What other lies have I been told? Is my name really Jane Williams? Did I really talk about coming from a place where there was a big red bridge my mother called golden? Is there any truth to any of it?"

Noah heard the frustration in her voice, and he certainly could understand it. He turned off the country lane that had led them away from Nadine Belford's place and headed up one that twisted around the majestic mountain they had followed to find her farm.

They drove for a while in silence, up the steep, two-lane road. Sheer drops into a wonderland of color spread out below them. In the distance rose more green mountains, interspersed with the glorious gold and crimson coats of fall.

But Noah could see his companion was no longer aware of the spectacular scenery. She had retreated deep into

thoughts that wrinkled her forehead and brought her tongue
out to moisten the side of her mouth.

It was crazy, but that unconscious characteristic was the
most seductive thing he'd ever seen a woman do. He longed
to kiss the side of that mouth, capture that tongue with his.
Forcibly, he wrenched his eyes and mind away from images
he must forget. Noah knew his only salvation lay in setting
his mind to the problem at hand.

"Okay, let's try to work backward to figure out what
things we know have to be true. One, you're sure who your
adoptive parents are because you lived with them. Fact?"

"Fact," she agreed.

"You know Walton Fitch was the New Jersey attorney
who handled your adoption on that end. Fact?"

"Fact."

"And you know that Desmond Edelson is the San Francisco attorney who handled your adoption on that end.
Fact?"

"Fact."

"And you know these things are facts because you either
have personal knowledge of them or have seen documents
attesting to them. Agreed?"

"Fac—agreed."

"All right. Have you ever seen anything *in writing* that
connected you to that bus accident here in Vermont?"

"Yes. When I was eighteen and I requested my adoptive
parents have a new search done to see if my parents could be
identified. Walton Fitch contacted Desmond Edelson, who
in turn contacted the San Francisco child-welfare department. I distinctly remember the papers that came back from
Edelson referred specifically to my being that child from the
bus accident."

"But was the information on child welfare stationery or
just on Desmond Edelson's?"

Her eyebrows furrowed even deeper as she concentrated
on recalling images of that stationery stored away in her

mental files. "Come to think of it, I don't ever remember seeing any documents on child-welfare stationery. Just the attorney's transmittals and synopses of the findings."

Noah glanced in the rearview mirror to see a large logging truck looming up behind them on the mountain road. Ever since his accident with Eric, large trucks made Noah nervous. He speeded up a bit to get out of range on the curving narrow road.

"And maybe that's because San Francisco's child welfare agency didn't have anything to do with your adoption. What if yours was a private adoption, handled solely by attorneys? And to make sure no one ever found out who your parents really were, suppose one or both of those attorneys decided to pretend you were that child who survived the bus accident?"

"Yes, I see what you're saying. Those Associated Press versions of the accident were probably distributed all over the U.S. If my adoptive parents were told they were getting the child from that bus accident, one whose parents had been burned beyond identification, that would have been easier for them to accept than a child with no past. You know what this means, don't you?"

Noah watched as the logging truck got right up on his tail. The next stretch before them on the mountain road was fairly clear. He slowed, moved as far to the right as he dared on the narrow road and waved out his window for the truck to pass.

"What do you think it means, Jane?"

"Almost anyone could have been my parents."

"Almost anyone in San Francisco during 1966, you mean. Otherwise, why involve a San Francisco attorney?"

"That's a point I hadn't considered. Maybe we should also consider—"

Noah never found out what else she thought they should consider. Suddenly they were both knocked forward as the logging truck behind them slammed full speed into the bumper of their green Gremlin.

It happened too hard and too fast for Noah to have any hope of regaining control of the car. One moment they were skirting the edge of the precariously twisting mountain road, the next they were sailing off its cliff.

Chapter Twelve

Noah fought against a solid, heavy blackness, like the lead slab of a coffin lid nailed down on his mind. It was an old enemy he had battled before, a powerful one that gave no quarter. But an urgent feeling told him that if he didn't challenge it, he'd never know something desperately important.

And he had to know. He strained with a fierceness of will. Slowly the blackness lifted into a gray, granite texture. The acrid smell of smoke burned his nostrils. The thickening pulse of pain hammered through his body. He knew if he gave up, the pain would go away. He didn't give up. He pressed through it until he heard her husky voice edged with urgency.

"No, no! I can't go on with it anymore! He's hurt! Oh, God, he's hurt!"

She's alive.

That reality beat through him in a wave of profound relief. He knew then that this was what had been important for him to know. *She* lived. He didn't need to fight the heavy unconsciousness anymore. He stopped struggling against the weight and the pain and fell thankfully beneath the lid of its ponderous blackness once more.

When Noah next opened his eyes she was bending over him. Her cheeks were smudged with ash, her eyes filled with worry. Her fingers felt cool against his scalp as they feathered through his hair.

Even as his mind still fought to push away its clouds, inside his chest his heart felt the release of a lingering weight.

"Noah. Finally you're awake. How do you feel?"

He smiled and warmth replaced the worry in her eyes. "No time like the present to find out."

He moved his arms and legs. They cooperated, but not without registering a bevy of new complaints. He raised his hand to nurse a bump making itself felt on his forehead. He coughed as the smell of smoke on his sleeve assailed his nose.

"To answer your question, like I just got hit by a truck. Which, if memory serves, is exactly what happened. You okay?"

"Fine."

"What's that smoky smell?"

"Our car was set on fire. We got out just in time."

Noah slowly rose to a sitting position and found himself on a faded blue handmade quilt. The rest of the small bedroom had much of the same homey, rustic feel. The walls were shades of lemon over taupe. A crisp white lace-edged curtain had been tied on either end to a tree branch that expanded across the small window. Old books, daguerreotypes and a miniature document box sat upon a wall cupboard above a William and Mary dower chest. An ancient hand mirror rested on a red blanket chest at the foot of the bed.

His surroundings did nothing to clear Noah's disorientation. "Last thing I seem to remember is us sailing off a cliff. Where are we?"

"A small Vermont inn. You've been out almost an hour. Are you sure you're okay?"

The throb in his head had begun to subside. He swung his legs over the bed, finding himself fully dressed except for his shoes. He felt more aware by the second—and more perplexed. "Not that much the worse for wear. How did we manage to survive?"

She stood beside the bed looking at him, her eyes suddenly grave. "The car landed in some thick tree branches."

"You said something about a fire?"

"A passerby pulled us out in time. He helped me to carry you here. He went to get a doctor."

Noah was trying to take it all in as the lingering haze over his eyes and thoughts slowly lifted. "So what you're saying is, this Good Samaritan saved us and is going to be returning with a doctor soon?"

She turned from him and began pacing around the small room in quick, agitated steps, her hands clenching and unclenching by her sides.

Noah knew then that despite their apparent escape, something was wrong—very, very wrong.

Gone was the cool, controlled woman he had come to expect. The person before him suddenly had the look of a stranger. That fact registered like a sharp slap across his face, bringing his mind forcibly back to crystal clarity.

"Jane?"

She stopped and swung around to face him, flinging her words out with an anger that stunned him all the more because he recognized it as inward lashing.

"He's not a Good Samaritan, Noah. Scott Lawrence has been following us since you drove me to Riddle Investigations days ago. That's why he was on hand to pull us to safety after witnessing our car being forced off the road."

Her words made no sense. Noah found himself repeating them like a parrot. "Who's been following us?"

She exhaled, a deep, sad sound that seemed to tear down her anger as quickly as it had built up. For the first time since he'd met her, Noah saw her shoulders slump.

"Scott Lawrence. One of the owners of Riddle Investigations. Scotty's been looking out for us, thwarting Marty and Vance wherever he could. He was the one who got in the way of Marty's aim that time we were pulling out of the garage around the block from the Hotel Triton."

"But I thought you told me Scott Lawrence's plane had—"

"That's the story Scott and Sam had their receptionist giving out in order to throw off Marty and Vance. We were trying to make them think I was on my own and an easy target so they'd come out in the open as they pursued me."

Anger rose in Noah's throat and spread over his tongue, hot and thick. "You... you were *deliberately* trying to be a target? I can't believe this! How could you agree to something so stupid? And how could you keep this from me?"

Her voice was sad, but there was no apology in it. "You were threatening to go to the police, Noah. I couldn't let you do that. When I could tell you the truth, I did. But, on occasion, I had to leave out an important... detail or two."

Noah's heart began to beat in sick, thickening thuds as he read the new look on her face. There was more. He took a breath, almost afraid to ask his next question.

"So Scott Lawrence never was missing in some plane crash but, in fact, has been tailing us."

"Yes."

"Any other *details* you've been keeping from me?"

"Just one."

She looked at him and forcibly straightened her shoulders, as though getting ready for a blow. He just wasn't sure whether she was preparing to accept it or give it. He soon found out.

"I'm not Jane Williams."

Noah sat there and stared at the woman standing before him while her words whirled within his brain, bringing with them absolute chaos. If he had blinked and she had disappeared right before his eyes, he couldn't have been more astonished.

"Not..." Something thick congealed in his throat, leaving him with no voice.

She stepped forward, stiff, mannequinlike. She dug into her beige Windbreaker and brought out an identification card.

"I'm Tara Bishop, a private investigator. I work for Scotty and Sam at Riddle Investigations. Scotty's been holding on to this identification card. I asked him to give it back to me when I...I made up my mind to tell you the truth. I wasn't sure you'd take my word by itself, considering...everything."

Noah looked at the identification card without touching it. The picture of the woman with the dark silky hair and azure blue eyes stared back at him. A familiar face...a stranger's face.

His eyes raised to the flesh-and-blood woman holding it out. His initial stupefying surprise had begun to metamorphose into a strong, sharp feeling of betrayal that sliced into his gut. He rose to his feet as he found his voice. It had become deadly quiet.

"This is the...*detail?*"

Tara read the dangerous new emotion in his clear amber eyes and quickly looked away. She withdrew her identification card with shaking hands and hastily shoved it into her pocket. She spoke quickly, almost desperately now.

"Jane Williams wanted us to help find her biological family because of this illness that has struck her son. But after she got that threatening letter and suspected someone was following her—watching her every move—she called to say she thought it might be too dangerous for her to fly to San Francisco."

Noah had taken a step forward. "How could you let me think...all this time...when you knew how I—"

Tara cut him off, nervously pressing on with her story as she physically retreated from his advance.

"So I flew east and changed clothes with Jane Williams in the ladies' room at the airport. I got on the plane for San Francisco to draw off her tail. She got on the one for Boston to be with her son."

Tara glanced at Noah, then looked quickly away from the continuing anger in his eyes. She retreated another step, rushing to complete her explanation.

"We're about the same age, height, coloring. That's why we decided to take a chance with the switch. She faxed Riddle Investigations a huge file about every aspect of her life so I could be convincing. And it was a good thing, too. Because Marty and Vance were waiting at the San Francisco airport for Jane. They sent that phony message to the hotel. They tried to kill her by throwing her into the bay."

Noah fought to get his anger under control. He had no hope of keeping it out of his voice.

"But it was *you* they threw in. It was *you* in danger all the time. Damn it, Tara. Why didn't you tell me the truth about who *you* were?"

Tara stopped backing up. "Because I knew that as Jane Williams you couldn't argue with my right to discover the secret that hung over the head of myself and my sick child. But as Tara Bishop, a private investigator, you could—and probably would—have argued that someone else could do the job."

"You're damn right I would have! How could you put your life in such jeopardy?"

She stood her ground, looking him squarely in the eye. "Because it is my life, Noah. And it is my job. And they are both very important to me."

That damn determination was back in her eyes, that square jaw sticking out at him.

"Noah, I didn't want to deceive you, but you left me no choice. I had a job to do, and I knew if you learned the truth about who I was, you would try to stop me from doing it. I just didn't know how else to play it."

His hands cupped her shoulders, feeling both the strength and warmth of her. This woman who stood before him so defiantly, despite all they'd been through, had still managed to hold such an incredible secret from him.

A maddening woman...an infuriating woman...the most exciting damn woman he'd ever known. His heart began to race.

"So the job is all that matters? To hell with truth. To hell with trust. To hell with the fact that you've almost been killed several times? You're going on with this charade of being Jane Williams?"

Something flashed through those azure eyes, something her slipping guard could no longer hide. For the first time he realized her voice had lost its hardy, husky tone. It was barely a whisper.

"No."

"No?"

She swallowed. Hard. "It wasn't an accident. Scotty recognized Marty behind the wheel of that truck, and Vance was right beside him. After they ran us off the road they got out, descended into that ravine and doused our car with gasoline. Then they set it on fire. If Scotty hadn't driven up then, scaring them away, they might have stood there and just watched us burn."

Noah saw her fighting for control. Her hands balled into fists by her side.

"Tara."

Her voice disintegrated further into a sad, fierce whisper. "Despite the fact that I've been on guard every minute, and despite the fact that Scotty has literally been in the wings every second, they got past us both, and you...you were almost..."

Her voice just stopped. He could see it in her eyes then, what she hadn't said. And then it came back to him: her voice raised in anger and pain those few moments after he'd fought his way to consciousness.

No, no! I can't go on with it anymore! He's hurt! Oh, God, he's hurt!

He...him...she was quitting because of him. Because of the way she felt about him. Something swelled inside his chest, something so big the pressure from it felt as though it would burst his heart.

A door opened. In his peripheral vision Noah caught a glimpse of a sandy-haired, rugged-looking man. He heard a surprised deep voice say, as though from a distance, "Uh, sorry, doctor. Looks like we won't be needing you, after all."

The door closed again. Noah ignored it and everything but the woman before him. Her unguarded eyes swam before his, azure jewels sparkling with one less secret.

He gathered her fully, possessively, in his arms. The impact of her body against his and her small cry sent shock waves through him. His mouth took hers, firmly staking its claim. She melted into his kiss with a force that told him all he ever needed or wanted to know.

He was full of her. Her scent, her warmth, her softness, the sweetness of the cries escaping into his throat as his hands found their way beneath her blouse to the silk of her skin.

Her arms were wrapped around his waist, her fingers frantically kneading the muscles on either side of his spine, pressing him closer, ever closer.

When he'd imagined making love to her, it had been fast and furious, with the biting edge of desire to spur on the images. But now that she was really in his arms, and he was finding substance to the dream, his hands moved slowly over her, savoring every sensation ricocheting through him, every delicious moan and quiver his touch drew from her.

Now he could afford to take his time—and he would. He had a lot of things to say to this woman, things that had been held back too long, things his actions could convey far more eloquently than mere words.

His hands skimmed over her back and across the contour of her shoulders—he was fascinated by the firm muscles curving into her spine. His fingers released the strap of her bra, then they followed her spine down to the lean slimness of her waist. And with each sweep, he felt her tremble beneath his touch.

He exulted in his power to arouse her, craving more and more of it in instant addiction. Eagerly he circled his fingers outward to her sides, then upward until they just feathered the edge of her breasts. He felt the shiver run through her body, the quick catch of her breath.

She was so sensitive, so incredibly responsive. He released her mouth and circled his body around behind her, planting a bed of moist kisses across her face as he went. He tasted the scorch from the fire on her cheek, and its flavor mixed with the sweet creaminess that was her, combining into a heady, exotic sensation.

He wrapped his arms around her, cupping her breasts and gently rubbing at their satin tips as he nipped at the back of her neck through the smooth dark silkiness of her hair. Her nipples swelled in his hands as she arched back against him.

He ached with such exquisite torture in his need of her then, that for a moment the heat of their passion pressed down on his eyelids with a red-hot intensity, momentarily blinding him.

By touch alone he dropped his hands to her slacks, unzipped them, pushed them over her hips and let them fall down her thighs. Then he slipped his hand inside her pink nylon panties. He could hear her labored breathing and feel her moving beneath him as one hand feathered her nipples and the other caressed the silk of her tummy, his fingers gradually inching their way lower.

He deliberately let the tension build in her as he drank in every one of her quick, desperate breaths. Then his fingers found and stroked her.

She moaned and arched against him, melting and shivering at his touch.

He turned her to face him, and, not wanting to waste time on the buttons of her blouse, he impatiently drew it over her head and threw it, along with her bra, to the floor. Then he sat on the bed, pulled her into his lap and removed her slacks and panties. These, too, he threw aside as his mouth closed over her taut nipples and his hand once again sought the sweet, moist heat between her thighs.

He kept his eyes open, watching her head fall back, seeing the deep flush of her face, hearing the moans he extracted from her with every lick of his tongue and stroke of his fingers.

He saw and felt her crest again and again, tasting the passion building, shuddering, releasing through her body. But he wanted more for her—he wanted everything for her.

She was on fire. He'd set off a torch inside her, and he wasn't about to let it go out. What's more, she didn't want it to go out.

Tara didn't know she could be this greedy, so wantonly taking this pleasure he gave. But she had never been made love to like this before, and the unbelievable passion and energy of it rocked her past all control. If her brain had been functioning, that realization might have bothered her.

But her brain wasn't functioning. There was only him and these incredible sensations he brought on. Then there was this agonizing, tantalizing burning and yearning in her breasts and belly that only his touch could build, then release in shooting stars of enormous pleasure, blazing, then winking out over and over again.

Until suddenly a deeper, overwhelming ache told her of her need to be filled with him...only him. He needed to know this and what he had done for her. She would show him.

Her hands fumbled with the buttons on his shirt and then slipped it over his shoulders. Her fingers followed her exploring eyes as they moved appreciatively over the strong, lean contours of his upper body. Her tongue darted out.

He shuddered as her moist, wet tongue slid over his nipples. Her breath quickened with new impatience. Her hands dived to release his belt and then the zipper on his slacks. She pushed him back on the bed and pulled off both his slacks and his briefs, working her way back up his legs with sensitive, exploring fingers, bringing every hair on his body to attention.

He was magnificently aroused. The heat and hunger in his eyes had always been there... for her. Now it was time to show him the hunger that burned inside her... for him.

She poised herself just above him. His hands wound around her silky thighs. She lowered herself over him in a slow, deliberately sensual snake.

Then he was inside her, and he felt so absolutely glorious that the breath broke from her lungs, and she felt his thrusts stoking the fire within her yet again. They moved together, rolled together, and she opened more for him and he filled that more.

And when at last he could hold back no longer, her name broke from his lips into hers, and she was exploding with him in a release that rocked through her blood, her bones, her very being.

"TARA."

She raised her head from where it rested on the solid warmth of Noah's chest.

"Hmm?"

"I was just trying out the new name. This is going to take some getting used to. I've just realized I'm in love with a woman I know very little about."

Love. Tara sighed. His eyes had told her of his love so many times over the past few days. But hearing him say it after what they had just shared made her absolutely dizzy with happiness. Her fingers played with the soft brown mat of curls across his chest as the thought of his words brought a smile to her lips.

"I love you, too, Noah."

She felt his arm tighten around her as he firmly kissed the top of her head, as if he was placing his brand upon it. A warm wave lapped through her at the proprietary gesture. She didn't know why. All her adult life she had fought to be free of such rites of ownership placed on her by another. But now ...

"I should be angry at you for lying to me, Tara. I even want to be. But finding out you're not really a married woman has me so relieved that—" She felt the slight stiffening of his body. "You aren't married, are you?"

She lifted her head to smile into the worried look on his face. "Fine time to ask."

Seeing the mischief in her eyes, he rested his head back on the pillow. "Of course you're not married. Crazy men aren't allowed to marry, and no sane man would have you."

Tara's fingers tightened around one of his soft brown curls and gave it a tug.

His reaction was immediate and exaggerated. "Ow!"

"And now that I have your attention, Mr. Armstrong, I'll have you know I was once engaged to a perfectly sane man by the name of Mitch, who owned several portrait studios and was the proverbial pillar of the community."

"What happened? Did he run out of chest hair?"

She giggled, a happy gurgle deep in her throat. "Actually, he learned I was someone completely different than who he thought I was."

Noah shook his head. "Boy, do I know how that feels."

Tara's gurgle erupted into a husky laugh as she circled her fingers warningly around another curl of chest hair. But instead of giving this one a tug, she leaned down and kissed it.

And with the kiss came a heavy sigh. "I'm twenty-seven, Noah. And I'm finally beginning to feel as though I'm controlling my life and living it on my terms."

Noah's hand wove its way into her tangled dark hair. His fingers stroked her scalp, his tone probing as gently.

"When you told me about being injured when you were nine, and your parents instilling fear in you afterward, that was true, wasn't it?"

"Yes. My mom and dad are pretty much as I described, except of course for small details, like the fact that they are my biological parents, they are still very much alive and they're not at all rich."

He shrugged, smiling. "Those annoying details again."

She sent him a good-natured grin. "I lived a lot of years with that timid image, despite the mental dissent that welled within me. I knew I didn't want to be hesitating and afraid all the time. But I think I became a cautious, fearful child because that's what my parents seemed to want. Does that make any sense?"

"Perfect sense. Children strive hard for their parents' approval. To deny your naturally daring nature was a way to show them your love. I'm just surprised the real you was able to reemerge. How did you break out of all that negative conditioning?"

"Getting engaged to Mitch did it. I was twenty. We had a disagreement a couple of months before the wedding. A minor thing. He took me in his arms after I agreed to do as he asked, then he kissed me and told me how much he loved me. Then he said that he could tell we'd have a happy marriage, because I was the kind of truly feminine woman who would be content to follow her husband's lead.

"What he was saying, of course, was that he loved the fact that I was submissive and therefore controllable. I didn't realize—I mean, really realize—what the fear instilled inside me all those years had made me become until that moment when I saw myself through Mitch's eyes."

Noah could feel her body stiffening. He could see by the look on her face how distasteful that picture had been.

"It was the jolt I needed. I gave him back his ring."

Noah drew her closer, inhaling her sweet fragrance. His voice teased in her ear. "And soon became San Francisco's female version of Dirty Harry."

She relaxed again in his arms. "Not hardly. At first all I knew was that I wasn't who I wanted to be."

"So how did you go about finding yourself?"

"By getting out of the small Nebraska town in which I'd been reared and where everyone had learned to treat me as that timid little mouse. In order to be different, I needed to be around people without a preconceived notion of who I was. So I moved to Los Angeles and found a job as records clerk at the police department. That's where I met Sergeant Samantha Turner. She was smart, capable, professional and in control of herself and her life."

"And your instant idol, I take it?"

"And mentor. Despite my being too short to make it as a policewoman, she recognized my enthusiasm for detective work and encouraged me to pursue it. I took courses in criminology, self-defense and investigative techniques. I also began an ambitious workout program at the gym. For the first time since I was nine, I began feeling really good about myself. I began to really feel like ... me."

"Next step—daredevil investigator?"

"It's taken years, with lots of setbacks along the way. One was when Sam met and married Scott Lawrence six years ago and left the L.A.P.D. to join him at Riddle Investigations in San Francisco.

"Still, it was good for me that Sam left. I'd begun to rely too heavily on her for direction. It became totally up to me to keep pressing ahead and making my own decisions. I left the L.A.P.D. and went to work at an L.A. detective agency. I didn't forget Sam, though. And she didn't forget me. Two years ago she called to say that she and Scotty were thinking of hiring another investigator and asked if I would be interested. I jumped at the chance.

"I'd handled mostly surveillance and record searches up until Jane Williams contacted the firm again. This was my first big case. I talked Sam and Scotty into letting me run with it, overcoming their objections following the incidents at the bay and the hotel room with Marty and Vance. At that point they thought it might be better to have them arrested and play it safe."

"And I agree. Why didn't you?"

"Because we had a client to protect, Noah, and bringing in the police could have jeopardized the secrecy surrounding the search for Jane's past. Besides, I knew Marty and Vance were professionals. If they had been arrested, I very much doubt they would have talked. And whoever hired them could have just turned around and hired two more. At least with Marty and Vance on the loose, we knew who to watch for."

"And so that was the reason you convinced Scotty and Sam to let you continue to be decoy?"

"That, plus the fact that I knew if I backed down then, I'd lose the chance to really prove what I could do."

"Did Scotty and Sam doubt your abilities?"

"No, Noah. It was me who still doubted myself. So many years of negative conditioning are hard to undo. I had to prove myself to me."

Her voice trailed off. Noah suddenly remembered that night they had walked through the airport and that yearning look on her face when he'd described some of the more adventurous exploits of his youth as he tested his skills and daring.

He realized then that the wings of her adventurous spirit had gotten tied before she'd ever had a chance to spread them. And she wanted to spread them. He understood this in her because he understood it in himself—that yearning to define one's limits, and then the exaltation of discovering that you can sail beyond what you thought to be those limits.

Noah was also beginning to understand what she was giving up by walking away from this case. She was doing it because she was afraid—not for herself, but for him.

He couldn't deny that part of him was relieved. It was a selfish part, the part that wanted her safe. But among his deep and complicated feelings for this woman he was amazed to discover another even stronger part—the part that told him he couldn't let her give up now.

She needed to complete this case in order to get those wings fully spread. Only afterward, when she had proved what she could do, would she be content to tuck those wings back around her and discuss what the future might hold for them.

He knew he had to give voice to the words, but still they did not come easily, and he found himself tightening his hold on her as he said them.

"Marty and Vance and whoever hired them mustn't be allowed to continue stalking Jane Williams. We can't let them."

Tara immediately shifted in his arms so that she could see his face. Noah recognized that deep, sharp scrutiny that appeared in her eyes. "Noah, are you saying—"

"I'm saying we've yet to discover this secret about Jane's birth. I don't really see that we have any choice but to keep digging, do you?"

If he'd had any doubt as to whether he was doing the right thing, he lost it when he heard the rush of relief in her voice and saw the shine in her eyes. "You mean it, don't you?"

"Every word. So, Ms. Private Eye, what's our next step?"

She leaned over and gave him a hot, quick kiss—a salute that curled his toes.

He drew her close, burying his lips in the sweet, soft skin of her neck. "Hmm. I like this step." But before he could pursue the new heat that coursed through him, she pulled back and jumped off the bed.

"Noah, we can't waste time lying around like this."

"Waste time?"

Tara smiled at the new hunger in his eyes while grabbing for her clothes. "I thought you were still on the mend."

"I am. You ain't seen anything yet. Wait until I get my full strength back."

She sighed in regret as her eyes feasted on his newly aroused body. "I'm afraid we will have to wait, Noah. Come on. If we're really continuing this pursuit, it's up and at 'em."

"This minute?"

"Of course this minute. I have to find Scotty fast. I have to tell him I'm not resigning from the case after all."

He watched the tantalizing view of her bottom as she bent over. Him and his big mouth. He let out a very long sigh, wishing he'd kept this bright idea to himself for a while longer.

Reluctantly he swung his feet off the bed and reached for his clothes.

"It must have been Scotty who walked in on the beginning of our...uh...discussion earlier. You may find he'll have some questions about that for you."

Tara flashed him a grin. "I doubt it. He guessed that was the way it was with us about the time I fell apart when we couldn't bring you around at the crash site. Just before he left to get the doctor, he gave me a hug and said he understood, something about having been through it himself with Sam."

"Where is this Sam? Back in San Francisco?"

Tara had just fastened her slacks and was reaching for her bra. Noah forgot his question as his eyes filled with the sight of the lovely globes fitting into the wisps of pink lace.

"Sam flew to Boston to watch over Jane the morning I returned to Riddle Investigations and explained about the attempts on my life. She's been keeping a watchful eye out for Jane ever since. When I called the Boston hospital back at the Hotel Triton, it was Sam I spoke to. She was the one who discovered the bogus message called in to the nurses' station, the one the person behind this madness was using to try to lure Jane to Boston."

Tara turned her back to Noah as she slipped on her blouse. Noah exhaled in regret as he zipped up his pants and reached for his shoes and socks.

"Does Jane know Sam's shadowing her?"

"No. Sam didn't want to alarm her by explaining why Riddle Investigations felt it necessary to send in a bodyguard. She reasoned Jane already had considerable worries over her sick child. Sam's staying in the background and keeping her eyes open—insurance just in case the men following me find out I'm not Jane Williams and head for Boston after the real Jane."

She was dressed now and came to stand beside him as he reached for his shirt.

"Scotty will be wondering what's happened to us."

"I don't think he'll be wondering at all, Tara."

She smiled as her fingers brushed tantalizingly against the skin of his chest as she took over the task of buttoning his shirt.

She smelled so sweet, so warm, so near.

His hands cupped her shoulders. "Tara, are you sure we have to go right this—"

"Minute," she finished for him firmly. "I've got an idea. It's one I think even you are going to like."

SCOTTY SAT BACK in his chair in the inn's tiny dining room, surrounded by rustic warm wood paneling and the intimate treasures of old bronzed baby shoes and antique pewter oil lamps that sat on the mantelpiece. Age-darkened portraits of the stout, hardy people that had called this Vermont farmhouse home for two centuries watched him from the walls. But Scotty had eyes only for the couple sitting across the table.

Scotty had decided he liked Noah the moment he'd felt the man's solid shake and had seen the openness in his eyes. His respect had grown when he'd learned that not only had Tara filled Noah in on what they were really up against, but also that he wanted Tara to complete the case.

That decision was the hardest kind a man could make—how well Scotty knew that.

And if he had needed any more of a recommendation, the soft, liquid shine that came into Tara Bishop's eyes every time she looked at the ex-tennis star clinched it. Their chairs were purposely drawn close together, their thighs and arms frequently brushing in a lover's communication.

This glowing creature before him was quite an overlay to the serious, driven, all-business Ms. Bishop he'd come to know over the past two years.

It brought to mind Sam and their recent nights of separation. It never got any easier to be apart from her. But he knew it never would.

"So, tell me, Tara, what is this idea you and Noah have cooked up between you?"

She replaced a delicate china coffee cup onto its saucer. A sharp spark of that familiar driven look pierced her eyes.

"As you know, we've hit a dead end here. This story Jane was told about being the child who survived that bus accident simply isn't true. As we see it, Scotty, we need a new approach."

"Which is?"

"Do Marty and Vance know we're alive?"

"My arrival ran them off the scene of the crash. They have no way of knowing the extinguisher I carried enabled me to put out the fire and pull you to safety. At the moment they probably aren't sure."

Tara nodded. "That's good. Do you know where they are?"

"Earlier when you were...earlier I traced them through the license on that logging truck they were driving. They rented it from a company in the next town. I learned they've already returned it and checked in to a nearby inn. They told the landlord it would only be for the night."

Noah rested his arm on the back of Tara's chair. Tara rested her shoulders against it as they looked at each other. "They must be waiting for news of our demise or survival before deciding what to do next. That's perfect."

Scotty looked at the couple before him. "Perfect?"

Tara leaned forward and lowered her voice, despite the fact that they were the only ones in the small dining room.

"We have a plan for misleading these two into thinking they succeeded in killing us."

"And this plan is?"

"Ichy, the newspaperman we told you about, is a guy who believes in fighting for a just cause. We thought we'd have him dummy up a special edition of his newspaper with the story of our deaths and deliver it to our pursuers."

"You think Marty and Vance will fall for it?"

"They're not from Vermont, Scotty. They can't know when the newspapers really come out around here or how such a local story would be handled."

"They may wait for verification on the radio or TV news."

"They may, but I'm betting they won't."

It was Noah's turn to sit forward. "They want to believe we're dead, Scotty. We think they'd accept it as confirmation if they see it in print by a local newspaper. Two visiting tourists, who lost control of their car, crashed into a ravine and died in the resultant fire."

Tara nodded. "The driver carrying identification as one Noah Armstrong. His female passenger as yet unidentified. Two truck drivers apparently stopped to help but then gave up when the car became engulfed in fire. Another passing motorist called authorities to the scene. They managed to put out the fire, but it was too late to save the couple."

Scotty leaned back in his chair and fingered his coffee cup. "And if they believe you're dead, then what?"

"Then we follow them to find out who hired them."

"The plan has merit, Tara, but it also has problems. Even if you're able to fool Marty and Vance into thinking they've succeeded in killing you, there wouldn't be any reason for these two to personally meet with whoever hired them. You see that, don't you? All they'd have to do is phone in the news of their success and arrange for the payoff to be delivered."

Noah smiled. Scotty saw a momentary flash of the same kind of driven light in his eyes that he'd just seen in Tara's. "Unless they got a congratulatory telegram on the heels of our phony news bulletin, telling them that in order to collect their money and a nice bonus for the job, they have to come in person immediately."

Scotty nodded. "I see. And that telegram will be from us, of course. Not a bad idea. Might just work."

His approval was greeted with smiles from the two faces across the table.

Scotty looked at his watch. "It's going on two o'clock. Providing this Ichy is agreeable, how fast do you think he can get out that special bulletin?"

Tara rose with Noah at her side. "He's printing it up right now. He should have a few copies run off his press by the time we reach Northrock."

A smile lit Scotty's eyes. He should have known that the inventive and energetic Tara Bishop would have already insisted on putting the wheels in motion. These two seemed to have thought of everything. Well, almost everything. Only the excitement of the chase and each other could have caused them to forget they had been pulled out of a burning car mere hours before.

"Uh, what are you going to do for transportation?"

Tardy awareness flashed through both their eyes as they exchanged glances. "Is there a rental place around?" they chorused.

Scotty dug into his pocket. "Not for miles. Take mine. It's the bronze Chevy Blazer parked in front."

He threw them the keys. Noah snatched them out of the air, his hand a mere blur. Scotty nodded approvingly at the man's lightning-fast reflexes. Tara had already moved to the doorway and halted there, waiting.

"Don't worry," Noah called over his shoulder in a voice deliberately too low for Tara to hear, "I'll look out for her."

"Look out for each other," Scotty called for both of them to hear.

Scotty walked over to the window to watch them leave, a frown puckering his forehead. Noah Armstrong's pledge to keep Tara safe told him that the man didn't yet know the lady. If these two were really going to end up a team, Noah had something important to face and accept about Tara. But could he?

When Scotty was satisfied their departure had gone unnoticed, he left the inn and headed for the nearest telegraph office.

Less than thirty minutes later he had accomplished his objective and reentered the inn to wait for Tara and Noah's return from their trip to Northrock. He was walking by the desk on his way back up to the room when he heard his name being called.

"Mr. Lawrence?"

Scotty stopped and turned toward the innkeeper, Mrs. Giusti, a hefty, fiftyish lady with a dimpled chin, ready smile and small, alert eyes that darted with gossipy goodwill. He strode up to the small desk that she had set in the entry hall of the old farmhouse to greet the guests and welcome them to her rustic inn.

"Mr. Lawrence, a lady just called for you. Said it was urgent. She had a very nice voice, 'cultured' my mother would have said. Mother loved to comment that English spoken through most lazy lips sounded like the unfortunate garble of sick cows. That's why she appreciated anyone who—"

"Mrs. Giusti, the call?" Scotty cut in, aware of the innkeeper's propensity for verbosity and eager to cut to the chase. There was only one person other than Tara and Noah who knew he'd checked in to this inn. That she would call him here spoke quite strongly of the urgency.

"Oh, yes, the call. Well, I'm sorry you missed her, Mr. Lawrence, but I did my best. I knocked on the door to your room and walked through the dining area and I even—"

"I went out for a walk," Scotty explained quickly. His growing impatience had his fingers tapping on the counter.

Mrs. Giusti frowned a bit at Scotty's drumming digits and interruption. She dutifully raised the reading glasses sitting upon her ample chest to set them upon her equally ample nose and consulted the papers stacked on her small desk.

"I wrote down the message. Let me see. I had it just a few moments ago. Oh, yes, here it is."

Her short, blunt fingers drew out a yellow slip full of scribbles. She raised it a bit closer to her glasses.

"Her name was Sam. She said it wouldn't be any use trying to call her back because she wasn't going to be there. She wanted you to stay by the phone here. Said she'd try you later. Urgent she speak with you, she said."

"Did she say when she would call back?"

"No."

"You're sure?"

Mrs. Giusti's small, alert eyes darted at Scotty over the rim of her glasses. Her look told him that she was not used to being questioned in this abrupt fashion. Not used to it at all.

"Well, Mr. Lawrence, your friend was speaking rather hurriedly. I wrote down what I could. I am not a machine."

Scotty gripped the counter, trying to keep the impatience out of his voice. "There was nothing else you can remember?"

Mrs. Giusti was getting more defensive by the second at what she took to be an ungrateful and unwarranted attack on her not-too-inconsiderable efforts. Her lips tightened as her sturdy arms crossed her chest. "No."

Scotty deliberately took several deep breaths. He leaned forward slightly and forced his mouth into a smile.

"Mrs. Giusti, you've been very patient with me. But if you can remember anything else, anything at all, it would be such a help. It's so very important, you see."

His altered tone and smile seemed to mollify her a bit. Her arms uncrossed. "Well, I do seem to recall an odd comment she made. But I thought it was just a muttering to herself, you understand."

Scotty's grip on the counter tightened as the innkeeper paused. It took all the control he possessed to keep his small smile in place.

"A muttering to herself?" he coaxed.

"Yes. Something about having made a mistake. A very big mistake."

Chapter Thirteen

Tara's husky voice rose as her eyes flashed to her wristwatch. "Only five o'clock and they're already checking out of the inn. See them over there shoving luggage into the trunk of that bluish Chrysler Concorde."

"Less than thirty minutes after we put Ichy's special edition underneath their door and their innkeeper delivered the telegram right on its heels. And look at those smug expressions on their faces. I'd say they've taken the bait."

"I suppose the next question is whether they'll head for the airport or the highway."

"I doubt Burlington Airport would have any flights to New Jersey going out tonight. They must intend to drive down. Good thing we've got a full tank. Too bad we don't have time to call Scotty and let him know."

"Yes, but he's got to stay there, anyway, until Sam calls back and clears up the mystery. Maybe we'll get a chance to telephone him if they stop along the way."

Tara paused to check the safety on the pistol Scotty had passed to her earlier. "How does it feel to be the hunter, Noah?"

"Lot better than it did being the prey. You sure you don't want me to carry the gun?"

"I have a sharpshooter qualification with this forty-five. What do you think?"

He smiled at the challenging glint in her eyes. "I think I'll just do the driving."

She leaned across the seat to brush his cheek with her lips. "You drive exceptionally well, in case I haven't mentioned it. Hey! There they go!"

"And look at them, Tara. Laid back, windows open, radio blaring. No attempt at all to be cautious. They obviously think they're safe. Well, let them wallow in that congratulatory security for a while. It's not going to last long."

SCOTTY PACED the small lobby of the inn. Every time the phone rang next to Mrs. Giusti he was instantly beside the desk, hoping it would be for him. It wasn't. Every few minutes he checked his watch. Five...six...seven—the hours dragged by.

And with every minute of them, Mrs. Giusti's anxiety seemed to be rising, too. The look on her face told Scotty that she was definitely questioning this decision she'd made to convert her home into an inn, inasmuch as it led to her having to play hostess to such a clearly unstable person such as himself.

But at the moment Scotty gave the innkeeper and her concerns very little thought. He had too many of his own.

Sam's message kept ringing in his ears. *Made a mistake. A very big mistake.* What could that mean?

Should they have stationed an operative at the New Jersey estate of the Tremonts? Should they have put tails on the family members? Had the person behind these attempts on Jane Tremont's life finally realized Tara was a decoy and gone after the real Jane in Boston?

Come on, Sam. Give me a call. Tell me what's going on. Where the hell are you?

The phone on Mrs. Giusti's desk rang.

Mental telepathy seemed to be working this time—it was Sam. Scotty eagerly tore the phone out of Mrs. Giusti's hand.

"Sam, what's going on?"

"I'm calling from the airport, Scotty. We've got trouble."

"THAT MUST BE the Tremont estate," Noah said to Tara as they watched the bluish Chrysler Concorde with Marty and Vance inside pull up to an electronic gate.

They had stopped their Chevy Blazer half a block back, its headlights out. Noah watched through special infrared binoculars Scotty had left in the glove box as Marty communicated with someone through the electronic voice box of the security system.

There was a smile in Noah's voice as he handed Tara the binoculars. "Look at his face, Tara. I don't think he's getting the reaction he was anticipating. He seems to have resorted to yelling."

"Good. I hope these paid assassins get so angry at their employer that they decide to storm the— Hold on. Who's that driving up?"

A Mercedes pulled up behind the Chrysler.

Noah and Tara watched Marty and Vance get out of the Chrysler, lit by the headlights of the Mercedes. They walked to the driver's door. Marty yanked it open, reached inside and dragged out the driver.

"Oh, God, Noah! It's Jane Tremont!"

Noah saw a flash of dark hair as Marty dragged the struggling woman to the electronic voice box. Vance, meanwhile, was slipping into the driver's seat of the Mercedes.

"Tara, I thought she was in Boston. What in the hell is she doing here?"

"I don't know. Something must have gone wrong. I don't see Sam anywhere. Oh, hell, Jane couldn't have arrived at a worse time. Look, Marty's literally putting a gun to her head. She's reaching into her purse for something. He's obviously going to use her to gain entry to the estate."

The ornate, wrought-iron gate began to swing open.

"They can't know who she really is, or they would be doing more than just using her to get inside. Damn. Too bad this Chevy doesn't have a car phone. We need the police here."

"By the time we drive back to a phone to call them, it could be too late. Noah, it's all up to us."

Tara took the safety off the gun and snapped a cartridge into its chamber. The competence in her movement both assured him and sent a small nervous chill up his back.

She turned in the seat to face him, that determined look back in her eyes. "It's a slow-moving gate. Once they drive through we're going to have to slip inside before it closes again."

"We'll never make it with the car."

"I know. We'll have to do it on foot. We'll be less conspicuous that way, anyway."

"Did Jane ever mention if the estate has guard dogs?"

"I seem to remember something about Victoria Tremont forbidding their use. The driveway is obscured behind those trees as it angles off to the right. We should wait until they get to that point to be sure they don't see us. Come on, let's get as close as we can."

Silently they exited the car. Keeping as close to the shrubbery as possible, they angled their way toward the entrance to the Tremont estate. The Chrysler drove through followed by the Mercedes.

Fortunately the gate proved as slow as anticipated. Noah and Tara slipped through just before it clicked closed. Running now to catch up, they followed the dark, twisting driveway that led to the entrance of the Tremont estate.

A half mile later the enormous mansion came into view, its lights a beacon against the night sky. The Chrysler and Mercedes were parked out front. There was no sign of their occupants.

Tara stopped beside Noah as they both caught their breaths. "They've gotten in. This is one hell of an explosive situation, Noah. They have to be blazingly angry at whoever hired and now seems to be ducking them. It's not going to take long for them to be told they've been fooled into killing the wrong woman. And there Jane will be—totally at the mercy of her would-be executioners and the person who hired them.''

"Which means there's nothing left for us to do but storm the citadel. Do we beat down the door or find an open window?''

"Well, as Sam is fond of reminding me, when you've only got surprise on your side, be sure to use it. Let's go find that window.''

Easier said than done, of course. The Tremont estate was enormous and the windows were not only securely fastened but also advertised the fact that they were wired with a sophisticated alarm system. Tara and Noah circled around the back. Finally they followed the muffled sound of voices through the flower garden to the open French doors leading into a well-lighted study. Noah immediately recognized the man standing behind the desk. His raised voice droned angrily, like a buzzing wasp on the soft September night breeze.

"How many times do I have to tell you men? You've made an error. A very grave error. And one you will live to regret, I promise you! Bursting into my home, brandishing guns, threatening—''

"Shut up, Tremont. You may be impressing the woman here, but you're not impressing us. Now let me make this simple for you. You hired us to do a job, and we did it. If you don't pay us the two hundred thousand as agreed, right now, in cash, we're going to blow you away. Now you got the message?''

Marty was pointing his gun at Loren's chest. Vance held Jane securely, his forearm across her neck, the barrel of his gun grazing her cheek. Noah saw that she was an attractive, delicately featured woman who, except for general coloring and size, didn't really resemble Tara. Jane Tremont looked very white and very afraid.

Loren Tremont didn't look much better. Noah watched as the blood literally drained from his face. He seemed to collect himself from the blow of Marty's threat only with great difficulty.

"I don't have—"

"No excuses, Tremont. I'm tired of your games. Get the money. Get it now."

With stiff, robotic steps, Loren Tremont jerkily made his way to the bookcase. He pressed the titles on two volumes, and the shelf sank into the wall, revealing a hidden safe.

Noah knew it would be foolish to think that Marty and Vance would just take the money. Far more likely, they would leave no witnesses. He watched as Marty followed Tremont to the safe. His back was now to them as he closely observed Tremont working the combination.

Tara had a clear shot at Marty. But Vance still stood in the middle of the room holding a gun to Jane's cheek, her body blocking a clear shot at him. Noah knew if Tara took out Marty, Vance would have time to take out Jane.

He had to think up something, and fast. Just beyond them, near the mossy path on which they crouched, Noah spied a small hand spade, a tool that had been left by a forgetful gardener. Noah reached for it at the same time his hand drew out the tennis ball from inside his pocket.

Noah looked at Tara, gave the spade a small swing at the tennis ball and pointed to Vance. Tara nodded in understanding and trained the .45 on Marty.

Noah took a deep silent breath and let it out carefully. This was one serve he couldn't afford to miss. He grasped the wooden handle of the spade in his left hand, the curved side of its blade facing outward. He bounced the tennis ball in his right palm, testing its feel.

Loren had opened the safe and was reaching in for the money. Noah knew it was now or never.

Adrenaline pulsed through his arteries as he bolted up, threw the tennis ball in the air and swung the spade toward it. He felt the firm connection, a strange sensation with this

unorthodox racket. The tennis ball flew through the air on
its unerring path to Vance's temple, striking him a popping
blow.

Vance dropped like a rock to the carpet, taking Jane with
him.

Marty heard the sound and whirled around. Tara fired.
The bullet caught Marty just above the elbow of his right
arm. He let out a howl, his gun falling to the carpet. Tara
leapt up. Four quick steps and she was standing over the
dropped weapon, swooping down to pick it up, then rising
again as she slipped it into her Windbreaker.

Marty grabbed at his wound, blood streaking down his
arm. He fell to his knees before her, his voice incredulous.

"You're dead!"

Tara smiled. "If that were true, you'd be in even more
trouble than you are."

Loren Tremont stepped to Tara's side. "I don't know who
you are, but I've never been more glad to see anyone in my
life."

Tara backed up, keeping the gun trained on both of the
men before her. "Be that as it may, Judge Tremont, I would
appreciate your staying where you are."

A look of absolute astonishment flashed over the fine
features of the judge's face. "You can't be serious."

"Never been more so. How is Jane?" Tara called over her
shoulder.

Noah came to Tara's side. "She's dazed a bit from Vance
falling on her, but I think she'll be okay. He's out cold. I've
laid her on the couch. Time to call the police."

"They've been called, sir," a quiet voice announced from
the direction of the door.

Keeping one eye and her gun trained on Marty and the
judge, Tara turned her head to find a man whom she assumed was the butler, standing in the open doorway. He was
an elderly man with an expressionless face.

"I took the liberty when I heard the shot," he explained
in that same quiet voice. "An ambulance is also on its way."

"Mansard! What was that awful noise?"

Victoria Tremont swept the servant impatiently aside as she rushed into her husband's study, Gerard right behind her. Her eyes widened when she saw the man bleeding on the carpet and the gun pointing in the general vicinity of her husband.

"Loren! What on earth—"

Before Victoria could finish her exclamation, Gerard Tremont had charged past her in a direct line for Tara and the gun. Noah quickly intercepted him, bringing him up short with the threat of the spade in his hands and the look in his eyes.

"Let's just stay cool, shall we? The police will be here soon to straighten this all out. Until then, I suggest everyone take a seat and try to remain calm."

"Ohh."

Tara glanced briefly toward the noise to see Jane Tremont coming to on the couch. At Noah's nod, she handed him the gun to keep an eye on Marty and the rest of the Tremonts, while she went to the woman's side.

"Jane, are you all right?"

Jane opened her eyes and blinked in surprise. "Tara? It can't be you! They said you were dead!"

"'Reports of my death have been greatly exaggerated,'" Tara quoted with a smile.

Victoria Tremont swept over to the couch. "Jane, finally. We've been frantically trying to reach you. Charles is in the hospital."

Jane waved Victoria away as if she was an annoying fly. "Yes, yes, I got your messages. Charles's illness is why I came back. What are you doing here, Tara?"

"We arrived just in time to hear your father-in-law bickering with his hired assassins over the payoff money. The police are on their way here now to arrest him for your attempted murder."

Victoria stiffened by the couch. "Attempted murder? Loren? Are you mad? Jane, who is this woman?"

Jane twisted on the couch to face her mother-in-law, the blood rapidly returning to her cheeks. She slowly got to her feet.

"This woman is Tara Bishop, a private investigator. She switched places with me to draw off these assassins Loren sent to kill me. He gave these men orders to kill her, thinking she was me."

Gerard took a step in his sister-in-law's direction, his hands clenched fists at his sides. "That's not true!"

Jane stood before him, her face rigid in anger. "No? For all I know you were in on this with your father. And maybe your mother, too!"

"This is preposterous, Jane!" Victoria screamed from behind Gerard. "None of us would harm you."

Jane skirted her brother-in-law to come face-to-face with her mother-in-law again. Tara felt suddenly very uncomfortable with the look on her client's face.

"Oh, no? You did your best to dissuade Charles from marrying me—the nameless, nothing orphan. And you've done everything you could since to find fault with me and turn him against me."

"You turned him against you, Jane. Your behavior was not—"

"Acceptable for a Tremont. Oh, yes, I've heard it all! But how about your behavior now, Victoria? Were you in on the scheme with Loren, and maybe Gerard, to kill me before I could reveal the scandal surrounding my birth and really tarnish the Tremont name?"

Victoria's glacial eyes stared like frozen lakes at her daughter-in-law. She drew herself up, her voice full of dignity. "Jane, nothing about your birth, scandalous or otherwise, could have anything to do with Loren or Gerard or me."

Jane's lips lifted into the kind of smile that sent a small warning chill up Tara's spine.

"Not even the fact that I'm Melissa's daughter?"

Victoria's tall, statuesque frame swayed. "No! It can't be true! No, no, no!"

Something like delight danced in Jane's eyes. "But it is true, Victoria."

"Impossible! You can't be—"

"A Tremont? Oh, but I am, Victoria. Ironic, isn't it? You who fought my marriage to Charles because you didn't think my pedigree was good enough. You, who have been harping at me every damn day these last six years to be more like a Tremont. And now here I am. More of a Tremont than you will ever be."

Loren stepped toward his daughter-in-law, his face ashen, his jaw so clenched it looked wired. "Melissa never had any children."

Jane swung toward her father-in-law. "You mean you wish she never had any. What turmoil it must have caused! Old-maid Melissa having a fling with the Tremonts' young, handsome chauffeur. And then fleeing with him to California to have her child and avoid her family's disapproval."

"No. Melissa couldn't have—"

"Of course she could have. And did! She left this estate thirty years ago. For two and a half years. When she came back, you and your father had her ostracized to the cottage in the back. Didn't even want her eating with the family, did you, Loren? And now you're trying to tell me you didn't know about the child you made her give up?"

Loren's sharp words were clipped and precise. "My father and I knew about the indiscretion with the chauffeur. But there was never any child that—"

"The chauffeur's name was Williams, remember? Just like mine? No, of course you didn't know I was his and Melissa's child when I married Charles. You definitely would have prevented our marriage then. But you sure as hell knew it when Edelson called a year ago. And you've been covering it up ever since."

"What?"

"Surprised I know? Yes, I bet you are. You thought you could hush it all up, didn't you? You never figured on Edelson calling back."

"But he never—"

"No wonder you panicked and hired these thugs when the Supreme Court nomination came up. You had to stop my searching into the past. You had to stop my learning that I was your first cousin joined to your son in illicit marital bliss. What a juicy little tidbit for the tabloids! Too bad I took that second call from Edelson a year ago when he asked for you. Too bad he repeated everything to me he'd told you on the first call."

Everyone in the room had grown still with shock as Jane's words echoed through their ears. And then into the deathly quiet broke a new voice.

"No, you're wrong, Jane. It wasn't Loren he spoke to on that first call. It was me."

Tara swung around to the study entrance to see a stout, formidable-looking lady amble in. Hers was a craggy face, a face that had gathered many unhappy lines in her seventy-plus years.

"Melissa!" From Jane's lips the call sounded almost like a hiss.

Melissa stepped up to Jane, leaning heavily on her cane. There was pain in her face, but Tara didn't think it came from the swollen ankles she favored.

"Jane, I'm so sorry. I never knew that fool Edelson had called you, too. The man was raving. Off the deep end. I'm so sorry he told you and brought you this unhappiness."

Jane's eyes flashed angrily. "You think keeping it a secret brought me happiness?"

Melissa sighed, long and deep. "It's clear I have no choice now but to tell you the whole story."

"It's too late to tell me anything."

"Yes, perhaps it is, but it still must be done. Forgive this old woman, but I think now that I must sit down while I do it."

Melissa hobbled over to a chair and sank into it. Tara saw profound regret, along with a substantial amount of worry, etched on the weathered face. Melissa's faded green eyes glazed over with a distant memory.

"I was born with a plain face, no money and the burden of being under the thumb of an elder brother, Roland, who worshiped at the altar of the Tremont name. The only young men I was ever permitted to be around were the wealthy and privileged of my so-called class, who could afford to cast their affections on those far prettier and wealthier. My affair, when I was in my mid-forties, with Bill Williams, our chauffeur, was a desperate, pitiful bid for a little happiness before the chance completely passed me by.

"Bill was more than twenty years younger and incredibly handsome. I was completely captivated. He told me he loved me and that we must run away and get married before Roland tried to separate us. It was all like a dream.

"Only, like all dreams, the time came to wake up. We fled to Sacramento, California, where he finally asked the kind of probing questions that opened his eyes to the fact that I had no money of my own and that my marriage to him would cut off all support from my wealthy brother. We were sitting in a restaurant, having dinner. I'll never forget how ugly his handsome face suddenly turned as the truth dawned on it. He said not another word, just got up and left. I knew he wasn't coming back.

"I just sat there and cried, a silly, middle-aged woman with a broken heart. Finally, a young woman in the next booth came over to comfort me. She had overheard my discussion with Bill. She said she, too, had been left by her lover, so she knew how I felt.

"Her last name was Janae. I couldn't pronounce her first. She was from Eastern Europe, in the U.S. on a student visa. Only she'd gotten herself pregnant, and the father had disappeared as soon as he'd heard. She wanted to remain in the United States to have her baby so it would be a citizen. Unfortunately, her student visa had expired, and the authorities had already sent her notice that she had to return home.

"She was six months along. Without funds. Without friends. All she had in the world was an old suitcase that held a few articles of clothing and the determination that her child would be born a U.S. citizen.

"My heart went out to this young, brave woman. My problems seemed small in the face of hers. I told her I would help. I got us an apartment. We streaked her hair with gray, and I sent her to the doctor for prenatal care using my identification to prevent the authorities from locating her. Caring for her gave my life a new and welcome focus. We both eagerly looked forward to the birth of her baby."

Melissa's voice grew soft and sad.

"Only Janae died right after her baby was born. When they asked me who I was, I lied and said I was Janae's sister. I told them to put Jane on the birth certificate of the baby, which was as close to her real mother's name as I could come. Since I never knew the real father's name, I had them enter Bill Williams."

Jane charged over to where Melissa sat on the sofa. "It can't be!"

Tears welled in Melissa's eyes. "Your mother was willing to give up everything to ensure your citizenship. In memory of her bravery, I had to carry on. I moved to San Francisco with you and called myself Mrs. Williams. For the next two and a half years I raised you just as if you were my own. I couldn't work because the death certificate in my real name had invalidated my social security number. So I sold all my jewelry to get the money to support us.

"We lived very frugally. Still, inevitably the money ran out. I had to provide for your future, so I went to Edelson and told him I wanted you adopted by this older New Jersey couple I knew who so desperately wanted a baby. I showed him my identification and your birth certificate to 'prove' you were mine. I directed him to arrange for things through Walton Fitch, my old lawyer. Together we agreed to say you were the baby from the bus crash. None of the survivors had ever been identified. We reasoned that story would curtail further inquiries into your past.

"With you safely adopted and close by, I returned to the Tremont estate. My brother, Roland, made nasty, holier-than-thou remarks at my expense and relegated me to the cottage in back as punishment for the moral pimple my affair had brought to the lily-white Tremont cheek.

"But it didn't matter, Jane. Because I knew you were safe. Then when the time came, I purposely arranged to bump into you so I could make you a part of my life again. I was delighted when you and Charles married. You see, dear, there was never any common blood between you."

Jane's fists clenched at her sides. "You're lying!"

Melissa looked taken aback by the anger in her tone. She obviously thought her explanation should have relieved the woman's mind.

"Jane, I told no one this, except Walton Fitch and his daughter, Judith. Taking a child who is not one's own is kidnapping. I did not intend to live what was left of my life behind bars. And then there was the terrible guilt. For two and a half years you were my child, my love, the only living thing that had ever completely captured my heart. I can't even begin to describe to you what it felt like when you cried and clung to me that day that I had to let them take you away."

Tara felt a small constriction in her throat as she read the incredible sadness on Melissa's face. But when she looked over at her client, she was shocked not just to find Jane Tremont's eyes dry, but also to see the fire of a blazing anger lit within them.

"You...you...you've ruined everything! Everything!"

"No, Mrs. Tremont. You did that all by yourself."

Tara's ears picked up that familiar voice instantly. She swung toward the newcomer who had quietly entered the room, a tall woman with black braids wrapped around her head.

Samantha Lawrence's voice was as steady and deadly as the gun she pointed directly at Jane Tremont.

"You lied to us when you hired our firm to search for the truth about your birth. You already knew, or thought you knew. But you had no proof, just the frantic words of a mentally disturbed lawyer, who hours later lapsed into a catatonic state after burning his records.

"You wanted us to get the proof for you, then make us expose it. That's why you hired these thugs in Judge Tremont's name to kill Tara, while she was posing as you. You thought that once she was murdered we'd be forced to put the matter into the hands of the police and Loren Tremont would be blamed, with the blood relationship discovered as his motive."

Sam's words whirled like a fierce tornado through the still air of the study, snatching away Tara's remaining confusion. Jane Tremont did not have to answer Sam's accusation. The angry, trapped expression on her face broadcast its truth for all to see.

Victoria Tremont sucked in a shocked breath. Gerard Tremont muttered an angry oath. And Loren Tremont stiffened into a rigid post.

Tara was emotionally reeling from the full implications of what Sam had exposed about their client. She felt Noah move beside her. She leaned into him, grateful for his solid, steady warmth in light of these earth-shattering revelations.

From the corner of her eye she watched Melissa raise herself shakily to her feet, her arthritic hands clutching tightly to her cane.

"But why, Jane? If you really thought you were my daughter and Loren's cousin, exposing the truth should have been the last thing you would want to do. Think of your child!"

Jane suddenly laughed, high and wild and chilling.

"Think of my child? I never wanted that child. I only had it because Charles insisted. Charles was all I ever wanted. He's the only reason I put up with any of you Tremonts."

"But then Edelson called and told you of your supposed relationship to Charles," Samantha coaxed. "And he said he'd called before."

Jane's eyes were wild as she twisted toward Sam. "I thought he'd talked to Loren. At first I was so afraid that Loren would tell, and I'd lose Charles forever. But Loren said nothing.

"I felt so relieved! Only then I overheard Loren urging Charles to divorce me, assuring Charles he could have his son without having to put up with me anymore. And Charles was going along with it. He told me he wanted a divorce.

"I loved him so. He should have loved me! I begged him. But he betrayed me. Told me it was over. Well, it wasn't over. I vowed right then and there that neither he nor any of you Tremonts would get rid of me so easily. I'd give you all what you feared most. Scandal! Hot, juicy scandal!

"And I had the means already in my hands. But I needed proof of my blood kinship with Charles, and Edelson was dead. So I made the kid sick so that they'd eventually run DNA testing on him."

"Sick?" Victoria repeated the word, barely managing a wobbly whisper. "You made your own child sick?"

Jane's voice was wild, high, unbalanced. "Except Loren talked Charles out of being tested and screwed that up. So that's when I decided he'd just have to get sick, too, with the same symptoms."

"Jane, no. You couldn't—"

"Shut up, Melissa! When I think how close I came to having them all in my hands. These hands! I could have made them squirm on their bellies forever. And you ruined it! You're nothing but a worthless old hag."

Tara had never wanted to strike another woman before, but her arms ached to knock Jane to the carpet when she saw the pain she had inflicted reflected on Melissa's face. The elderly woman dropped to her chair, her gnarled, misshapen hands covering her face.

Sam handed Tara her gun. Tara thought Sam was giving her too much credit for self-control. While she pointed it at the woman, Sam grabbed hold of Jane's hands and yanked them around to her back, clicking on the cuffs. Jane immediately struggled, trying to pull away.

"What do you think you're doing! Get those off me! Who do you think you are?"

"I'm the one who's going to muzzle you in a minute if you don't shut up, Mrs. Tremont. And I mean it."

"You wouldn't dare! You have no authority!"

"Maybe not. But I don't know of anyone in this room who'd try to stop me. Do you?"

Chapter Fourteen

"So, it's really true? Jane Tremont was behind this whole business, even going so far as to deliberately make her own child and husband sick?"

Tara nodded as she slipped her arm around Noah's waist, happy to finally be alone with him after a very long and difficult night with the police. They moved as one away from the dark, ugly things they had learned in the Tremont study, following the garden path as the first rays of the sun lit the eastern sky in the promise of a new day.

"Sam just told me that's how she caught on to Jane. The tests that little Charles was going through at the Boston hospital revealed an abnormal and mysterious fluctuation in his potassium levels. When they were elevated—which just happened to occur right after his private visits with his mother—he had limb paralysis, nausea and a whole slew of other symptoms. Sam got suspicious and stole a sample of some baby food Jane had been feeding her son. That's why she was late in getting to the estate tonight. She was having it analyzed."

"So the analysis proved Jane had added potassium."

"Awful to imagine, isn't it? She thought her son's mysterious illness would force Charles into genetic testing and, in that way, expose their blood relationship. But Charles wouldn't submit to DNA testing. So that's when she decided to make him sick, too."

"How'd she do it?"

"She's been slipping potassium into his food for months. When the doctor misdiagnosed his condition as emotional and gave him pills for the pain, she substituted more potassium for the pain pills. Finally he took such an overdose of them the other night that he passed out in near respiratory failure and had to be rushed to the hospital."

"How is he now?"

"Last report from Scotty was that both he and little Charles were doing fine now that the potassium in their systems is almost back to normal."

"What a nightmare it must have been for them both. She never got a threatening letter like she told you, did she?"

"No, that and the business about the New York private investigation firm were just more lies. She was the one who had sent notification to her bank and credit card companies that she was dead so that they'd cancel her cards and freeze her account and she'd have more evidence of the supposed conspiracy against her. She wanted to take the Tremonts down, and she was willing to go to any length."

"Did she also send that bogus message to the Boston hospital about the results of the tests on her son?"

"No, that was Melissa. She was trying to get Jane to leave San Francisco in order to curtail what she thought was Jane's delving into her past."

"It's hard not to feel sorry for Melissa. Whatever she did, she seems to have done it with the best of intentions. Actually, none of the Tremonts seem nearly as bad as I had imagined."

"Jane's lies about them colored all our thoughts. From the moment Sam exposed Jane's scheme, Judge Tremont looked like a man with two tons removed from his shoulders. He's insisting on paying Riddle Investigations' fees, plus a big bonus."

"What are they going to do with... her?"

"Psychiatric evaluation, Sam says. I'd be surprised if she was ever brought to trial."

"Because of the prominence of the Tremonts?"

"That, plus the fact that I can't see how she'd pass the test differentiating between right and wrong."

"Yes. Well, she certainly picked the wrong investigative firm to help her perpetuate her nasty scheme. I can't tell you how relieved I am this case is over, Tara. Now you can leave this business riding high on your success."

She stopped dead in her tracks and turned to face him. "Leave the business?"

He rested his hands on her shoulders.

"You've done it, Tara. You've proved what you can do. And it's mind-boggling. When I think of the times that your ingenuity and expertise got us out of some very tight places, I'm still amazed. This case has certainly had some exceptionally close calls."

Her husky voice was even softer than usual. "It's also left a lot of questions still unanswered."

"Things Sam and Scotty can pursue. We have other questions to consider. Tara, I love you more than anything. I can't imagine a future without you. Do you understand the question I'm asking?"

He looked into her eyes and saw very clearly that she did. He also saw the question she, in turn, had for him.

And it was at that moment that he knew he'd been kidding himself. This case had never been a one-time shot for her. This was what she wanted to do. A cold chill shot up his spine.

But she loved him, and that love had made her willing to walk away from her first big case for him.

He could ask her to walk away from her career for him, too. No, not just could, he *had* to. He loved her too much to allow her to risk her safety again. He was just a normal man, after all, a man who instinctively wanted to protect his mate.

And he would protect her. He'd build a home for them anywhere she wanted. He'd do everything to make her happy.

Except, how happy would Tara be when she didn't become all she wanted and needed to be?

Noah's palms were moist. His heart pounded. Suddenly he knew that the question in Tara's eyes was the most important he'd ever been asked—and one of the most difficult he ever had to answer.

Less than a week ago he'd stared out at the Pacific Ocean, admiring its symmetry and purpose, contemplating what the new directional signal to his life might be. And then out of those waves she'd emerged—a virtual tidal wave, carrying him forward with astonishing force and excitement every moment since.

How could he strip her of those very things that had drawn him to her?

Noah's hands tightened on her shoulders, his voice hardly more than a croaked whisper.

"So which one do you want us to tackle first? The disappearance of Ina Dusart's daughter or Ichy's mysterious survivor from the equally mysterious passengers of that bus crash?"

Tara couldn't keep back the tears of happiness that caught in her throat and spilled onto her cheeks.

She looked up into Noah's clear amber eyes and saw herself there—captured within them and yet also so wonderfully free. And she knew then that this was the way love was meant to be.

"Noah, I love you so much I—"

He broke off her declaration by drawing her to him in a tight, fierce hug, his words a savage whisper in her ear. "Then marry me, Tara. Before we get shot at again."

She held him close as her chest expanded with happiness. She could hear the beat of his heart and feel the warm strength of his body flowing through her.

She exulted in those glorious feelings of union in that embrace for several moments before slowly drawing back. His clear eyes told her he knew that she had already given her answer.

Mischief immediately entered hers. "You're sure, Noah? Didn't you once say that only a crazy man would marry me?"

He smiled, a brilliant smile that melted her heart. "How true, my love. But then, since meeting you, I've begun to think that maybe sanity's overrated."

He brought her to him again, wrapping his arms around her, exulted in the incredible feel of the force in her response.

She was his magnetic pull now—this crazy, reckless, stubborn, wonderful woman—and his life would never be the same.

HARLEQUIN®

I N T R I G U E®

Are you a word sleuth? If so, find the hidden clues and
uncover the truth about a twenty-year-old murder for
rancher Danielle Baylor, and her sexy foreman, Tyler, in
THINGS REMEMBERED by Kelsey Roberts!
(Harlequin Intrigue #294, coming next month)

```
T B E D A N I E L L E K L A
S Q U A R Y X B N N O P R T
A U F N S V H M C S X S W F
P L J G M M N Q O E O E I T
E G A E I I E U M N N C S O
R I N C R N E S M Z R T E K R
I K R O O X P S O E R A E S
L E E U V E L X I R A L N O
E M R S I E Y P A N Y I O A
U I E L D F R R I T G T V C
T R T O H Y K U L B D E B O
H C A V U W M P R D E R L
Z D C E F L A S H B A C K I
H C N A R O L F G H E A T Y
```

CLUES:

DANIELLE	COVER-UP	PAST
TYLER	MONTANA	PERIL
MEMORY	RANCH	DANGEROUS LOVE
FLASHBACK	ARREST	CRIME
MISSING	ARSON	

WDF-2

Answers

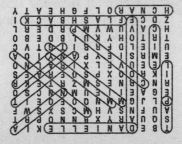

HARLEQUIN®

I N T R I G U E®

Outside, it looks like a
charming old building near
the Baltimore waterfront,
but inside lurks danger...
and romance.

The "true master of intrigue," Rebecca York returns with...

TANGLED VOWS

It was as if she'd come back from the dead....For investigator
Jo O'Malley, nothing was the same after she'd been ambushed
and almost fatally shot. Not even her husband, Cam.
Suddenly there was a ghost from her past between them in
the present—and the future held the most haunting test of
their love....

Don't miss #289 TANGLED VOWS, coming to you in September
1994...only from Rebecca York and Harlequin Intrigue!

LS93-5

This summer, come cruising with Harlequin Books!

In July, August and September, excitement, danger and, of course, romance can be found in Lynn Leslie's exciting new miniseries PORTS OF CALL. Not only can you cruise the South Pacific, the Caribbean and the Nile, your journey will also take you to Harlequin Superromance®, Harlequin Intrigue® and Harlequin American Romance®.

- ◆ In July, cruise the South Pacific with SINGAPORE FLING, a Harlequin Superromance
- ◆ NIGHT OF THE NILE from Harlequin Intrigue will heat up your August
- ◆ September is the perfect month for CRUISIN' MR. DIAMOND from Harlequin American Romance

So, cruise through the summer with LYNN LESLIE and HARLEQUIN BOOKS!

CRUISE

HARLEQUIN®

I N T R I G U E®

Harlequin Intrigue invites you to celebrate
a decade of danger and desire....

It's a year of celebration for Harlequin Intrigue, as we
commemorate ten years of bringing you the best in romantic
suspense. Stories in which you can expect the unexpected...
Stories with heart-stopping suspense and heart-stirring
romance... Stories that walk the fine line between danger
and desire...

Throughout the coming months, you can expect some special
surprises by some of your favorite Intrigue authors. Look for
the specially marked "Decade of Danger and Desire" books
for valuable proofs-of-purchase to redeem for a free gift!

HARLEQUIN INTRIGUE
Not the same old story!

DDD